The second
BLACKSTAFF
book of
SHORT STORIES

The second BLACKSTAFF book of SHORT STORIES

THE
BLACKSTAFF PRESS
BELFAST

ACKNOWLEDGEMENTS

Some of these stories have already appeared in *A Bad Day to be Winning* (Oberon Press, 1991), *Cyphers*, the *Guardian*, the *Irish Press*'s 'New Irish Writing', the *Irish Times*'s 'Summer Fiction', the *London Magazine*, the *Midland Review*, and *Panurge*; some have also been broadcast on BBC Radio 4 and RTE Radio 1.

First published in 1991 by
The Blackstaff Press Limited
3 Galway Park, Dundonald, Belfast BT16 0AN, Northern Ireland
with the assistance of
The Arts Council of Northern Ireland

Typeset by Textflow Services Limited

Printed by The Guernsey Press Company Limited

British Library Cataloguing in Publication Data
The second Blackstaff book of short stories.
823. 0108 [FS]

ISBN 0-85640-473-X

CONTENTS

GEORGE MCWHIRTER
A Bad Day to be Winning 1

ÉILÍS NÍ DHUIBHNE
The Flowering 17
The Garden of Eden 31

MICHAEL CARRAGHER
The Loanen 40

DAPHNE GLAZER
Passing Through Bombay 51
Nothing to Offer 61

CIARÁN FOLAN
The Lights of a Town in the Distance 68

JANET SHEPPERSON
Green 78

JIM MCCARTHY
Balloons 92

GERARDINE MEANEY
Counterpoint 105

PATRICK SEMPLE
The Pass 111

AISLING MAGUIRE
Oppression 117

MONICA TRACEY
It's the Living that Kills You 126

HARRIET O'CARROLL
At Arromanches 133
Chinchilla 143

EMMA COOKE
   The Bridge 153

EDWARD POWER
   Elderberry Wake 165

SIMON KORNER
   Force 174
   Yuri Gagarin 184

JOHN MACKENNA
   The Fallen
   a novella 193

BIOGRAPHICAL NOTES 231

A BAD DAY TO BE WINNING

George McWhirter

Often I ate champ at their house, where they lived in Cupar Street, near the meadow. Mostly they ate sausages and champ, or plain champ, and had the greyhounds been fed the same mashed potatoes, chopped scallions and butter as the family, they would have fattened into canine pashas in their pens. Their kennels were built on the grand scale, up to a ceiling as high as that of a Regency house and open into the back yard. Concrete foundations with runnels and raised bowls were fitted into the lower walls.

The dogs never looked to be impressed. Strapped into their horsehair blankets for the wintertime, their backs were as skinny and bent as safety pins. They were muzzled to stop them nipping at anything that passed by, or to keep the bitches' maws off their whelps, or the stud from snapping at the bitches. Like miserable mendicants, the lot of them wandered in constant solicitation of somebody or something to put the bite on.

Andy had put in a huge window between the kitchen and the enclosure. Eating at the table with the family, we could watch the dogs, and the three-pack of greyhounds could watch us.

'It tortures the animals,' Lena moaned.

'It makes them run,' said Andy. 'They see what they get when they win.'

'And what's that?'

'Fed!'

'They'll bloody well forget then, for they never bloody win.'

At a distance, walking up Cupar Street to a card at Dunmore

or Celtic Park, their tartan race blankets over the numbered vests gave them a glamour, the status of diminutive Derby horses. But there were, too, the lacquered numbers on the torn betting tickets that Lena had stacked into ragged cairns for all their competitions lost. 'I suppose we'll be riding six Rolls Royces when we win,' she used to say.

The dogs were as sulky as she was. Going out the back door with the sons – Hughie and Joe – to play in the bare meadow, the greyhounds would either ignore you completely or, as neatly as needle-nosed pliers, their jaws would begin to chop at the wire.

Money had been kept back from her and the house; a pair of hounds was bought to start the kennel, and their habits learned the hard way. Overfed, underfed, they changed from being too much the family pets into savage beasts turning in ever-leaner circles behind tall window and high mesh. By the time Andy had finished with them their bent backs could have scaled the walls as easy as the fleas springing out of the furniture indoors to feast on any piece of passing visitor. The insects had retreated from the cold of the outside pen, the gales of flea powder, the tempestuous and sullen bathings, into the body of the house that Lena neglected altogether, left in some illusion that the relentless groomings on the dogs kept the house clean for her as well.

And Andy changed handlers as regular as Lena had hairdressers in the early going of their marriage. He spent more and more, but something was always crippling the beasts, delaying their sure-fire winnings: the diet, the weather, the handlers; latterly, the pedigree. And this notion that Lena was secretly sabotaging them with sausages, thwarting him, out of jealousy, leaving her own family with not one banger to go in the champ.

One time when I was sitting in their house Andy looked her hard in the face and shouted, 'Go and wash your dirty dial with soap.'

'When did you ever give me the money to buy sausages, never mind soap to wash my face?' she yelled.

'Aye, done in with sausages,' he repeated. 'You won't do me a rasher of bacon because of that bad temper you have, yet you'd fry them fillet steak on the sly.'

'With what money?' She let him have her main complaint again. 'They'd eat a pig off its hocks. They're as hungry as ever, the miserable bastards. Did they get into something when you walked them to the track?'

Then she would clam up completely and leave Andy to rave on. It all began to turn on the handlers. 'You don't find the good ones in a backstreet pub. These fellas wiping their noses on a paisley scarf and thinking that's class are useless. The boyos in the camel-hair coats on the far side of the track, the ones standing in the G-r-a-n-d S-t-a-n-d-s . . .' He paused to appreciate these two words he'd lately comprehended.

'Can I have a black suit?' Lena asked dreamily.

'Pinstripe would do just as well. Black's for funerals, you stupid bitch, and black would show off every bit of dust you forgot to brush up.'

'But that's what I would wear. That's what *I* think quality is. So there!'

'Righto, Lena, when I win you'll have a black suit for every day of the week. The house will have to be kept spotless then so as not to ruin your suits.'

Then he could be heard lecturing the dogs through the back window about learning to do right by him and about all the time he had put into their training. The beasts yapped and traipsed round the kennel till he left, their claws scraping at the concrete like vicious aunties scratching angry notes of their own at *his* ignorant intrusion.

When he wasn't straining to get rich, my cousin Andy talked like a scathing Stalinist about camps for the Backstreet Brigades of Chancers. 'Uncle Joe would have the lot in kennels,' he would say, looking at the greyhounds, then at Lena.

'What about you?' Lena asked. 'If I wasn't so soft, I'd have *you* in one.'

Then, tall and excruciatingly thin, Andy would smile at her, his height as spectacular and unmanageable as her beauty. Anyone could see how it had drawn them together on the ballroom floor – among the tall American and English men of war – the sally-rod sweep of his body, the light swipe of his tongue. And Andy could dance, his legs flicking like whips, driving her own.

The one thing Lena had kept good was the suit she had been married in. Wearing it, she felt tidied up and ready, just sitting or standing, without ever having to do a hand's turn. When Lena learned from Andy, through my aunt, that I had been confirmed and had started going to Holy Communion at St Stephen's, she arranged for me to link her down the road to Millfield. I was fourteen by then and had stopped going up to their house. Once my taste for the dangerous dogs and the filthy meadow waned and this other one for Lena waxed, I felt ashamed and kept away. Now I was to be her Lord's Day date, sport for smart remarks.

Sometimes, walking down the road, I would peel myself off her arm, saying I wanted to see something in a shop window. There I would stare at Lena's reflection, then at my grey Sunday suit, which was too small but my mother refused to throw it out because I was growing so much. After a year of that suit, with no more turn-down in the sleeves or trouser legs, I started to understand the ill-fit of Lena. I realised Lena could only pull herself together if she was done up properly and had someplace special to go, even if it was just for someone to shake her hand, like the minister at the church saying, 'Glad you were able to come.'

When I told my mother about this, she gave me a cold, older woman's look. 'Don't be that smart that you fool yourself over the likes of Lena. Dig under Lena's dirt and you have your modern woman. Even if she had money for fish and chips every

4

day, she'd be drooling for them club sandwiches,' she said, as if Lena were an instant relic, a warning to me.

Right enough. Marriage as a social calendar, making dates for breakfast, dinner and tea with Andy and her kids (a notion of life she first picked up from the GIs) would have been heaven for her, but to tell the truth, most of my growing observation of Lena was physical. At 8 a.m. on the Sabbath day the Shankill was utterly empty, and the juggle of Lena on her high heels on the hill, like the tilted bottom of a bowling pin, exaggerated the roll of her hips. Anyone else who saw her followed her the longest way down that whole lobe of the hill. Lena alone with a boy, able to ignore him because he was so much younger. The boy's eyes climbing the slope of her calf, the back dimples and culverts of her knees, beginning to absorb more and more of her body as the Sundays passed.

None the less I did learn that the first day in the new week was her earliest chance to clean up after Andy's Saturday nights, when his talk turned vindictive and he tarred her with his regret at marrying, a regret blacker than any grit or grime that she let cling to her week-long for want of places to go.

At the service, like all Church of Irelanders, she took her absolution general, nothing too specific. After her church and his lie-in, Andy would look at her arriving back, dressed up, and promise to emulate me next Saturday by going to Celtic Park, in duds spectacular, with Lena on his arm. Maybe, said he, if they all dolled up, the dogs would win.

The premiere of this hoped-for upward motion came in a Humber that skidded to the curb early one Sunday morning. Lena had got herself together for going down the road. The driver knocked. He wasn't clad in camel hair, but an Aran sweater, cavalry-twill trousers, red scarf, boots and cloth cap.

'That's a smashin' car,' said Lena, looking across his shoulder in the doorway.

'Black's very hard to keep clean. Do you want to try it out while I talk to Andy?'

She could hear him thumping downstairs behind her into the front room. 'You didn't say there would be somebody here this early. Lucky I'm respectable.'

'Very respectable. Andy knows class,' said the man. 'But go on out and give that car of mine a go.' He handed her the keys. She held them, wriggling them like the legs of a little octopus. 'Go on,' he said.

'Can I really do that?' she asked.

'She'll drive it to desolation – like me,' Andy said behind her, and the remark appeared to thrust her outside.

She got into the back seat. The man's head reappeared to look in at her there. 'You didn't get in the front and start her up. Do you want to take a spin with us?'

'I'd love to. I'd really love that, Mister. . . ?'

'Cairns,' he informed her, 'Norman Cairns. You sit on then. I'll drive you up the hill with us. You'll love the jaunt, dressed up there as you are. Is it a wedding or a funeral?'

'Church,' she said.

Norman Cairns stepped back and Andy dragged open the door, whirled a rug at Lena and unleashed the muzzled dogs into the back. Getting in, the lead dog's claws tore her legs. Now there was a scrape across the bottom of her thighs as if she had been got at by a three-prong toasting fork or Old Nick himself.

'What hill are you taking *them* three to?' she wailed.

'Wolf Hill.'

Lena glanced out the window while the dogs curled beside her, the nearest nosing her leg and dropping its jaw on her lap.

'Cupboard love,' Norman Cairns, the handler, laughed.

'Your poor upholstery,' Lena lamented, pushing herself back in the seat and looking down at her suit.

'Aye, Lena. Pull the rug under you,' Andy shouted.

Going up into Lawnbrook Avenue, she waved weakly at me

6

coming the other way. She looked out the window as if she had just been kidnapped by the Holy Order of the Canine Brothers.

On the mountain she waited hours for them. The sun forced her to open the door of the car and sit on the bank. A mile away she saw them shuttle through gates, in and out of fields, the shadows of clouds racing ahead of them, up one slope, down another. Their shouts bolted after the muzzleless dogs; now they could vent their hunger to their hearts' content on hares and rabbits and unsuspecting rats.

'They need to taste the racing meat often enough to remember what they chased,' Norman Cairns had started in to Andy. 'By the time some handlers shake their hangovers of a Sunday morning, the world and their wives are up here and it's the rabbits that are back in their burrows, like good Christians, singing hymns and hallelujahs at being saved.'

Lena laid her jacket in the car. Then she got out, rolled up her sleeves and raised her skirt over her legs to sit on a clean stone that was half buried in the bank. The sun dried out the last trace of grease on her hair that washing hadn't got, the wind flannelled her face. People passing up the road now nodded to her, taking her to own the car. She played out their mistake, climbing down to pretend she was looking for something in the glove compartment. Then she got back onto the bank with the car blanket.

When the walkers were well past, she shook off the dog hairs. Their greyness blended with the dead grass and the sheeps' wool snagged on the barbed wire. A feral anonymity – like the grey-brown mallard ducks' who clung together near the drakes, shining emerald-blue on their own, in a pond that had gathered under the gate to the sloped field behind her.

The men passing on the road turned to look at her longer, and the women accelerated uphill in a cluster of complaints about their legs and their shoes, and 'some tarts having the luck to *swally up* the country, sitting on their arse in a motor car'.

One woman noted this in passing. Another said: 'The poor

7

sod of a driver must be off somewhere picking her a posy of pee-the-beds.' Then the last woman, but not the least, remarked: 'Look at the legs on that trollop!' – they had all seen the claw marks on her thighs. 'From the looks of thon, she's been in bed with the auld beast hisself.'

This was her marriage to Andy, being left on a bare bank until the day turned to a sour reek and a running commentary on her growing dinginess and distraction.

Lena had been shunned by my Aunt Alice, who blamed her for all of Andy's weaknesses and addictions. Whenever I met her in my Aunt Alice's house, she would say, 'You know, Barney, ever since I married your Andy, your Aunt Alice hasn't stopped sighing or let herself sit down where I'm in a room with her. I just pop by because Andy says she likes to count heads in the family, even if she doesn't like some of their number. Andy says she's like a farmer's wife with her poultry, and I suppose Andy ought to know – his dogs have demolished enough of them.'

My aunt's house was next door to our own, and if my mother and her had been inseparable sisters in health, they were like Siamese twins in her sickness. Ever since Aunt Alice had contracted cancer of the throat my mother acted as her medium, conveying messages the way an older sister would, interpreting the wishes of a younger who had no desire or hadn't yet learned to talk.

This went on until my aunt's dying day, when my mother took it upon herself to send for Andy and Lena to pay their deathbed visit to her beloved older sister. Lena was to come down with him after he finished work, and I was sent before my first lecture at the university to deliver the message and told to be back by the afternoon. I was to be there to prevent any rows between Andy and his father, or between Andy and Lena. It was only logical that they'd elect me as Andy and Lena's intermediary. Whenever she was about they saw the shame-

fondness creep up from my neck and around my eyes like a rash.

Afternoon to early evening I sat downstairs with my uncle, waiting, while my mother stayed upstairs with the aunt. I swivelled in my chair by the door and glanced up at Lena as soon as she came in at seven. As usual her skin was that clear, glazed white, but greasy, like a plate that hadn't been properly washed. But through-other and all as she was, she did put in her appearance. On the other hand . . . 'Andy couldn't come,' she told my uncle.

My uncle just stared at the fire and separated this bony cathedral he had made by pressing his fingertips together, which was as close to church and prayer as the uncle ever got. 'Barney, let Lena have that seat,' he said, still not even gracing his daughter-in-law with a glance.

Lena edged onto the chair, waiting for some more sourness from him or for him to take a swipe at her, but he just got up and went in behind the stairs for his coat.

'Which track has he his greyhounds at tonight?'

Lena jumped when he stepped back out and asked her that. 'You're not going there?' she bleated.

'No, I'm not,' my uncle assured her. 'There would be no help in my getting him. The damage is done. You know, Lena – Maggie, Barney's mother, has been up there nights on end, and *he* hasn't seen her the once.'

The uncle did as he was wont. He spelled out the members of the family to Lena, as if to a stranger freshly arrived. Her look didn't dispute her confusion on the matter. Then he leaned over to drop a departing word in her ear: 'I'll be in Heddie Garvin's for a minute. You'd better go up on your own.'

'Do I have to?' she asked.

But he had skipped out, leaving her to the decision herself. Sitting there inside the door of her in-laws' house, she kept on touching her dress and the ends of her hair. The fidgets of Lena, at having to face my aunt, would have made anybody feel sorry for her.

Again I thought about her during the war, the best-looker in the Plaza ballroom. How she must have spun out of the arms of the American soldiers and stuck to my cousin's spidery embrace: a buzzing blond fly in an impeccable gossamer whir; her head turning, the smut of the family's gossip already beginning to cling. She still bore that blurred resemblance to Virginia Mayo – a Hollywood star I liked, who jerked her high cheekbones away from the likes of lean Randolph Scott, the navy-blue jaw of Rory Calhoun, or dimpled Audie Murphy, the cherub in a stetson. I saw Audie as something of myself, a good guy whose sullen innocence didn't go with Virginia Mayo's angry turning away from the indignity of his lips and embraces, in this one picture I saw them in together where Audie played the villain.

Lena motioned me toward her, but I had scared myself into standing where I was, by the fireplace, too well-aware of the legs she had left splayed in her dejection. Hadn't I been studying them for years? They were fine legs: the skin, flawless and smooth. The stubbled hair stood out above its sheen, I imagined – in that half-boy, half-man, half-mad way of mine – like scruffy reeds, bristling in an evening tide, measuring a depth of water as it swells into a river mouth where a boy might want to swim, pretending at commandos, or Indians.

My aunt was dying upstairs and there I was gawking at Lena's lips and legs, making coarse excursions out of her parts, wondering what was the right way to convince her that I supported her in her suffering, even if nobody else did.

'I can't make Andy come or go anywhere,' Lena confided. 'He thinks they'll win this time for sure. "If there's a God in heaven," he says, "they will this night before she goes." Those bloody dogs. You know he forgets all about me since he's had them. I might as well be dead or dying along with your aunt up there.'

Lena twisted in the seat. I felt deserted too, dreading the call to participate upstairs.

'Is that Angelina?' my mother's voice curled down the stairs to us.

The stairwell had this single turn at a window, the size of a porthole, that spied out onto the back yard; the stair crest and short landing broke the other way, into the front room. My mother was still standing there on the landing, looking out through the window, when Lena and I came up. Lena turned to see what she could be watching in the yard before going into the curtained room and I went no further than the landing.

During the afternoon, when the doctor had come, I had watched the streams of spring sunshine shining outside, avoiding the dark that lay dammed inside my aunt's room. Inside I imagined the illness accelerating toward bloom along with everything else, node by node, like a constellation of poison mushrooms in my aunt's throat.

'Is it you, Lena?' My aunt pushed away the wreath of grey hair clinging to her sweating forehead. Her body looked like it had disappeared, leaving only this small grey evidence of its fullness on her brow. 'He's not with you, is he?'

'He's at the dogs. Barney's Bite is a favourite.' Lena passed on this simple information. My aunt and my mother nodded; Andy had called one of the dogs for me.

'I have to tell you I am heartily sorry, Lena,' said my aunt. 'I have thought ill of you and not him. It's the devil himself that gets by you with a chuckle. You know that well enough, Lena. A glass of whiskey, a flutter on the horses, their hand on your leg stopping you from moving anywhere.'

'Ssh, ssh.' My mother wiped my aunt's brow.

'He says he'll have something to bring this time.'

'Lena, what has he ever brought to me or you but grief?'

'Don't say that, Alice,' my mother told my aunt in the dark. 'Andy is Andy. It takes all sorts to make a world.'

11

Unable to listen to any more, I crept back downstairs, only to see the Humber draw up, the door open and Andy step out like a lanky apparition. He shook his fist at the windows of his mother's house and reeled around the front of the car, across the road and into Garvin's. For a moment I thought it was a sheaf of huge razor blades he was wagging between his fingers, then I realised it was fivers. I needed to let them know upstairs, before Andy blundered in with the trainer and his father, who would surely meet up with him in Garvin's.

I stood on the landing behind Lena. I had come up the second time slowly, suffocating the creaks on the stair. 'He's here,' I said and Lena jumped to let me by as soon as I spoke.

'Take Angelina down,' my mother told me.

'He's across the road. His fist is full of fivers,' I whispered to Lena.

'Oh dear bless us.' There was shock and no elation in her face.

When he came in with his father not five minutes later, Andy's own face was as clenched and white as a fist. The fivers were folded tighter. He must have rolled them over and over while he was drinking and inserted them so that they now butted between his fingers like the stumps of a fan or a mangled knuckle-duster.

'This is just a couple,' he announced in his lowest voice, his Adam's apple jumping.

'Andy, for Christ's sake!' said Lena.

Andy ignored Lena's alarm. 'She'll have to see the good in this. It was your namesake won.' Andy McCabe was challenging me to share a bitter smile at this piece of information on Barney's Bite.

My uncle was back on his chair and sucking the dregs of Garvin's whiskey off his teeth. Outside the window we could see the Humber driving off.

'Well, what have you got to say *this* time, big fella?' Andy challenged me.

Over the years, how often had Andy and I argued over things I was learning at the university? Faster than rats at a string of rotten sausages he would go at my big words. Or he would glide in, as if I had just asked him to take the lead onto the waxed floor of the Plaza ballroom. The family would listen to him spiral into a vortex of drunken fancies with me, waltzing the same as he must have once waltzed with Lena. If it hadn't been for the peace it afforded on their Saturday visits to his mother's, she might have been jealous.

At the bottom of the stairs, when Lena looked into my eyes, I saw she sensed the electric shock of recrimination circuiting between her father-in-law in his chair, Andy tramping up the stairs, and his mother about to damn her son's good fortune with her dying. God help us, it could be no other way. Their leanness, their loveliness, was like their dogs': a pedigree hopelessness, as distracted as it was hungry.

Around the downstairs room Lena wandered, wringing her hands, waiting until Andy came back down, zombified. My mother led him to the front of the fire.

'Warm yourself,' she told him. 'You look like you haven't eaten a bite. You know your mother shouldn't have said that. It was wrong.'

But Andy left the fire and planted himself beside his father instead. He knocked him on the shoulder with the fivers in his fist. 'This'll pay for the bloody funeral and a gravestone,' he said. 'That should please her.'

His father ignored the money, leaned forward and placed his head between his hands as if to warm its bald top at the fire that my mother was relighting with paper and fresh kindling from a twopenny bundle of sticks. The cedar sticks crackled like a burst of ventriloquised coughing from my uncle.

Downstairs none of us had heard anything, but we knew the gist of it. Andy was prodding me now with the money, boxing my chest the way he did when we were joking on some matter of philosophical contention.

'Take it, take it. That'll do another year at Queen's. Make yourself Dr McCullough with it.'

'No, Andy. No, I'm all right.'

'What'll I do with it? I can't give myself a scholarship. I'm too old. They didn't have the Eleven Plus when I was passing through the Northumberland Street school. Anyway, she cursed me to hell. "The fivers can light the fire," she said.' Andy waved the money across the hearth and the brass rail.

'Give it to me,' Lena cried out at him. 'This isn't anybody's money, give us it! We've earned this piece of scratch rearing your fleabags.'

There was double desperation on Lena's face – that they would lose the fivers in his hand to the fire, and that her grabbing his wrist would be seen as greed, robbing the grave.

'Come and help me make a cup of tea,' said my mother. 'You can hide the money from him in the kitchen.'

Andy waved his empty hand in the air, reached up the other and turned, throwing his palms down on the mantelpiece to weep full-faced into the fire.

'Christ,' said his father. 'Christ, you'll burn your bloody coat off.' Then his father's own head fell down between his hands.

'When my mother went she weighed a ton. Alice is as light as dust already,' said my father, whom Lena liked and who was burly and open with everybody. Two funeral attendants lifted the coffin off the polished wooden horses and set it on the bearers' shoulders. Andy's height knocked the rest out of step.

The other men fell in behind the hearse and Lena stepped into the lead limousine, another Humber. She didn't object that they hadn't put her there as principal female mourner, but to be shot of her while they set up the sweetmeats in the cluster of kitchen houses on the corner belonging to the McCabe and the McCullough families, or that they forced me to ride chaperone with her. I was ducking my head as I climbed in. I sat half bent, inspecting the fold-down seats and other gadgetry.

The women in the doorways wouldn't give Lena the benefit of their attention. Tear-tangled, lingering stares were trained down the street at the brasswork and the flowers choking the chrome railings on the hearse's roof. The immaculate black of Lena, in bellboy hat and veil, nagged me. Her skin shone beside me; mine, in my grey suit, reddened, my right arm hooped with its mourning band.

As we turned the curve at the bottom of Northumberland Street, circled past the back wall of Andrews' flour mill and Northern Spinning and Weaving, I dared a more direct look at Lena. Her lips were perfect, her legs, everything, for this one trip to the graveyard. She swallowed my mangled admiration and leaned toward me.

'Men always have to be up to something other than what they should,' my mother told Lena once. 'A woman's job is to show them *should*.'

But hadn't Lena done that?

'It wasn't wrong,' she said. 'It's the best suit I've ever had. He didn't even notice. Not a word out of him about where his winnings went.' She looked at me and lifted her hand to my armband. 'Barney, can you give me a kiss?'

'Why?' I asked, trembling beside her at this wish of mine turned into her request.

'Just to let me know that I'm not dead and sent to the City Cemetery myself,' she said. 'Her curse has put him up there in the hole with her already.' She pointed ahead at Andy and the coffin tilting and tossing like a shipwreck.

The driver's ears were locked away behind the sliding windows but his eyes came and went from the rear-view mirror. How did we appear to that chauffeur who knew nothing about us?

And what did I know . . . ? Goodness that goes unrewarded, lets in the badness. My mother never did thank Lena for leading me in the direction of church, to the altar where I shared in Holy Communion, not matrimony, with her. Any word of appreciation was always withheld from her – even by me, out of shyness or lust. And walking by, Lena spent Sundays learning how beauty in Belfast is a curse that needs to be covered up after marriage, because plainness is holiness. And the one true church – the dismal company of other married women.

Past my uncle's, then ours, past the windows of the neighbours' row, houses with the men standing rigid to attention and the women with their arms folded in the doorways, whispering the niceties of memory required for an old neighbour, Lena rode beside me, dressed up better than she ever was of a Sunday, with never a compliment to record her going. The men's clumsy and ornate efforts to please their wives and other dowdy women were still denied her. Through the smoky mourning curtains, even their sly appreciation of her figure was tugged away with a leer, like another pair of knickers Lena never knew she wore.

It was terrible for her. To be done up to the nines and then have her desire to be adored stripped bare, while under quilts and curlers the pudgy torsos of her peers stayed tucked in and treasured, twisted away under the layers of irritations at little details, a million petty neatnesses they paid attention to about the house in compensation for what Lena possessed and they did not: glamour.

The chauffeur couldn't have heard my raving but he must have seen the sudden thrust of intimacy; my tongue following hers, then bolting back into platitudinous chatter after breaking through the shining trap of her teeth. The limousine jerked forward. Lena turned her face away. Rewarded with this outrage of affection, it had hardened into certainty and closed off, her beautiful anger as marbled and remote as her mother-in-law's tomb.

She watched the tow dust swirl from the Northern Spinning and Weaving mill, where she had worked as a girl, pursued by the fingers of love-struck apprentices and managers. The dust fell on the shining black of the limousines behind, aiming to dull even the glittering passage of the dead.

THE FLOWERING

Éilís Ní Dhuibhne

Lennie has a dream, a commonplace, even vulgar, dream, and one which she knows is unlikely to be realised. She wants to discover her roots. Not just names and dates from parish registers or census returns – those she can find easily enough, in so far as they exist at all. What she desires is a real, a true discovery. An unearthing of homes, a peeling off of clothes and trappings. A revelation of minds, an excavation of hearts.

Why she wants this she does not know, or knows only very vaguely. It has something to do with a general curiosity and more to do with wanting to know herself. Why is she as she is? Why does she look this way? Why does she like some things and not others? Do some things and not others? If she knew which traits she inherited from whom, and those which she did not inherit from anyone, surely she would be a better judge of what she is herself or what she can become?

When she begins to ask these questions she becomes excited, initially, then dizzy. The litany of queries is self-propagating, it grows and grows and there are few satisfactory answers. And the longer it grows, the more certain is Lennie that the answers are important. The promise, or rather the hope, of solutions glows like a lantern in the bottle-green, the black cave of her mind, where Plato's shadows sometimes hover but more often do not make an appearance at all. Drunk on questions, she begins to believe that there is *one* answer, a true, all-encompassing answer that will flood that dim region with brilliant light for once and for all, solving all mysteries. The final solution.

17

Of course when Lennie sobers up she knows, above all, that that is impossible. The only thing she has learned about the truth – she believes in its existence, that is her one act of faith – is that it is many-faceted. This is as true of the past as it is of the present and the future. Knowledge of the ancestors would not tell her all she needed to know in order to see herself, or anything, clearly. But it would provide a clue or two.

Clues. To them. There are a few. Place is one and a strong one. The same place for hundreds of years, if popular belief holds any veracity – the documents suggest that it does. Wavesend. Low hills swoop, black and purple and bright moss-green, into darker green fields. Yellow ragweed and cow parsley decorate them. Royal red fuchsia, pink dog roses, meadowsweet and foxgloves flounce in the ditches that line the muddy lane leading down to the shore. Leonine haunches of sand roll into the golden water of the lough. Golden lough, turquoise lough, indigo lough, jade lough. Black lough, lake of shadows. The shadows are the clouds, always scudding across the high opalescent sky. The terns, the oystercatchers, the gulls swoop into those and their own shadows, after shadows of herrings, shoals of shadowy mackerel. Shadows on the other side of the shadowy looking-glass of the water.

The house of stone, two storeys high, with undersized door and windows squinting like small eyes in the grey walls. Cross-eyed, short-sighted house, peering at the byre across the street – the name they gave the farmyard. A cobbled path brings people limping there to milk the cows or – if they are women and usually they are since cows are women's work – go to the toilet. The milk bounces into wooden buckets, the other flows through a neat square hole into the stinking green pond. The midden. A ridiculous word which always made Lennie laugh. Piddle, middle, midden. Riddle.

Inside, dark is relieved by bright painted furniture. The blue dresser displaying floral tea bowls, willow-patterned platters, huge jugs with red roses floating in pinky-blue clouds on their bellies; the jugs came free, full of raspberry jam, that's why there are so many of them. A special clock, known as an American clock, with a brass pendulum and a sunray crown. Red bins for corn, layers' mash.

The stuff of folk museums. Lennie gets it from textbooks (*Irish Folk Ways*) and from exhibition catalogues as well as from her own memory. The exhibited model and the actual house overlap so much that it is difficult to distinguish one from the other now. In her own lifetime – she is in her thirties, neither young nor old – real life has entered the museum and turned into history. A real language has crept into the sound archives of linguistics departments, folklore institutions, and faded away from people's tongues. In one or two generations. In *her* generation. It has been a time of endings. Of deaths, great and small. But this she finds interesting rather than painful. She was, after all, an observer of life in Wavesend, someone who had already moved on to other ways of living and speaking before she came to know it and its ways, before she grew to realise their importance. She was never really part of the Wavesend way of life and so she was not confounded or offended by its embalming and burial while some of its organs still lived on, weakly flapping like the limbs of an executed man. Saddened she was, but not bewildered.

Other clues to her past are folk-museum stuff, school history stuff, too. The Famine. Seaweed and barnacles and herrings for dinner. A bowl of yellow meal given to a tinker caused her immediate death – ate the meal and dropped dead on the hot kitchen floor, glory be to God, she hadn't eaten in a month, the stomach couldn't take it. Lennie's ancestors had yellow meal and seaweed and barnacles, so they survived, or some of them survived. What does that tell her about them? The litany goes on: O Mother Most Astute, O Mother Most Hungry, O Mother Most Merciful, O Mother Most Cruel. Give us our gruel. The

Lennies turned, became Protestant, and later they turned back again. Some of them went to America and later came back again. A U-turn it's called. What that tells U is that U are a survivor. Is it?

Wolfe Tone passed by the house on his way to France. Drugged. Red Hugh passed by the house on his way to Dublin. Drunk. Lennie's great-great-great-grandmother saw the ship and waved. Hiya, Wolfie! We're on your side! (Forget chronology. It doesn't reflect significance, usually.)

The Great War. Artillery practice on the shores of the lough. The guns' roar reverberated across the night-still water. Boom. Men stirred in their heavy sleep. Boom. The baby woke up and howled. In the daytime soldiers visited the house to buy milk and eggs. So were they friendly? Did they chat? Did one of the girls fall in love with one of them? They gave Lennie's father a ride in a car. His first car ride. That's the sum total of it. It must have been exciting, Daddy! It was. It was.

A personal experience tale: when Daddy was seven he fell off a bike, a man's big bike that he had been riding with his legs under instead of over the crossbar. Ten months in hospital in Derry followed the experience. The wound on his leg would not heal. Home, with the abscess, to live or die. Philoctetes. Folk belief: the miracle cure. A holy stone from the holy well, the well of Saint Patrick, was taken by his grandmother. You shouldn't take stones from shrines or ancient sites of worship, from open-air museums, but people did not know that then. She took the stone home with her and placed it on the wounded spot, and the next day she took the stone back again. The wound healed. He always limped but he was healed by whatever was in that stone. And what was it like in hospital for ten months all alone? Not a single visit for the little seven-year-old boy. Not a single visit. He forgets. He doesn't remember it at all. Perhaps he cannot afford to remember.

It's enough to drive you crazy. Archaeology, history, folklore.

Linguistics, genealogy. They tell you about society, not about individuals. It takes literature to do that. And since the Lennies couldn't write until Lennie's grandparents went to school, and not very much after that, there isn't any literature. Not now, anyway. The oral tradition. What oral tradition? It went away, with their language, when the schools started. Slowly they are becoming articulate in the new language. Slowly they are finding a new tradition. If there is such a thing as a new language or a new tradition. Do you have to invent them? Like you have to invent history? Invent, discover, revive? You too can transform yourself. Must transform yourself. Utterly.

Sally Rua was Lennie's great-aunt. A tall girl with long dim hair and green eyes and a mole on her chin and two moles on the sole of her right foot. Gentle sometimes, sometimes sharp and impatient. She lived in that house in Wavesend, slept in the bedroom at the back of the house with the window that has to be propped open with a stick and the green wardrobe with cream borders that her own father made for her. In the mornings she went to school in the low white cottage beside the church; the rest of the day she was engaged in all the busy activities of the house. Baking and boiling, feeding and milking. Teasing and carding and spinning and weaving and knitting and sewing and washing and ironing. And making sups of tea for the endless stream of callers. Rakers, they called them, those who shortened the day and the night and stole the working time. A hundred thousand welcomes to you. Just wait till I finish this skein.

When Sally Rua was thirteen a lady from Monaghan, a Miss Burns, came to Wavesend to open a lacemaking school there. The Congested Districts Board had sent her and her brief was to teach twelve likely girls a craft that would help them supplement their family income. The craft was embroidery. The people of Wavesend, and Miss Burns too, called it 'flowering'. Twelve girls, including Sally Rua, assembled in a room in the real

21

teacher's house, which had been kindly lent to Miss Burns. There she began to teach them the rudiments of her craft.

Miss Burns was thirty-six, pretty and mellow, not sharp and cross like Miss Gallagher, the real teacher who was lending them her room. She wore snow-white high-necked blouses with a dark blue or a dark green skirt, and her hair was fair. What they called fair. Leafy brown, fastened to the nape of her neck in a loose bun. Her face was imperfect: there were hairs on her upper lip, quite a little moustache, and Sally Rua thought that this softened her, made her gentler and more pleasant than she might otherwise have been. More cheerful, more enthusiastic about her work of teaching country girls to embroider.

The atmosphere in the chilly room where they worked around a big table was light-hearted. An atmosphere of well-aired orderliness, appropriate to the task in hand. It had less to do with the embroidery, or even with Miss Burns, Sally Rua thought, than with the fact that boys were absent. This resulted in a loss of excitement, of the difficult but not unappealing tension that tautened the air in the ordinary classroom so that no matter what anyone was doing they were vigilant, aware that extraordinary things were going on all the time under the apparently predictable surface of lessons and timetables. Here in the single-sex embroidery class there was none of that; only peace and concentration.

The first thing they learned to work was a rose. Sally Rua had sewn the clinching stitch and severed her thread by the end of the first day, although most of the other girls spent a week completing the project. By then Sally Rua could do daisies and shamrocks, and had produced a border of the latter for a linen handkerchief. She worked at home as well as at the school on her embroidery, gaining extra light at night by placing a glass jug of water beside the candle, a trick Miss Burns taught them on the first day. (She had also told them that a good place to store the embroidery to keep it clean was under the pillow, unless they happened to have a box or a tin. Nobody had.)

22

'You've already learned all I'm supposed to teach you,' said Miss Burns at the end of the week, smiling kindly but with some nervousness at Sally Rua. She had encountered star pupils before and was not afraid of them but there was always the problem of what to teach next and the suspicion that they knew more than the teacher already. 'You could stop coming here if you liked. You can already earn money.'

Sally Rua did not want to stop coming. She was finished with her primary education now – the flowering was by way of finishing school. The prospect of spending her mornings sitting outside the house at home, working alone in the early light and being called upon to do a thousand and one chores, was not immediately appealing. She'd be doing it soon enough, anyhow.

'Maybe you can show me how to do that?' She pointed at a large piece of work lying on the table. It was a half-finished picture of a swan on a lake. Miss Burns had drawn the picture on a piece of paper and pinned some net to the paper. Now she was outlining the shape of the swan with stitches.

'That?' Miss Burns was confused. 'You won't be able to do that. I mean, you won't be able to get rid of it. The board wants handkerchiefs, not this type of thing.'

'What is it called?'

It was Carrickmacross lace: appliqué. Miss Burns, who came from Carrickmacross, or near it, was doing a piece for her sister who was getting married in a few months' time. The 'picture' was to form the centrepiece of a white tablecloth for the sister's new dining room.

Sally Rua offered to finish it for her if she showed her what to do, and after some deliberation Miss Burns agreed to this, although it was not strictly ethical. However, Sally Rua continued to do her roses and daisies and was earning twice as much money as any of the other girls already, so the aims of the Congested Districts Board were not being thwarted completely. And Miss Burns was finding the swan tedious.

It was slow work. Sally Rua spent over a week completing

the stitching, which looked anaemic and almost invisible against the background of its own colour. Then the paper behind was cut away. Miraculously, the scene came to life, etched into the transparent net with a strong white line.

'It's like a picture drawn on ice,' said Sally Rua. In the centre of the hills behind Wavesend, which were called, romantically but graphically, the Hills of the Swan, was a lake, the habitat of several of those birds. Every winter it froze over; the climate was colder in those days than it is now in Donegal. The children of Wavesend climbed the hills in order to slide. Sally Rua had often done that herself and had seen crude pictures drawn on the ice with the blades of skates. Once, she had seen something else, a swan frozen to the ice, or rather the skeleton of a swan, picked clean by other luckier birds.

Miss Burns gave her cloth and net to do a second piece of appliqué. She allowed her to make her own pattern and suggested a few: doves, stags, flowers. Sally Rua drew some foxgloves and fuchsias in a surround of roses, and this was approved of. It was a complicated pattern to work but she managed to do it. Miss Burns said she would send the piece to a shop in Dublin that sold such embroidery, and gave Sally Rua more material. This time she did a hare leaping over a low stone wall. There were clouds in the background and a gibbous moon.

'It's beautiful,' said Miss Burns, 'but I'm not sure . . . It's very unusual.'

'I've often seen that,' said Sally Rua, who had never seen a stag or a dove and had already done the flowers. 'It's not unusual.'

'Well,' said Miss Burns, 'we'll see.'

The shop in Dublin wrote back three weeks later, Miss Burns's last week, and said that they liked the appliqué and were going to send it to Chicago where it would be on exhibition at the Irish stand at a great fair, the World's Fair. They enclosed a guinea for Sally Rua from which Miss Burns deducted nine and a half pence for the material she had supplied.

24

'You should buy some more net and cambric with some of that money,' Miss Burns advised. 'The address of the shop in Dublin is Brown Thomas, Grafton Street. Do another piece of that Carrickmacross and send it to them. You are doing it better than they can do it in the convents.' And she added, because she was a kind and an honest woman, 'You can flower better than me now, too, you know. You should be the teacher, not me.'

Sally Rua, who had known she was better than Miss Burns on her first day's flowering, took her teacher's advice. She walked seven miles to Rathmullan, the nearest town to Wavesend, and bought some yards of net and cambric. She created appliquéd pictures of seagulls swimming on the waves of the lough, of an oystercatcher flying through the great arch at Portsalon, and of the tub-shaped coracles her father and brothers fished from. Each of these pictures was dispatched to Brown Thomas and for each of them she was paid ten and sixpence, half of what had been paid for the first, and, it seemed to her, inferior piece. She heard no more about that or about how it had been received at the World's Fair.

The time required to do the appliqué work was extensive, and in fact it did not pay as well as the ordinary flowering. Sally Rua continued to do a lot of that, although she did not particularly enjoy it. However, she could turn out a few dozen roses or daisies a week and that was what the merchant who called to the school in Wavesend every Friday afternoon wanted. For every flower, she received four and a half pence. The money formed a useful contribution to the family economy, and so the aim of the Congested Districts Board was fulfilled and Sally Rua's life settled into a pattern that she found rewarding: flowering and housework by day, appliquéing (and some other forms of entertainment) by night. She was happier than she had ever been before.

It did not last. In September, Miss Burns had left Wavesend

25

and the lacemaking school had stopped. In March – six pictures later – Sally Rua's father and two brothers were drowned while fishing on the lough during a storm. When the wake and funeral were over and the first grieving past, the practical implications of the disaster were outlined to Sally Rua by her mother. She could no longer afford to live on the farm at Wavesend unless her daughters went out and earned a living (the only son, Denis, was married himself). The flowering would not be enough. Sally Rua would have to get a real job, one that would support her fully and leave some money over for her mother.

She went to work as a maid in a house in Rathmullan, the house of the doctor, Doctor Lynch. She was the lucky one; Mary Kate and Janey, her sisters, had to go to the Lagan to work as hired girls for farmers. Sally Rua's polish and her reputation as a skilled needleworker ensured that she had the better fate.

The house in Rathmullan was a square stone block on a low slope overlooking the roofs of the town. It was called The Rookery because it was close to a wood where thousands of crows nested. Sally Rua's room was in the attic, of course, at the back of the house, above the farmyard and with a view of the trees and the crows which she would have been happier without. It was a small, cold room, but she had little time to spend in it. Her days were long, hectic rounds of domestic and farm routines. The Lynches kept other staff, but not enough, and there was always something to be done.

At first Sally Rua was not unhappy. Mrs Lynch was a reasonable woman who wanted her servants to be contented, if for no other reason than she would get more out of them in that way. She spoke Irish to them since she knew they preferred it, and also to her children, because really she felt more at home in Irish herself, even though the doctor, from Letterkenny, did not speak it and wished English to be the language of his household. That did not matter; he was not often at home and never in the kitchen where Sally Rua spent most of the time when she was not in the byre or the dairy. When she described her life in Rathmullan to her mother, whom she visited once a month, she painted a picture of a calm, contented existence.

This description began to change after about three months. Sally Rua, speaking in a voice that had become low and monotone and should itself have been a warning to her mother, said she was troubled. Her mother, legs parted to catch the heat of the flames, looked at her anxiously, shook her head and did not pursue the matter. Sally Rua, lying that night on her high bed in Rathmullan, watching the shadows of the giant oak trees gloom across the floor, wept. She told herself she was stupid. She told herself she was sad. She told herself she was miserable, lonely. What she was missing was the house at Wavesend, her sisters, her friends. Her mother. That is true. Homesick she was. She had been homesick from day one. But what made her cry with misery and frustration was the way she was missing her work. Her real work. The flowering.

She had hoped at first that there would be some need for that here. That Mrs Lynch would ask her to make some antimacassars for her big armchairs and sofa, which could badly do with them, or runners for the dressing tables and sideboard. After about six weeks she realised that such requests would not be forthcoming. There was plenty of needlework to be done in the Lynch household all right, but it took the form of mending sheets and underwear and nightgowns rather than of anything elaborate. Sally Rua was expected to spend every night working at the linen closet and wardrobe of Mrs Lynch and her daughters. She had been employed chiefly for her skills in this line, the other work she spent twelve hours a day doing was simply thrown in as a little extra.

There was, of course, no possibility of doing embroidery in her own room during her spare time, simply because she had no spare time. Every minute in the Lynch household that was

27

not spent sleeping or eating had to be devoted to Lynch work. The only free time she had was one Sunday a month, the Sunday she spent visiting her mother. She did a bit of flowering while she was at home, occasionally. But a few hours a month were insufficient. There was never time to get even one flower finished, never mind a whole picture.

Sally Rua got more and more miserable. She also got more and more cross. She snapped at the other maids and at the lads in the yard and even at Emma and Louise, the daughters of the house. Gradually her personality transformed and she became renowned for her bad temper as she had once been renowned for her skill at the flowering. She became so crotchety that sometimes on her day off she did not go to Wavesend at all, but wandered around Rathmullan, staring at the ruined abbey, at the boats moving across the lough to Buncrana, and at the seagulls wheeling over it. She stared at the crows who built their nests in the high scrawny trees that surrounded the Lynches' house. Once, on a winter's evening, when the moon was a full white circle behind skeletal trees, she saw a hare on the fence that divided the garden from the bog. Its coat of fur was brown and gold and yellow and purple, streaked with odd white patches. It had a small white bun of a tail. Never had she seen a hare at such close quarters. She was so near that she could see its tawny eyes gazing at her and its split, trembling lip. For minutes she stared and all the time the hare stayed as still as the fence it sat on. Then something happened. A twig fell, a scrap of cloud shadowed the moon. And at that same moment the hare and Sally moved. She bent, picked up a stone, and flung it hard at the hare's white tail. Before she had touched the stone, before she had stooped to the ground, the hare was gone, bounding over the moonlit turf at a hundred miles an hour.

A few days later Sally screamed at Mrs Lynch. Mrs Lynch had simply asked her to make a white dress for Louise's confirmation and had suggested that she do a little embroidery on the cuffs and collar. It was the first time such a request had been made. Daisies, she suggested, might be appropriate. Sally Rua had taken the material, a couple of yards of white silk, and thrown it into the fire. She watched it going up in flames without a word or a cry and then, as Mrs Lynch, having got over her shock, began to remonstrate, she picked up all the cushions and tablecloths and textiles that were lying about the room (the drawing room) and pitched them on the fire as well. At this point she began to scream. This helped Mrs Lynch to regain her presence of mind and she ran for help to the kitchen. John, the hired man, and Bridget the cook (all cooks are called Bridget) caught Sally Rua and pinned her down to the sofa while someone was sent for the doctor. There was a certain gratification in imprisoning Sally Rua in this way; it was a slight revenge for all the abuse she had heaped on them over the past months.

There was no lunatic asylum in Letterkenny then, as there is now. What there was was a poorhouse with a wing for the unsound of mind, and that is where Sally Rua went. Later it became a lunatic asylum and she experienced that, too, for two decades before her death. She reached the age of seventy-six and was completely mad for most of her life.

Sally Rua. She went mad because she could not do the work she loved, because she could not do her flowering. That can happen. You can love some kind of work so much that you go crazy if you simply cannot manage to do it at all. Outer or inner constraints could be the cause. Sally Rua had only outer ones. She was so good at flowering, she was such a genius at it, that she never had any inner problems. That was the good news as far as she was concerned.

Sally Rua. Lennie's ancestor.

Of course none of that is true. It is a yarn, spun out of thin air. Not quite out of thin air – Lennie read about a woman like Sally Rua. What she read was in a history of embroidery in Ireland, about a woman who had gone mad because she could not afford to keep up the flowering that she loved and had to go into service in a town house in the north of Ireland. The bare bones of a story. How much of that, even, is true? She might have gone mad anyway. She might have been congenitally conditioned to craziness. Or the madness might have had some other cause, quite unconnected with embroidery. The son of the house might have raped her. Or the father. Or the grandfather or the hired man. People go mad for lots of reasons, but not often for the reason that they haven't got the time to do embroidery.

Still and all. The woman who wrote the history of embroidery, an excellent, an impassioned book, which would be cited if this were a work of scholarship and not a story, believed that that was the cause of the tragedy. And Lennie believes it. Because she wants to. She also wants to adopt that woman, that woman who was not, in history, called Sally Rua, but some other, less interesting name (Sally Rua really was the name of Lennie's great-grandmother, but what she knows about her is very slight), as her ancestor. Because she does not see much difference between history and fiction, between painting and embroidery, between either of them and literature. Or scholarship. The energies inspiring all of these endeavours cannot be so separate, after all. The essential skills of learning to manipulate the raw material, to transform it into something orderly and expressive, to make it, if not better or more beautiful, *different* from what it was originally and more itself, apply equally to all of these exercises. Exercises that Lennie likes to perform. Painting and writing, embroidering and scholarship. If she likes these things, someone back there in Wavesend must have liked them too. And if someone back there in Wavesend did not, if there was no Sally Rua at all, at all, where does that leave Lennie?

THE GARDEN OF EDEN

Éilís Ní Dhuibhne

In the end Eric simply said, 'I am going.' And Carmelita knew what he meant.

'All right,' she replied. She had been waiting for this announcement for twelve years. She had feared it, postponed it, protested against it, and also – at other times of course – wanted it, craved it, paved the way for it. Now – this now, this minute, sitting, appropriately, at the kitchen table (*ad mensa* . . . what's the Latin for 'at'? she wondered idly), it was nothing but a bald fact, like the sun that shone on the lawn outside, like the marigold in the window box, like the wine glass of water on the blue checked cloth.

Eric stood up, leaving a little food on his plate, and went upstairs. Carmelita sat gazing absently out the window. The laburnum was dropping black pods on the yard. The lobelia had withered. A few montbretia bloomed, with their characteristic brilliance, in the euphemistically named rockery, but mostly the garden was on the wane. Middle August, and hardly a thing left in it. After nine years in the house. And garden. Eric usually did the latter. The split would be mainly *ad hortis*, actually, she thought calmly, pleased to remember this word, if not its cases. He'd never done anything much at the table except eat the food she'd cooked.

She considered the garden next door, as she often did. It was the horticultural *tour de force* of the neighbourhood: tender velvet lawn, bright but not gaudy borders, shrubs in all the right corners, flowering or leafing in a happy sequence of colours, scents and textures. Patio, arbour, roses clambering over trellis, geraniums in great carved terracotta pots. A conservatory. Carmelita envied them, those next door. She coveted that garden. She craved it passionately.

Eric popped his head in and said, 'I'm off now. Goodbye!'

His heavy step sounded on the hall floor. The door opened and then shut slowly and sadly, but firmly.

Carmelita stopped thinking about the garden next door. She got up and plugged in the kettle and made a cup of tea. When it was ready she carried it out to the garden, her own garden, and sat down at the table there. A white plastic table with a green sun umbrella and a few odd, mismatched lawn chairs surrounding it. She sat and looked at her shrubs, her flowers, her trees, and the sky. Evening in middle August. The sky, the little bit of western sky she could see, was pale pink. The sun had already disappeared behind the roofs of the houses on the next road.

The summer is over, well and truly over, she thought. A dreadful last-rose-of-summer sentiment of loss and bereavement overwhelmed her for a few minutes. But she did not wallow in it; she waited for it to pass, because she was so accustomed to it. Periodically, every year from about the tenth of August to the beginning of September, she got her last-rose-of-summer depression – she was very sensitive to seasonal cycles, like a lot of women who live in suburbs. The beginning of nice ones, like spring or summer, brought jubilance. The end of nice ones – and there is only one season that really ends – seemed like a great tragedy that experience exaggerated rather than assuaged. And in August it seemed much more over then, much gloomier than in September, which had its own character and self-confidence, which was the beginning of something again, even if it was something not very good. School, frost, long, dark nights.

Carmelita and Eric had been married for twelve years. Oh

yes, how time did fly. It seemed that no time at all had passed since their wedding. Since that time of being in love with Eric. There is no time as far as the emotions are concerned, perhaps. On the other hand it was aeons ago; its trappings belonged to history. That ceremony in the registry office in Kildare Street. The drinks afterwards in Buswells, with everyone dressed up somehow. The bridesmaid in white pants and a navy striped T-shirt had looked odd, certainly, Carmelita could have killed her, but most of them had made a respectable effort with flowery dresses and hats. Outmoded. Dated. Ancient.

Eric had been as always: smiling broadly, jocular and in full control. He was smart and quick-witted, Eric. She had basked in that, in his protection. He was never at a loss. His decisions were almost invariably the correct ones. And he never regretted them, as a matter of principle.

The decision to get married had not been his, of course, but hers, and her decisions were frequently wrong she had found out as her life progressed. Usually they were irrational whereas Eric's would as a rule be the opposite. It had seemed terribly necessary to marry him at that time twelve years ago, though. She had been pregnant, but that was not why. It had seemed necessary before the pregnancy, which was an effect, not a cause, of the need. Marriage to Eric had seemed to be her only salvation, the only course open to her in life. Life without him, she thought, was unthinkable. She would die without him, she would wither up and cease to exist.

And indeed her expectations had been fulfilled. Marriage had brought happiness and activity. Life had been full as a tick, it ticked all day, all night, there was never a moment's idleness. She had been so busy, so very busy, for several years. So busy that she had not time to consider whether she was happy or not. Now she knew she had been happy during that hectic time. Not having time to think of it, that had been her happiness, it seemed. Not having time to bless herself.

Now she was not busy any more. The garden was empty before her eyes. Friday evening, she had the weekend free, three nights, two whole days, for herself.

She walked over to the fence dividing her garden from the Garden of Eden. She did this every night, because the neighbours were away on their fortnight's holiday in Greece. There was a broken place on the fence – God knows how they had let it remain broken – over which she could peer and get a perfect view.

The first sight of it broke upon her like a peaceful oriental vision. There was a quietness in this garden, partly because it *was* quiet, there was nobody in it, but in greater part born of its perfection. The greenest grass. The fluid forms of the bushes. The pale pinks, yellows, lilacs of the flowers. It was in no way a busy garden, although it required much business to achieve the effect it created. Like a beautiful, rich room upon which endless attention and expense had been lavished, it looked natural and spontaneous.

Eric had driven off in the car. She had heard him starting it, she remembered, just after the door shut. He was possibly far away by now. The thought that there was no longer a car crossed her mind, like a slight shadow, and disappeared. Who needs a car?

She began to climb the fence. It was not easy because it was a thin Swedish fence. But it was not difficult because it had wires attached to it, a bit of broken chicken wire up which she had once tried, futilely, to grow woodbine. She swung herself over the narrow top and jumped onto the pale red paving stones of the patio next door.

At first she stood and looked around at everything she had seen so often from the other side of the fence: the palm and elephant grass just where the patio met the lawn; the green hose lying on the slabs; the pots of deeply pink geraniums all around. She breathed deeply and perfume from mignonette, honeysuckle and escallonia filled her lungs, along with a headier, more intoxicating air: something like incense.

She walked slowly along the lawn. The greenness of it soaked into her skin, she could feel her body absorbing it. It was like swimming softly, breaststroking through a long aquamarine pool. Or through a cloud. Although, naturally, she had never swum in a cloud. She sat on the grass for a minute. It was dampish. She could feel the wet seeping into her skirt. A ladybird came and crawled along her leg. It was a great year for ladybirds. All the gardens were infested with them.

She stayed there for a long time. Then she got up and left, using the same route and technique she'd employed in entry. Before she left she cut three slips from the pink geraniums, which looked like hot, fluttering butterflies resting on a turgid foliage. And when she got to her own side of the fence she potted the slips in terracotta plastic pots, in peat moss, and put them on the windowsill to root. She had heard from a woman she'd once met on a plane to London that stolen slips did best.

She went to bed. The house creaked a lot. Some doors banged because a window was open. She thought about burglars. She believed in burglars, but her image of them, like her childhood images of God and the devil, was vague. They were male, they would break glass, they would burst into her bedroom and . . .

Lulled by such creaks and bangs and ideas, she fell asleep.

The next day would have been long and empty had she not decided in the morning that she really must go shopping. So she took the bus into the city centre and spent the whole day walking around the shops, trying on clothes, examining furniture and rugs. Time passes very quickly in town and she remembered the Saturdays of her youth, her later youth that is, when she had lived with her mother and had had her job, the job she still had. Shop after shop, garment after garment. Bought, worn a few times, discarded.

She bought a white linen suit. And a bag of peaches. And a packet of incense sticks. And several small terracotta pots.

That evening she watched television and cut three slips of

escallonia in the garden next door. She burnt the incense, thinking how Eric hated incense or anything that seemed cheap and eastern, like curried eggs and the novels of Hesse and Indian rugs. She drank some red wine but it was sour, as it usually is if you buy a cheap bottle in a supermarket, and she couldn't take more than one glass.

Her thoughts were less of burglars, as she lay in bed, and more of the past. Not the past with Eric, which hardly seemed like past. But of her childhood, of her teenage years which seemed, in retrospect, serene and carefree. She also thought about her slips and planned the future of her garden. Every mickle makes a muckle, she thought, and eventually it will look like theirs next door. Patience is a virtue.

Carmelita was not an especially patient woman and on Sunday she went to a garden centre and bought a palm tree and a blue hydrangea (she'd never fancied the pink) and came home and planted them on the back lawn. And that night – after dark – she stole a large carved terracotta pot from the garden next door. But for the time being she put it in her bedroom where the next-door neighbours were not likely to see it.

That night as she lay in bed she thought of the next-door neighbours. They would not have seen the pot if she'd put it in the hall or the living room, she thought, because they did not visit her house. The reason was that she and Eric had had such fearful rows in the year or two after the accident. Carmelita had been given to screaming loudly in the middle of the night. She used to accuse Eric of all kinds of awful things: not caring about her, letting her waste her life, never doing any housework, not fulfilling her. She had ranted and raved and sometimes Eric had hit her. Battered. She had been a battered wife, according to a certain point of view. In her own estimation, in retrospect but even at the time, she could justify Eric's hitting her. They always say they've been provoked. But in his case it was, she suspected, true. Anyway, invariably she had hit him back and not infrequently she had hit him first. They had been like two boys scuffling in the school playground.

Except that the sound effects were higher pitched and more alarming. They heard. It was so embarrassing for them and for Carmelita. She hadn't wanted to speak to them. She didn't speak to them, or have cups of tea with them, or invite them in for a drink on Christmas Eve. It had all stopped long ago. There was no noise, no screaming. No fighting at all. But the pattern was set. No neighbourliness. No visits.

Lulled by these thoughts, she fell asleep.

The next morning was Monday and she was supposed to get up and go to work. She worked in a bank. She was a cashier. It was not as boring to her now as it had been when she'd started it; she enjoyed saying hello to the customers, she liked to be nice and friendly and make them feel at ease, which is not how most people feel in a bank. And also she had grown, over the years, fond of her colleagues and of her salary.

But this morning she did not go to work. She got up at the usual time of eight o'clock, went down and had her coffee, but when the time for leaving the house came she did not go. Instead she went into the garden. She examined the slips: none of them had withered so far, which she took to be a good sign. Now she had fuchsia, escallonia and geraniums on the go. She climbed over the fence and looked around. The garden next door looked even more wonderful than usual in the early morning light. The fresh, clean sunshine, the unsullied air of start of day, suited its own spic-and-span, cared-for character. It was in its element.

Carmelita walked all around it, simply admiring. She no longer felt any envy or covetousness, she realised, and supposed it must be because she knew that soon – or at least eventually – she was going to have her own beautiful garden. As beautiful as this. Or more beautiful? No. Just the same.

What would she take? She remembered that they were due home the day after tomorrow so her time in the garden was

37

limited and she would have to choose exactly what she wanted now. She looked at dahlias and lupins and tea roses. Broom and rose of Sharon and a shrub she did not know the name of, that had greenish-reddish leaves and huge fluffy red balls. She looked at elephant grass and marram grass and cordyline.

In the end she cried, 'Ah!' Because she saw it. Just exactly what she had wanted all the time. How odd that she had not seen it before, how very odd.

In the corner of the patio, propped up against the wall, a small tricycle belonging to the youngest child next door: there were three children, two girls and a boy. The boy was the youngest. He was four and this was his bicycle. She grabbed it and let it down over the fence as gently as she could. Then she climbed over herself and carried the tricycle up to her bedroom where she put it on the floor just beside the bed.

After the accident all Raymond's things had been given away. Absolutely everything; Eric had thought it was better that way. It was all as bad as it could be, they didn't need reminders, he had said, packing the toys and the clothes and the things, Raymond's things, into boxes for the travellers who called to the door every Saturday, regular as clockwork. There were the photographs, of course, but only in albums. None out on the sideboard, none displayed with the other photographs on the mantelpiece. They had to get over it. They had to forget.

She lay in bed for a while, thinking about her slips and glancing at the bicycle from time to time. Then she searched in the drawers of Eric's desk for the albums. She selected three of the nicest pictures, showing Raymond at one, three, and seven and a half, just after he'd made his First Communion and just before he'd died. She propped them up on her dressing table where she could see them at night before going to sleep and in the morning as soon as she awoke. She'd get some frames for them later. Later today, or maybe tomorrow, or maybe she'd ask Eric to get them.

Because of course he was going to come back. They always come back, Carmelita knew, unless . . .

And Eric came that very night, because he'd rung the office and she hadn't been there and because he couldn't cook and for various other reasons. His decisions were usually rational, Eric's, and usually correct, and he hardly ever regretted them, on principle.

THE LOANEN

Michael Carragher

Packie Balfour squatted in a corner of the field away from the loanen and hummed a tuneless air with uncommon violence. He reached into a pocket and took out the pouch of tobacco and papers, rolled and gummed another cigarette and lit it. He didn't smoke much as a rule and the tobacco was dry and dusty since he had last been to a public house, and he had neither ear nor liking for music. But he sucked on the skinny cigarette relentlessly, and coughed and hummed until his throat was sore. The tobacco would not stay lit but that was no great drawback – the opposite, in fact, as long as his matches lasted. He knew that the heifer was fretful and trying to settle, and to be able to stay quiet for her sake and to concentrate on the job in hand would have mightily pleased him.

But there were men beyond the hedge, waiting in the loanen. Packie cursed under his breath. All day he'd been cursing softly, with no real spleen, but by now his wry patience and good humour were deserting him. Men behind hedges were not to be laughed at, not after dark, not in south Armagh.

At first he'd assumed that a routine army patrol had stumbled upon him, so he coughed and struck up a match and a tune to advertise his presence and prepared answers to the questions they might ask him. If he was challenged he had nothing to hide. He was an honest man, a farmer who couldn't choose his working hours nor tell his heifers when to calve. He did know Foxy Murphy, certainly, but only to say hello to. He hadn't seen the man in years and didn't care if he never saw him again, as long as he kept his eyesight.

Then he recalled that there had been only a distant hum of helicopters in all the hours since he'd left home. That suggested that it might be 'the Boys' instead, especially as there had been some activity about Murphy's place.

But it could always be the SAS. The SAS kept none of the rules honoured loosely by the common soldiery. Not for them the decent warning of the helicopter descending in a roaring swirl of wind and dust and belching frightened squaddies from its belly. No. Them lads could lie out like bullocks for weeks at a time, eat stones to sharpen their teeth, and catch rabbits better than dogs could. And like rogue dogs after sheep, you never knew where they'd turn up.

But whoever it was that was lurking in the loanen, soldiers or IRA men, Packie was too close for comfort, and could not get away. His lips twitched mutely as he cursed the Provos and the army, the heifer for coming to her time just now, and the scrub-bull for serving her nine months before. Then he cursed his own stupidity for not having properly dressed that calf and his folly for not having brought the heifer back to the home farm when he'd known her time was near. But he'd been busy with the harvest and had assumed or hoped that she would not calve till it was saved. He'd hardly thought it necessary to bring the rope and torch and other things, and had been made feel almost foolish by his fastidiousness.

His day's misfortunes had begun when the van broke down, a sorry victim of neglect. He'd had to trudge across the shoulder of the mountain to the outfarm on the Ballinoga back road, and Packie was slow with age now and soft with upholstered van seats. What's more, the breakdown had caused knock-on delays, so that the evening was well advanced by the time he got away, taking to the fields and then to the heather when his own lane petered out above the house, until the rocky upper reaches of Caipín Dubh's loanen began to lead his steps downhill and give his legs and lungs a break.

Then, as his bad luck would have it, he fell in with the Poet

Flanagan pushing his bicycle, and he raised a martyr's eyes to heaven. For the Poet was an odd oul' eejit and Packie resigned himself to putting up with long-worded, windy nonsense for the remainder of the trek to the road. Not that the Poet was anything but a civil, harmless craythur. A smart fella too, a mass o' brains. He'd been on the television once and spoken very well, and though it had been double Dutch to Packie, the audience had clapped and there'd been professors and various breeds of clever men and women there. But for all the good the brains did him, his head might as well have been full of mad dog's shite. Personally, Packie was convinced that he had too much brains, which could be just as bad as not enough. Who but an *amadán* would live in that forlorn shanty on Slieve Brackan, with neither chick nor child to share it, when he could have a nice wee council cottage in the town? And of course the drink was a curse on the poor fella too. He'd been in and out of dry dock in St Luke's for years. He was more to be pitied than laughed at.

The Poet said he was going to Crossmaglen.

'Headin' in for the few pints, Poet?' Packie said agreeably.

You'd swear he'd asked if he was going in to rob the wine from off the altar. The Poet stopped so suddenly he all but fell over his bike and threw the two hands up at the sky in horror.

'Perish the thought, Packie! Never, never, never again. After the last skite I vowed against the loathsome stuff and may the gods forsake me if I be forsworn', the hands going good-o the whole time, of course, as though the flies were at him, long bony fingers raking through the wild grey hair as he described some of the sufferings he'd gone through.

'Oh no no no no no! I am indeed going to an alehouse, Packie, but there I shall have nothing stronger than Perrier' – whatever that might be. 'The committee has asked me to give a reading as part of the south Armagh festival.'

'Oh?' Packie stole a glance at his companion. A quare-looking tulip, wouldn't ye think, to be going anywhere except a circus. All he was short of was the greasepaint. The head was like a hoarfrosted whin bush, he hadn't stood very close to the razor, and the rigout he was decked in would put you in mind of a flag on a short pole. If you met him on the street you'd give him a penny. 'Oh,' Packie said again, 'that's ah . . . that's very good, Poet.'

You couldn't even talk about the weather to the Poet. Yet Packie tried. 'Grand spell o' weather, Poet.'

'I quite agree, Packie. The gods are well disposed. We must give thanks to the Great One who sustains us all when the harvest's home.'

Wouldn't ye think by the crack he had a field full o' gods to keep great with? He must be some class of a Protestant now. Packie didn't know a great deal about Protestants, beyond that they didn't believe in the One True God, had harvest thanksgivings in September and said that Our Lady was a whore and Christ himself a bastard – God forgive them! And that was enough for Packie. Civil enough craythurs, mind, the few of them he knew, and he said the odd prayer for their conversion. But a man could never trust them.

He cast another sidewise glance at the Poet and tried again. 'Another good day the morrah,' nodding westward.

That really wound the Poet up. He went on and on about the colours and the shadows and reflections, and the miracle the sunset was, and how privileged they were to see it. Privileged, note. A miracle, no less! As if the same sun hadn't been rising and setting every day since God was a *gasún*.

'Right enough, it's lovely,' Packie agreed, glancing towards the spectacle above the Cavan hills.

The Poet didn't seem to hear. He actually stopped the bicycle and stood to watch the last rays die, and only that Packie had been well brought up, he thought he would have walked on and left him standing there like a stoogie. Eventually the Poet fell into step but he looked so woebegone that Packie felt obliged to cheer him up.

'Sure ye'll see it again the morrah night, Poet.' By the look he got, you'd think that it was *his* head was cut.

That was almost all of Packie's input to the clever bullshit that passed for conversation. The Poet could keep crack with a haggard of sparrows and was supposed to be powerful value with a few drinks in him. But sober he'd put years on a banshee. The constant chatter and the enormous words got on Packie's nerves. He interrupted gladly when they passed the only other house along the loanen, and saw the open door.

'Is yer neighbour home, Poet?' he asked with heavy irony.

Foxy Murphy hadn't been in south Armagh for years, except on very fleeting visits, and it was known that the house was used for unquestioned purposes from time to time. After escaping from Long Kesh in 1975, Murphy had lived for some time in Dundalk. Later, after the SAS began their cross-border raids, he fled further south. Since then he'd fallen foul of the *gardaí* as well, and it was rumoured that even some of his erstwhile comrades were against him now, alarmed by his maverick recklessness and the flurries of security that slipstreamed him and threatened their own activities. He lived on the run all the time, snatching a night's sleep here and a day's rest there, with whoever there was left who would shelter him.

'I know little, Packie, and I care less.' The genteel accent slipped a little under the weight of contempt. The Poet was no lover of men of violence and made no secret of the fact. He'd written a poem once, 'Two of a Kind', about an SAS man and a Provo, spitted head to head over the same fire in hell, condemned for all eternity to meet each other face to face, as impotent as their victims had been. It was a powerful poem. Packie had heard it. An English singer had put it to music and made a record, but it had displeased a lot of people. Certain radio stations refused to play it because it was supposed to be an insult to the upholders of law and order, and many shops were afraid to sell it because it was supposed to be an insult to the Provos, so that it all came to nothing. A pity, Packie thought. It might have made the Poet a bit of money.

And that finished that attempt to escape from the daftest oul' codology about . . . whatever it was that the Poet was going on about; dust and volcanoes and stars, and things that had happened back in Oul' God's time, with the Poet blatherin' away as if he'd been around at the time and seen it all with his own two eyes.

'Probably the sister in,' Packie muttered by way of epilogue. Sorcha Murphy maintained the house, she said, against the day that her brother would be free to walk his own land without fear of the ancient enemy or of traitors and collaborators.

But there was no car at the road.

It was a good thing, after all, that he had come prepared. The bones had slipped the whole way and he wasn't an hour in the field when the heifer put out the bag. Packie investigated with hard, tough, gentle hands. Through the membrane he could feel the jellied hoofs and behind, the muzzle with the tongue inside the mouth. So far, so very good. But they could still have quite a way to go.

Time, like the calf, moved slowly. Restlessly the heifer roved, seeking sometimes the shelter of the hedges, other times the latitude of the field. Thus the last of the twilight's afterglow gave way to darkness and Packie waited patiently until he heard the surreptitious movements of the watchers in the loanen, and he began to smoke and hum and rehearse his answers.

The night was dark, the field almost as lonely as the stars the Poet imagined he'd seen born. It was a lonely old life he led, Packie reflected wistfully. It would be nice, at such a time as this, to have a strapping big son to wait up with a sick beast, or even a small grandchild at whose fear of the darkness he might laugh, and thereby lose his own fear of the skulking men behind the hedge. But any regrets for his bachelor's barrenness were, like his desires, no more than dull aches now. It was the will o' God. Packie felt a sudden surge of shame and guilt. Who was he to be rearing up against that? He took out his beads and said the full fifteen decades of the rosary. It passed the time. He might be in the field till dawn and after it, because the half-castrated rig had been a Charollais-cross, and Charollais throw big calves, and the heifer was still an undersized yearling. He prayed that the wee craythur wouldn't get too much hardship.

Inexorably, the heifer's labour slowed her down, though for long she fought off settling. Even when she did so she could not seem to decide whether it was better to stand humpbacked with extended tail, or lie awkwardly down. After the bag burst, Packie investigated again. He was pleased enough by her progress, though he wished she had settled somewhere else. She had chosen the shelter of the hedge that marched along the loanen, behind which he had heard the watchers. Packie listened again, now. His matches were all gone but the torch batteries were still strong. The troubled panting of the heifer and the beating of his own heart seemed to be the only sounds. He held his breath. No stir of life came from the loanen. He let the breath out in a gusty puff. The watchers must be gone.

There was a thump as the heifer dropped to the ground, then a soft scraping noise as a painfully outstretched hoof tore up thin turf. Packie switched on the torch and approached her from the rear. He heard her grunt, and then, with a surprising sud- denness, two tiny, shiny hoofs sprouted like wet buds. The heifer groaned and laboured. Packie dropped the torch and took a rope from his pocket, got onto his knees and slipped a loop around each foot, reaching inside to place it high up on the foreleg. He tightened the loops carefully, took up the slack in the rope and waited for the animal to push again.

46

An alien sound intruded, mumbled conversation from the road. No, a single voice singing drunkenly – 'Take me for a night in Dundalk . . .' – a send-up of a song sung on the wireless. Packie nodded cynically. God help head-o'-wit – the Poet had broken out again. Though come to think of it, it didn't sound like him. The voice was a thick, slurred, south Armagh brogue, and the singer was on foot, with no clicking freewheel to betray a supporting bicycle.

Surely it could never be . . .? No, Foxy couldn't be staying at home – could he? If he was, and the watchers were SAS men. . . Packie strained once again to hear sounds from the loanen when the singing stopped. There were none. If it was Foxy, he could be the luckiest man in the country. Unless, of course, the watchers had been friends of his . . .

'Take me for a night in Dundalk, take me for a night in Dundalk . . .' the tuneless voice began again and went on monotonously. It was closer now, almost at the foot of the loanen. Suddenly it broke off in a mad bellow, 'Take me drunk, I'm home!' The heifer flinched nervously. The singer roared hilariously and repeated, 'Take me drunk! I'm home, I tell ye! Somebody take me drunk. Somebody, take me, take me!'

The heifer flinched again. I'll take ye by the throat if I lay hands on ye, ye noisy bollocks, whoever y'are. Aloud, Packie soothed the heifer: 'Sook-sook-sook-sook, poor wee pet.' It mightn't be Foxy at all, it might be someone else entirely, someone who lived further along the road. But for the life of him, Packie couldn't imagine who that might be.

The calf was well into the world by this time. The head had been born. It was going as well as Packie could have hoped. The drunk lapsed into silence again, and quickly receded from Packie's immediate awareness, and whether he was the Poet or the Provo or another ceased to matter. Packie tensed with the heifer and pulled as she pushed, and half a yard of new life slid into the world. It balked at the loins. A good pull now could finish it, but the kidneys could be a tricky spot too. Packie waited for the heifer in his role as nature's servant.

Into a cranny of his consciousness slipped a dull, heavy sound, as of a body falling. It came from the loanen. Was it Foxy or the Poet? A mumbled curse, and then a shout, from only a few yards away.

'Divil shoot ye for a moon! If it was a bright night ye'd be there!' And then the bray of a lunatic laugh.

God's curse on ye an' the moon. Would y' ever shut up! But the heifer seemed to be beyond distraction now. She moaned in pain and uncomprehending fear, her head twisted round to look at the man and what was happening to her. The whites of her eyes were wide in the misdirected beam of the torch lamp lying on the ground. Packie heard the voice, low, slurred, indistinct. Whose was it?

The heifer shuddered, clamoured in pain. Packie heaved on the rope, and the calf seemed to move a little. But the contraction quickly passed, and the heifer drooped in exhaustion.

An unaccountable worry took hold of Packie then. Something wasn't right. He checked the calf. It was alive, and seemed vigorous and healthy. Could it be the heifer that he might lose? Surely not. She'd had an easier time of it than she had any right to expect. She'd lost little strength or blood. Surely she wasn't going to die on him at this stage? But an instinct born out of a lifetime of daily communion with the earth insisted that something was terribly, terribly wrong.

Suddenly there was a deafening report, close at hand – beside him. Packie gasped in fright. The heifer startled, tried to scramble to her feet, in vain. She bawled again, her bass note rising to a thin high pitch of panic. Her body convulsed. Packie, as terrified as she, but only slightly less a captive to her confinement, tugged blindly on the rope. There was the sound of another gunshot. No short, sharp rifle crack, nor the dry wicked rattle of machine-gun fire heard in local skirmishes from time to time. This was the devastating, ear-splitting anger of a shot-gun. Packie shouted in horror, calling in a frenzied aspiration to the Mother of God. The heifer almost screamed. Her hoofs scrabbled on the turf. Something gave a little. Packie lost his footing. His heels skidded on the slippery grass behind her, but his hands held fast to the slimy rope, and as he tumbled back-wards there was a warm wet sluice and the calf was born.

The shotgun thundered again.

He pressed himself flat to the ground, reached for the torch and switched it off. He raised himself a fraction to feel for the muzzle of the calf in the darkness, and wiped the mucus from its mouth with hacked and blunted fingers. He waited with a different sort of anxiety until it breathed, and then sank back onto the ground, exhausted, shaking, drained. The heifer rested for a moment too, then grunted as she staggered to her feet. She turned to nuzzle the strange, wet, silent, hardly moving thing between her and the man. The calf raised its head slowly, still dazed by its trauma. It moaned throatily. The heifer replied. She lost her hesitancy, licked her calf.

Packie began to recover, though terror remained master of his emotions. Still he trembled. Still he prayed, but silently now, to Our Lady and his Guardian Angel to deliver him safely this night. But a lifetime's practices and generations of hunger as-serted themselves. He fumbled in his pockets for the raw egg, cushioned in newspaper, and the oatmeal. He shredded the soggy insulation, knowing that the egg had smashed. He scooped the sticky remains into one hand as best he could, and wiped the pulpy, shelly mess into the mouth and closed it, massaged the shivering gullet until he felt it convulse. He scat-tered the oatmeal over the damp body, but the heifer was not in need of encouragement. 'Good wee craythur,' almost aloud.

Only then did he approach the hedge, stealthily, apprehen-sively, the torch in one hand, still unlit. There had been no more sounds after the third gunshot, but when he was close to the hedge and silent he could hear phlegmatic, ragged gasping, and he knew that somebody was dying.

And now he felt an altruistic worry more than concern for danger to himself, dread more than fear, and it was this dread –altruism that made him run to the gateway onto the road, and then along the road, the torch beam zigzagging on the mossy tarmac. He slowed slightly when he came to the loanen, but out of respect for its broken surface rather than fear of anything he might find there, and he quickened his pace when the beam picked out the prone form on the ground.

Rage fought with pity for a place in Packie's heart. The poor unfortunate harmless eejit. God damn the bloody bastards! The silver hair – what was left of it – had told him who the victim was, but that would not have mattered. He would do the same for the Provo or a stranger in an army uniform. They were all somebody's rearing, all children of God, all entitled to enter God's glory if they repented at the end and made their peace. Incredibly, breath still rattled in the throat, and gory froth bubbled in the nostrils, but a glance was enough to tell that the body was destroyed beyond all hope of salvage. All that remained was the soul.

He tore the rosary beads out of their purse and dropped onto his knees. With ungentle urgency he grasped the bloodied hair and raised the shattered ruin of a head close to his lips. The stench of scorched hair and brains and cordite rose like a miasma to his nose. He swallowed back his gorge. He pressed the image of the slaughtered Saviour to the slack red lips of the dying man, and as the catechism had instructed, intoned into the deaf ear, 'O my God, I am heartily sorry for having offended Thee . . .'

Of the killers, not a sign remained.

PASSING THROUGH BOMBAY

Daphne Glazer

Sushila lifted the lid of the gold and ivory box and removed a Black Russian cigarette. She gazed at the gold tip, fitted it into a tortoiseshell holder and then flicked her gold lighter. Inhaling, she stared out at the brown sea. It was August, almost the end of the monsoon. She rose and went to the window to get a better view and stood gazing down at the scrawl of waves. Two women in tattered saris were walking along the thin rim of sand. They didn't look up at the frontage of those prestige flats.

So, he would come. She inhaled again. Her right hand shook. Distractedly, she examined her scarlet nail varnish which was chipped at the edges. Lulu, her favourite Pekinese, a mothy bundle of cream feathers, tried to nestle between her feet and almost made her stumble.

'Lulu . . . you baby!' She stooped and scooped her up, trying to keep the cigarette away from her. The dog's black eyes bulged like moist marbles. She whimpered and exposed two fangs. 'Steady, steady, sweetie, but don't get under my feet.'

In anguish she turned now to examine her sitting room. Perhaps the answer lay in the French table with its scatter of gold boxes, silver and crystal vases, bowls of rose quartz and jade, the rugs, the lacquered furniture and the low divans. It was as though she were surveying the room as a stranger might. She had long since ceased to see the individual items.

'Passing through Bombay . . .' the letter had said, '. . . a sudden urge to see you.' There were things she wanted to think out, but it seemed impossible. A headache throbbed over her

51

left eye. What should she do? If she rang for her maid, what should she tell her? Which sari should she wear? Scarlet Benares silk? For a moment she saw the picture of a lissom eighteen year old with wide-open, dark eyes, a scarlet mouth and new-fashion, shoulder-length bobbed hair. Some of the excitement, the intoxication, fought through her muzzy head.

The letter lay on the table. She put the dog down and picked it up, so as to scrutinise the flamboyant pen strokes; black ink on thick white paper. 'Passing through Bombay . . .' Thank heavens he would not arrive until late afternoon – she needed time. Should she wear the diamond necklace, or the simple pearls? She must take a long, luxurious bath and prepare herself, rub her skin with sandalwood oil.

But things circled continually. Bobby and Samson, Lulu's brothers, growled ominously at each other; the sea heaved far below and in it she seemed to see massive water serpents, twining and elongating themselves. The sky was puffy with heat and moisture. She ought to have been at the monsoon palace, watching peacocks dancing in the rain . . . and not here.

She sat down again on a divan. A long grey tooth of ash had formed on the cigarette. It trembled and fell as she reached for her glass and drank. There was a small burn mark on her pale pink sari where hot cigarette ash must have fallen at some time. The muddle intensified.

She stroked Lulu's head. 'Sweetie, there, there, mm.' She let her face rest in Lulu's hair and smelt the dogginess. The others pressed around her toes and whined.

What on earth was she to do? She ground out the cigarette in a crystal bowl, bending its black stalk in the middle. Perhaps she should send a servant to the astrologer, her adviser. Panditji might tell her to perform a puja. But there wasn't time. She thought of Panditji in his white shirt and loin cloth, legs folded in the lotus. He had seen the scintillating white beam of Krishna. He knew. Really she was in a dreadful state. She took a swallow from the glass and reached for another cigarette.

The sea serpents twisted and writhed up. The sky bulged and became the colour of sulphur. Down on the beach hawkers passed. Of course she had seen his face in the *Times of India* on many occasions over the years. He was one of India's leading polo players, a playboy and an aesthete. He had a fine head and big brilliant eyes, was six feet tall.

In the bridal procession there had been two hundred elephants, who had set off months earlier from Bodrapur, whilst he, Shakti Singh, Maharaja of Bodrapur, had travelled up to Patrapur by private train with five hundred retainers. India's most expensive wedding, the newspapers had trumpeted. Her mother had sent away for two hundred chiffon and silk saris for her trousseau, and shoes and matching handbags from Ferragamo in Florence. The *mousseline de soie* nightdresses had come from Paris. Sheets and towels also from Florence.

Drifting through veils of memory, Sushila summoned her maid; she was to run a bath. While she lay in the sweet-smelling water she returned over three days of preparations: the bath in perfumed oils; her fingers massaging turmeric paste into her skin; the prayers and the twenty-four-hour fast before the marriage ceremony. As a bride, she had made her special prayers to elephant-headed Ganesha . . . and then the endless wait. And yes, the anticipation. Music had mooed and vibrated through the palace from conch shells, reed pipes and drums. Sushila watched the water pearling over her legs and it seemed to her that she could actually hear the thin-drawn notes of the pipes and see the benign head of the elephant god nodding at her. All the married women had twittered about her, painting her insteps with henna, holding up the heavy scarlet and gold silk of the sari, slipping ivory bracelets onto her wrists and the gold jewellery studded with rubies and pearls.

The dream floated on. Outside the palace gates they were distributing alms to the poor. Prisoners were being released. The entire palace was lit by thousands of earthenware lamps filled with ghee. The white leaping flames shed weird shadows.

And then the cannons thundered. The Maharaja of Bodrapur was arriving on his elephant at the palace gates.

How had she felt? She rose from the sunken bath and wound herself in a fluffy pink towel. Lulu and the others were whining and scratching to come in and periodically she heard their staccato yaps as one bit the other in irritation. She ought not to have dismissed the servant responsible for looking after them. 'Darlings,' she muttered, 'darlings.' She took another drink from her glass as she slipped into a satin robe and padded into her white and gold dressing room.

Shakti Singh's driver manoeuvred the Silver Shadow round munching-cow islands and shoals of scooters. Women's saris floated in the monsoon wind. Taxis horned. Bullock-carts stumbled and banged. All pulled aside in deference. Policemen blew their whistles and halted the blaring, raucous flood and then it broke loose. In the air-conditioned interior Shakti Singh was untroubled by the sultry day outside. Bicycles, motor-rickshaws and scooters surrounded the car for an instant and were then lost. He hardly saw them. For thirty years he had held her in his memory, his beautiful young bride. He had been forever seeking her image.

In the beginning they had sent him her photograph. She posed awkwardly, a very slim, elfin girl with a pointed face and huge dark eyes. There was in them an almost wistful expression, as though she were waiting for something miraculous to happen. It was that wistfulness that had intrigued him. She was said to be one of the most beautiful women in the world. Strange, strange how in their horoscopes the gunas had matched. All the omens had been auspicious, preparations had gone ahead. He was bathed in waters from the holy rivers of India. The mantras were chanted. He could almost hear their rhythmic cadence. Ghee and grain were sacrificed in the fire and rose in salutations to the gods.

Oh, what a triumphal entry it had been, with the band

playing and the troupes of girls dancing, then came the swaying elephants and clopping horses and finally he himself and his retinue. With regal slowness they had all passed up the long drive. Fireworks burst in silver and gold rain on the dark night sky. He experienced a fierce exultation at the memory. The drumming and the full-throated, dithering lilt of voices, the tinkling of bells and the hiss of exploding fireworks wove together, and he remembered whole sequences of those days. Seven days of feasting, of rituals. He saw her in her sari of scarlet Benares silk, with her eyelids lowered. She was achingly beautiful, more beautiful than he could ever have imagined. He thought of Parvati, the entrancing consort of Lord Shiva. Like some image of Parvati she had sat on the silver palanquin and was borne by her male relatives into the courtyard.

Later had followed the long train journey back to his estate, which she had to make in a purdah carriage with her ladies. He sat with his friends, other royal princes. For five hours the train had rumbled onwards and he had dreamed of the coming bridal night, and of his wife, the new Maharani of Bodrapur, and in between had talked of polo and horses, had laughed and drunk pink champagne and now and then played bridge with the princes. Refreshments were served on thals. Feasting and supping champagne, they travelled, and the wheels of the train thrummed as it snorted through miles of farmland and villages and scrubby, barren plains.

The driver turned into Sea View Road. On their right the biscuit-coloured sea squirmed; facing the sea were high white blocks. So that was where she lived. Suddenly Shakti Singh felt breathless. His heart throbbed. Why had he come? He was no longer a young man. But as the years had melted away, he had returned with increasing frequency to the thought of her unattainable flesh. And then there had been the dream, the dream in which he had gone searching for her and had at last come to a closed door that he knew he must prise open. She had been sitting on a throne with her back to him, and he, crying with joy, was about to rush up to her and look into her face, when he had woken up. It was then that he had determined to visit her.

'Stop here, please.' The driver drew up at the kerb. Shakti Singh emerged from the car's cool interior to the sticky Bombay heat. For a few seconds he stood staring at the sea.

Now they were approaching his palace with its white marble verandas and scalloped arches supported by slender pillars. The white onion domes stood out in the navy-blue sky. Palm trees guarded the entrance and lined velvet lawns. Veiled, she had moved through the courtyards with their fern-fringed pools.

He braced himself for the meeting, and turning, rang the bell. After he had given his name, the door swung open and he entered the lift, alighting on the first floor. A maid opened the door to him and he was ushered into a large white room facing the sea. He had expected, as in the dream, to find her sitting on a throne, but instead he saw a spread of divans upon which innumerable creatures appeared to be dozing. Now they had cocked up their ears and were regarding him with belligerent little black eyes. Some even snarled. And the air was laden with undertones of a harsh animal odour, something damp and canine.

From a chair in the far corner an elderly woman rose. Her mouth was a violent red gash in her tea-coloured face, but it was her eyes that really shocked him. They were dark and hectic, set in spiky lashes like spiders' legs and the flesh beneath them looked bruised and bilious. She was swathed in a red sari that had a broad gold border.

'Hah,' he murmured, trying to cover his discomfiture and wondering what might have happened to Sushila. 'The monsoon is almost over . . .' He seemed incapable of finding anything to say.

'Yes,' she said, 'yes. What would you like to drink? Champagne, perhaps?'

As she said it, he saw the slight, shrouded figure entering the palace. He smelt the intense pungency of white jasmine flowers. The diaphanous sari suggested areas of exquisite pleasure. There was a milky moon above the palm spears.

The woman's eyes winked at him in an ugly, knowing way. Some of the dogs growled and the sound gurgled in their throats.

'Shush, shush, Lulu – that's very naughty. Not with Mummy's visitors. No, not with visitors – very, very naughty.'

She rang a brass bell and the maid came.

'Madam?'

'Will you take champagne, then?'

'Thank you,' he said softly, though he would rather have drunk tea.

At the sound of his voice the lapdogs yowled and one of them leapt from the satin cushions and bowled up to his feet and began to snap at his trousers.

'Lulu, you naughty, naughty girl.' The woman swayed across the room towards him and caught up the venomous little creature. The dog's eyes bore a similarity to those of the woman, he registered.

The maid brought the champagne on a silver salver and offered a glass to him.

'Cheers!' he said, and their eyes met across the room. He sensed areas of frenzy and madness and looked away to the coils of slumbering livestock on the cushions.

'How many . . . er . . . dogs do you have?'

'Twenty,' she said, animation entering her voice for the first time. 'My pride and joy is Lulu, but I must say she's very badly behaved, aren't you, sweetie?' The little dog yawned, showing a curled pink tongue and white spiny teeth.

Sushila was trying to hide the wild surging of her mood. So many single frames passed before her eyes that she felt dizzy. He was standing before her in his jewel-encrusted dhoti and wearing a shining turban. At his side was his great sword. The

Maharaja of Bodrapur – and this was her husband. Perhaps they would be together on the journey to his kingdom . . . But no, the purdah carriage waited, and hours and hours of tension and boredom. She was a modern young woman who had been educated in England and gone to finishing school in Switzerland. She swam, rode, hunted, played badminton and tennis. The palace was a vast white building, glowing under the moon. Lights twinkled everywhere. Cannons fired a welcome. A fountain tinkled into a marble basin. Grecian statues reared up on plinths. It promised much.

Her wedding night. The ladies led her to the women's wing. She entered the zenana. Where was the maharaja? They would prepare her and lead her down a maze of corridors to him. What if she lost her way in that labyrinth of two thousand rooms?

She asked him about his work as an MP, for since the title of maharaja had been abolished he had begun a new life. She knew it all from the newspapers and television. He talked.

Dressed as she was in one of her fragile nightdresses and veiled in chiffon, she was conducted by the women on the journey to his wing. From behind the carved purdah screens she glimpsed the polished marble floor of the great hall far below, and the gigantic chandeliers seemed almost within touching distance from her. Terror and excitement choked her chest.

The calm voice went on, endlessly detailing. He finished his champagne. She rang for more. Her head reeled.

His bedroom was empty. Well, she must wait. One hour, two hours. The ladies delayed their departure. Life was suspended. People stifled yawns. Where was the maharaja? At the billiard table, they said, with friends, celebrating at the billiard table. That was a region which no female might enter. At the billiard table.

After the passage of two and a quarter hours she rose from the divan and silently indicated to the women that she would retire to the zenana and sink deep behind the fortress of purdah, never to reappear. For an awful moment, uncertainty flickered in her. What if he had already waited for her and then left?

'So that is how it is,' he was saying. The years had turned his hair from raven to ash and his body had thickened, but not unpleasantly. Charm beamed from him. Here was her handsome bridegroom, returned from his game of billiards to find her after thirty years. Old rapture tingled in her as she sipped another glass of champagne and smoked a cigarette from the gold and ivory box.

'Well,' – he seemed to emerge from a dream – 'I must go. You see, I just happened to be in the vicinity, so I considered it only civil to call.'

She seemed to start at that. He saw the claw of her hand with its ragged red talons convulsing on the creature draped upon her lap. It squeaked. He wanted to get away and could scarcely wait to leave that sour-smelling room behind.

On gaining the street, he got into his car and sank back, collapsing into the coolness. 'Bodrapur,' he instructed the driver. That was a whole day's journey away, but he didn't care.

He was at the billiard table, hearing the clink of cues on billiard balls, seeing the bright jade, and light glancing off intent men's faces. When might he decently go to her? Too quickly and they might jeer behind their hands. Another shot . . . Why must he always win? What an eternity as the cues struck balls and scores were announced. Just the circle of brightness and the waiting for the mystery.

The sea writhed and spumed on his right. Where had he lost her? Would the search never end? Monsoon and the peacocks sported in the rain. A time of love. As he fought to remember his beautiful princess the mad doggy eyes seemed still to be gazing at him from their spiky fringe. The two became indistinguishable; one overlay the other.

Sushila stroked Lulu's ears. 'You were very naughty to Daddy,' she whispered as she drew the cork from a fresh bottle of champagne. 'Very, very naughty. And now he's gone away to play billiards again.'

NOTHING TO OFFER

Daphne Glazer

On a day of strange reverberations Simon Johnson stood before the principal.

'Sit down,' the principal said. He was wearing a black suit and a white tie and his smell was expensive.

As Simon gazed at the other man's soft white hands he remembered Cathy Tremaine's remarks after the principal had first been appointed the previous year.

'God, his hands, did you notice? Little white hands. Did you see how they moved? You could imagine him . . .' And then she'd squawked with laughter in the way she did, leaving the men rather shocked.

'Well now, Simon, tell me where you see yourself in the plan of things.'

It was always first-name terms these days. The new style was instant intimacy, a winning of contracts, of confidence, an updating.

'Where I see myself?' Simon sat in his littleness, his V-necked heather-mixture sweater crammed under his tweed jacket. He gazed for a moment at his shoes. They had rims running round them like car bumpers – not quite in the same league as the principal's thin-soled, narrow black lace-ups. Words failed him. He never had been good at the dramatic.

'Yes. What have you to offer?' The grey eyes played pleasantly over him from behind the metal-framed spectacles.

'Er, I'd like to carry on as I have been doing, you know. After all, I'm a career-teacher.'

The principal's eyebrows shot up, he gave a short laugh and grinned. 'Career-teacher! Did you say you'd been teaching fifteen years at this college and you're still a Lecturer I?'

Simon continued to smile gently, though inside he was crumbling. Cathy would have known what to say, but he couldn't find anything in his own defence.

Somehow he waded through the next interminable minutes and then escaped upstairs, puffing as he climbed. He ought not to have been so breathless; after all, he played squash every week at the sports centre and managed a few laborious lengths up and down the swimming pool.

When he finally reached his own workroom he went to stand by the window. The place was empty. For a moment he surveyed the four desks all stacked with piles of course work to be marked and sheaves of memos from the head of department and other heads of section. They gave instructions about the writing of reports, the keeping and placing of registers, schemes of work, students' assessments – whole forests had been hewn down to produce those witterings.

His gaze lingered on Cathy's desk. In one corner several cracked and wrinkled copies of some Women's Press editions had been pushed in beside what looked like a carton of plain yogurt, some sticks of celery and a cottage-cheese salad that she must have bought prepacked from Marks and Sparks. The desk in its big carelessness was typical of her. He realised abruptly that he had been looking at her heavy colourless face and big aquamarine eyes every day for almost fifteen years. In fact he had probably spent more time with her than with his wife, Linda. Strange how the years had crept up on them. Fifteen years ago she had been wearing micro-miniskirts and bright T-shirts, no bra. Her shoulder-length hennaed hair had bushed out in great wedges about her face. He had stared through half-closed eyes at her endless legs as she draped herself about in intense conversation with some passing occupant of their room.

All sorts of liaisons had taken place over the years, he suspected. When she'd looked at Bill Brannagan in that exclusive way, with her eyes all inky pupil, he had guessed. Bill had long since cleared off and lots more, all worn out with trying to make their lectures on pollution and poverty in the Third World be heard above the effing and blinding of Gas Fitters II or Carps I. Occasionally one or other of them had been elevated to nice little admin jobs, where they sat in offices and had secretaries who smelt of hair spray and powder and underarm deodorants.

Then there'd been her arty phase – the tight blue jeans and black T-shirt or baggy black sweater and the Art Nouveau earrings with their aquamarine drops set in a fine thread of marcasite. That had been during the affair with Alan Cutts. She would come in at one o'clock after her morning in lieu, spreading an aura of sex about her which he had found very unsettling. Alan had sat at his desk, grey-faced and exhausted, talking about his ulcer or emigrating to riches in the US.

From time to time she had administered one of her questionnaires to him: 'Simon, what do you think Linda really thinks of you? Does she still love you? Would you go for a bit on the side if you thought nobody would find out?' She had that way of making you feel that if you were not strictly monogamous, you were a brute. And yet at the same time she'd be leaning over you so that you felt the shock of an unfettered breast or a slice of smooth thigh, and smelt her sweaty underarmpit odour – she didn't wear deodorant on principle, or shave her furry legs. He knew it all. Most women terrified him, and she both fascinated and appalled him. He had long suspected she would finish a man.

He usually spent his afternoon in lieu of his evening class at the sports centre, and in the foyer he would see the businessmen's wives, sun-bed beauties like roast Buxted chickens in leisure suits, toting Nike or Lacoste sports bags. Inside he would glimpse them again through half-open doors in electric-pink or icy turquoise body stockings, swaying and writhing in aerobics rituals. They were all bored, endlessly bored, waiting for the Saturday dinner-dance or barbecue, or the next love affair. His neighbour's wife was the same type too. He would wave to her nervously when he'd see her staring at him and gesticulating over the privet hedge and then he'd put his head down and get on with the lawn-edging so as to escape.

The day after the unnerving interview with the principal he felt oddly cast adrift, floating in dangerous waters. He turned to gaze out over the white stone charioteers and Britannia wielding her trident. The impassive face of the gigantic stone woman stared back at him knowingly. He could almost fancy that she winked a huge eyelid. Why, he wondered, had past sculptors placed statues on the tops of buildings where only giants would be able to see them? What an absurdity was looming everywhere.

At eight-thirty that morning he had stood looking at his face in the bathroom mirror, had straightened the knot in his tie, combed his wavy hair and thought: Not bad! He was used to his pointed, narrowish face with its blue eyes and the red veins across his cheeks and round the nostrils. Best V-necked sweater too.

There had always been a steadiness about him; he did the right thing. His kids depended on him, so did Linda. He could say, I love my kids. But he remembered those years of seemingly endless weekends when they were little and he couldn't even sit down to read a book because they must be entertained. Other people's lives had shown him awfulnesses: patterns that he must eschew. Linda's dad, a solicitor, had never been at home either evenings or weekends, and she had grown up expecting nothing of a father except his absence. Once his firm had gone bankrupt, he had died quickly of cancer. Simon had shared the parenting with Linda, everything together, and now . . .

The door behind him opened.

'Hi, Little Johnny!'

'Oh, it's you.' He spun round, smiling. Cathy had hung up her coat and was going to sit at her desk.

'Must get some lunch.' She was busy now, opening packages and prising lids off cartons. She liked food and ate hugely; he had watched her. When she reached the celery stalks he would want to jam his hands on his ears.

'Do you realise,' she announced, 'that this is the end of an era?'

'Yes, I was just thinking that before you came in. The principal's determined to split up the department.'

'All those years and years in here together.'

'Yes,' he said, and there flowed into him a sudden and irresistible urge to put his hand inside her 1920s slippery white blouse. He saw the poles of her legs. She wore camiknickers; he had once caught her showing them to a woman from Secretarial Studies. She would be massive of frame and cream-coloured with just pinkish, blunt-ended nipples marking the place where her breasts should have been. And then the heavy thighs, long and straight. A big hooking woman, with thick red lips and cool blue-green eyes. Some tawny lily with wide waxy trumpet. In her home, where bergère suites and cane chairs rested on blurred Persian carpets, he would let himself know enchantment.

She was chewing carrots and raw cabbage and spooning up cottage cheese which coated her lips white. The long stem of her throat contracted as she swallowed. Down she glanced with pleasure at the cottage-cheese carton.

'So what did he say, then, Simon?'

She expected nothing of him, he saw. He had answered her periodic questionnaires correctly, was a goody-goody; a nice, safe chap in front of whom she might hitch up her knickers and feel no embarrassment. At times she would deliver a heavy, playful swipe at him, if she happened to be in a good mood.

They might even wrestle a while – nothing too serious, because he had been he and she the woman who had shared fifteen years of groaning, hilarity, rage and boredom with him. It amused him to watch her as she continued to browse amongst the cartons, chomping, munching, wiping her mouth with the back of her hand, concentrating on her enjoyment, quite unaware of the change in him.

'Oh, he more or less said I'd have to go asking around in other departments – can't stay together, there won't be a department any longer for us.'

'Dreadful!' She was frowning now, and squeezing the cartons and paper bags together, she hurled them into the wastepaper bin, where they fell with a ping. 'Everything seems to be disintegrating.'

He shut off for a while, watching her lips; it was like gazing at a TV film with the sound turned down.

'So much disease . . . All those cancers around . . . Well, this girl in the . . . Leukaemia . . . You just don't know . . . Additives . . .'

When she had fixed her gaze accusingly on him, he tuned back in.

'Do you remember when we had those appalling storms in the winter? Well, my cousin and her husband were literally walled up in their house. Have you thought what would happen if there was a breakdown in public amenities? We'd have an insurrection.'

Her eyes were all black now with their pupils overflowing but, he recognised dimly, this was something else that he was witnessing.

'You get the feeling everything could fall apart very easily. You can imagine how it would be in a nuclear war. I've started stocking up my cupboards, you know, tins and things. Well you've got to.'

Simon's concentration shifted. The moment of decision was

postponed whilst the next two hours passed in the lecture room. But behind all he said, there still lay the pressure of his new awareness.

Back in the workroom, four-thirty.

'Thank God it's over,' she yawned.

He watched her stretch. The white silk blouse parted company from the Oxford bags. He glimpsed white satin – a button was missing on the trousers.

They descended the stairs together, side by side.

'I've stopped using the lifts. Well, I mean, you might get stuck. Anyway, it's much healthier to walk. A very unhealthy place this.'

Should he say: Cathy, as this is the end of an era and . . . let me come back to your place. Cathy, for fifteen years . . .

Her talk was returning to insurrections. 'And do you know, the girl had been aware of all this rubbing – you know, like someone stroking her arm – at the bus stop it was. And then – can you believe it – when she got off the bus, her coat was drenched in semen.'

Speechless, he nodded at her and made his way to the car park. She had declined a lift, saying it was healthier to walk. As he stood by his car he caught a long shot of her. She was walking with a curious gait, stiff down one side and flat-footed, in black plimsolls, her right shoulder lurching downwards under the weight of her stuffed shoulder bag, and her wide coat flapping about her. Her expression was heavy and preoccupied, and he saw how it was caught in a trance of disease and insurrection – whether from carcinogens or rapists or revolution, or the threat of nuclear war, he could not tell – but he drove home carefully, smiling slightly to himself.

THE LIGHTS OF A TOWN IN THE DISTANCE

Ciarán Folan

'I'm fed up telling people the bad in this relationship' is what Cathy says at some unearthly hour of the morning. She'd been talking about her life with Alan. She'd made no mention of anything very disturbing before this. There were none of the terrible revelations I've come to expect when people begin to open up, in that way they invariably do, in the small hours. But we'd been drinking and I suppose she believed she was saying something of interest. Or perhaps I just wasn't paying attention. I spent the time looking at her face and neck, imagining the whiteness of the rest of her body. And her sister Emer sat there, silent, and I wondered if she could realise what was going on.

It turns out that Cathy firmly believes Alan has been seeing another woman. He's been making a lot of trips to Dublin all through the winter months. Business trips of sorts. Cathy has no proof, but she has a feeling. 'And you know Cathy's feelings,' says Emer.

I met Alan once, a year or so ago, in the departure lounge of Dublin airport, when Cathy and himself were flying out for some kind of lovers' weekend in London. He was wearing a faded denim jacket and jeans and he had an earring in one ear. And although we did little more than exchange pleasantries after Cathy's bright-eyed introduction, it struck me that he was already elsewhere, working out an escape route to another life, perhaps.

'I don't know when we're going to see an end to Cathy's

unhappiness,' Emer says. This is how she usually brings up some story concerning Cathy and her life with men. There are many such stories.

Once, Cathy met a man while she was working in an Italian restaurant off Grafton Street. 'She must have known him for exactly the amount of time it takes to order a pizza and a cup of coffee.' Next thing Cathy was in London, ringing Emer, begging her to wire over one hundred pounds. That was in 1974, when Cathy was seventeen and a hundred pounds meant something. Emer managed to gather some money together to get herself over on the boat. She found Cathy in a place in Kentish Town. 'There she was in this kip with this sleaze-ball Arab.' It turned out to be a false alarm. Cathy wasn't pregnant like Emer thought she was and after a week of seeing the sights they both returned to Dublin.

Ten years ago Cathy took up with an acrobat. They toured the country in his brightly coloured caravan. Late one night, after he'd been drinking, he held a knife to her throat and forced her up onto the ladder leading to the tightrope. He told her he was God and that he could fly. Then he told her what he'd been trying to tell her for months. He was leaving this shit-hole country and going back to his wife and kids in Marseilles. 'Thirty feet above the ground, with a knife at your throat, is no place for feeling brokenhearted.'

In her late twenties Cathy fell for an estate agent she met in a Leeson Street nightclub. First he promised to dump his wife and their terraced Georgian home to 'set her up in a condominium in New York. She actually believed that for a year.' Then he said he would buy her a time-share in an apartment on the Costa Brava. 'In two years they spent four days in London and a rugby weekend in Paris.'

'Cathy attracts those kind of men,' Emer said once. 'It's some kind of masochism. I can't explain it.'

Sometimes Emer says she believes Cathy just has a very strong gallivanting streak. Sometimes she calls her a mad bitch. And Cathy is pretty. Emer has to admit that: 'I suppose that's part of her problem. But she's losing her looks. After thirty things start to go wrong with your skin.'

Now Cathy has moved to the country. She has taken a small house by a lake in the midlands. She lives there with Alan, whom she met when they were doing a ceramics course in Galway Regional Technical College some years ago. After graduating, they tried to get a business going in Galway city, but there was strong competition and they lost money. They wanted some place without many overheads or social distractions. Then Cathy remembered the lake houses. She had visited them as a child when they were 'white and gleaming by the waterside'. They had been built as potential holiday homes in the late sixties, but through one thing and another they never became viable. In recent years many of the houses had changed hands in quick succession. Nowadays, apart from a retired German doctor and his wife who live there all year round, nobody seems very sure who owns what.

Cathy and Alan are renting from a cousin of hers who spends most of the year in Dublin. They've fitted out an old boathouse as a workshop and Cathy has been working flat out, day and night, trying to finish a contract for the canteen of a local computer plant.

One day, out of the blue, Emer got a letter from Cathy to say that Alan would be spending most of August with his parents in England and wouldn't it be nice if both of us came down to stay. It was time we all got reacquainted, she said.

'Reacquainted is right,' Emer said. 'I mean, you know I haven't heard from her for almost a year.'

'Let's go down,' I said. We could bring the sailboards. We could swim and relax and do nothing for a few weeks. Besides, it would give Emer a chance to visit the places of her childhood.

'I want to see this country you're always talking about,' I said.

'Oh, I'm sure it's not anything like the place I remember.'

Sitting in the kitchen of Cathy's house late one evening, Emer talks about her father.

'The summer before Cathy was born Dad drove our Ford Prefect off the end of a pier out there on the far side of the lake. Mam used to say it was all the result of his drinking. But if you ask me it was other things as well. Anyway, he mustn't have been so serious about it. The water wasn't very deep and he managed to get out and up onto the shore. He sat there and waited for the sun to dry his clothes. He never got his shoes properly dried, though. He had to throw them out eventually. I think they must have taken the car out too but I don't ever remember seeing a Ford around the place. The first car I remember was a Volkswagen, a small black Beetle.'

I wait for Emer to finish this story, but the conversation drifts on to other matters and I sit and look out at the lake water as it glows and then slowly darkens.

The weather is too calm for windsurfing. All day the lake glints and refuses to stir. In the morning Emer and I go for long walks along the shore. One day I take a boat out and try some fishing, but it's too bright and the water is too clear to catch anything.

The next afternoon we row out to one of the islands and wander among the ruins of a seventh-century monastery. We have lunch, sitting on the grass by the water, and do our best to beat off the tiny flies that swarm in the heat. I try to get Emer talking about her parents. I want to know what happened back then.

'It's no secret. It's not something I'm trying to hide.' She twists a blade of grass tightly around one of her fingers and stares out into the shimmering distance. 'When I was ten and Cathy was seven, or maybe eight, my father just disappeared. Well, as far as we were concerned, he disappeared. Early one morning in the summer of 1965 he packed a suitcase and took off. Nobody had any idea where he'd gone to, although after a week or so people began to mention England or the States. For months, for the best part of a year, Mam contacted relatives on both sides of the family: in London and Liverpool and in Boston and New York and San Francisco. It was a terrible time. Every single day she cried quietly from morning to night. Eventually she stopped expecting news of any kind. Then she just gave up, in ways. As you can imagine, we had virtually no money. There wasn't much we could do about it, so after a year of this Mam sold the house and we rented a smaller place in town. But it wasn't just the money. It was people and the way they behaved and what they said. "I don't understand these people," she told me once. "How can they be so cruel? It's not natural." But it was natural. I've realised since that cruelty can come so naturally to people.

'Years later, after Mam had died, someone sent me a newspaper cutting from England. It was just this photograph taken at a union meeting of electrical engineers in Brighton. There was nothing else. And I knew, before I even examined that photograph, that my father was in it. He was right there in the back row, all dressed up and smiling, as if nothing had ever been wrong in the world.'

Emer stops and looks at me. 'I know you don't believe this.'

'It's a weird story.'

'It's a true story. It happened to us.'

Every morning the first thing I do is check for a sign of wind, but by early afternoon the same dull heat smothers the lake and soon the flies have risen in a fine haze across the water. Cathy spends most of the day in the shed. Wearing a T-shirt and shorts, she emerges late in the afternoon. She sits in the shade, drinking chilled beer shandy, staring out at the stillness.

'Oh, the dog days of my childhood,' she says, in her slow, languorous voice, 'when the midlands smouldered and vanished.'

72

Sometimes she lies on the back seat of the car, with all the doors thrown open, and plays tapes. She plays *Astral Weeks*, or early Bob Dylan, or, on particular evenings, any of those new batch of women country singers – Kathy Mattea, k.d. lang, Nanci Griffith. The sweet, whining sounds of these lovelorn country songs sends Emer into the kitchen, where she can be heard clattering about, pretending to be busy preparing dinner. Later in the evening we drink and talk and play cards – games where none of us can agree on the rules and which usually end without a winner.

'Alan would know the rules, I'm sure,' Cathy says on one of these occasions. 'Alan is invariably very good on the rules of things.'

'You know, Dad was responsible for bringing electricity to this part of the country,' says Emer. 'He was one of the men the electricity board employed to visit the villages and townlands to convince people that they would have a better life if only they allowed this great power into their homes. He would call a meeting in the local hall wherever he was sent and try to impress them with the miracle that could be available at the flick of a switch. These country people, mostly small farmers, weren't easily convinced. If it meant change to them it meant money as well, and they didn't want to know about it. Some people were genuinely afraid. And some were just backward, I suppose. Of course the women were more prepared to listen. They saw how it could help bring an end to some of the eternal drudgery. Even Mam, even after he'd gone, whenever we had a power cut, would come out with "May God bless your father. Without him places like this would still be in the dark ages." '

'That was just something she said to keep up appearances,' says Cathy. 'Deep down she hated the bastard.'

Cathy and Emer look at one another, neither of them prepared to go any further.

It's evening and Cathy and I are in the kitchen, drinking coffee. Emer has gone rambling – 'It means to go and visit other people's houses,' she explains, 'people used to do it a lot in the days before television.' She's gone to see a woman, an old primary-school teacher whom she's not sure will recognise her after all those years.

'Come out with me,' says Cathy. 'I'll show you the shed. I'll potter in the pottery for you.'

She pulls the bolt back and we step into the dimly lit workshop. The walls are lined on two sides by a double row of deep shelves on which are arranged various pieces of finished work – vases, jugs, pots, dishes. There's a table in the middle of the room covered in rows of unglazed cups. The kiln stands on a platform of bricks by the back wall. Cathy lights a cigarette and leans back against the table. Her red hair, pulled back off her forehead, is tied up with a bright purple scarf. Her white T-shirt is covered with stains from the clay she's been working with all day. Her jeans are rolled up along her calves. Suddenly she goes over to the small back window and points out.

'Look across the lake. Somewhere over there you should be able to see the lights of Athlone shining on the water. On clear nights we could see them from our bedroom window. Mam would come in to tuck us into bed and she would often take us to the window first to look at those lights. I used to imagine there were millions of tiny boats with lanterns, anchored far out on the water. I can remember wondering why a grown-up could get so excited about the lights of a town in the distance.'

Both of us stand there looking out, searching the darkening skyline for that twinkling from out of the past. It's almost quiet, but I think I can sense the movement of the water as it shifts about in the depths of the lake and we can hear the low waves slapping the shore. Then I realise I am listening to our breathing, close and rapid, and in no time I feel all of Cathy's body pressed against mine.

One night Cathy and Emer had a talk.

'We stayed up until God knows what hour and finished off the wine. We got a bit tipsy, I suppose. All the same, that Cathy gave me a fright.'

Cathy told Emer that there might come a day when she would walk out into the lake.

'Just like that,' she said. ' "Walk out into the lake." And she wasn't joking.'

Cathy had said that as far as she was concerned, Emer and herself could never face things the way their mother had. Their mother had faith. She had a belief in a certain order of things, despite all that had happened. That was lost on them. They were shiftless, restless people. They had no centre.

'Cathy never had the full story about anything. Mam wasn't perfect. She had her day too.

'I found these letters – oh, years ago. After Mam died I had to sort through her things. Cathy wouldn't go near the place. Her clothes, her few bits of jewellery, her cookery books and all these novels and old magazines, all that sort of stuff. I found this bundle of typed letters, wrapped in old newspapers, in at the back of the wardrobe. They were all addressed to my mother and had been posted in Dublin back in the early sixties, in the days before Dad moved away. I didn't know what to do. I wanted to throw them out and I wanted to read them. So I glanced through one and thought that would be enough. I didn't even intend reading the whole thing. I checked for the sender's address but there wasn't any. There was something scribbled at the bottom of the page that I couldn't make out. So I read a few lines.

'I sat on the edge of the bed in my mother's old room in the middle of a September afternoon and read all twenty-three letters. They were love letters, of course, though not very much was said in any of them. But you could tell by the tone. You could tell from the way the writer talked about things in his everyday life. You could tell that very easily. He would say, I did this today, or tomorrow I'm going to visit such and such a person, and you could see why he was telling these things to my mother. He was sending the story of his life to her. And I suppose she did the same. They were two people in unhappy situations and they just kept the good things to tell to one another.

'A few times a year Mam would go up to Dublin. She'd be back in a day or two, laden down with bags from Arnotts and Switzers and summer or winter outfits for Cathy and myself. While she was away Dad would cope as best he could with feeding and entertaining us. He would tell us stories and make colcannon for dinner and jam sandwiches for tea. He'd take us with him on walks to neighbouring houses to collect milk or eggs.

'One night he brought me in to the station to meet Mam off the Dublin train. It was so cold. It must have been in January or February. I remember waiting and stamping up and down the platform, wearing my big furry mittens and my big woolly hat and Dad standing at the top of the platform. And every so often he would stamp his feet as well and say, "It won't be long now." Well, the train came in and we walked along, hand in hand, Dad looking into the brightly lit carriages, expecting to spot her. But she wasn't to be seen.

'After the train pulled out we walked around, searching. We looked in the waiting room and even asked a porter, but she wasn't anywhere in the station. So Dad said she must have missed the train or else she'd already gotten off and taken a taxi home. But when she wasn't at home he said she must have been carried on to the next station. This was the story they both stuck to when she reappeared the following afternoon. Mam said she'd fallen asleep and had been overcarried all the way to Sligo. You're really better off never finding out about people's secret lives.'

Out the back Cathy is dowsing down the car. She moves to the shore and back, carrying a large yellow bucket. She's singing something and every time she throws the water over the car she whoops.

Emer lights a cigarette and turns to watch her sister. 'Cathy is like Mam. She has all this unhappiness hidden away.'

A wind has been rising on the lake since morning and I reckon it should be good enough to keep us out for the afternoon. I shift the sailboards down from the roof of the car and take the rest of the gear from the boot.

The women are in the kitchen, talking. I go to the window and give a few raps on the glass. They both turn and look towards me.

'Come out,' I shout. 'Come out and try this wind.'

But I can see they don't want to have to hear me. They've been going back over old incidents and occasions, memories that would mean little or nothing to you or me. They sit there, caught between words, and I am an intruder, a boy at the window who hasn't realised that the game has now turned serious.

'Don't bother,' I mouth, and shake my head. 'It's all right.'

As I turn and face out into the freshening wind I hear Cathy's laughter ringing out, carrying its joy across all these miles of land and water.

GREEN

Janet Shepperson

'Such lovely flowers, Ashley.'

Her aunt is perched awkwardly on the edge of a rustic garden chair, beaming at her. Ashley pours tea from the white octagonal teapot that Adam calls 'very *nouvelle cuisine*' and hands round slices of lemon on a white octagonal plate. There are Florentines and tiny scones with damson jam and a chocolate cake she has made herself.

'Take some,' she begs.

Her aunt and Geraldine are gazing out over the garden. Geraldine nibbles at a piece and leaves it on the side of her plate; the aunt dismisses it with 'I couldn't possibly. I'm just after my lunch.' Then she leans forward conspiratorially. 'But what I'd really like,' she confides, 'is to steal some of your flowers.'

Ashley takes two steps into the flowers. They tower up round her, great swathes of vibrant, blending colour, lilies and red-hot pokers and huge Californian poppies just coming into flower. She pictures herself holding out a bunch to the elderly woman, shyly, charmingly, the way the children she herself taught used to offer her armfuls of daffodils filched from the park. But these flowers have much thicker stems, resistant and hairy; breaking them feels like snapping bones. She pulls more and more, wanting to assert herself, feeling an interloper in this garden another woman has planned, struggling with flowers another woman has planted. She stands up, breathless, clutching the leaves of the poppies, disgusted by their hairiness. A thick liquid, pale yellow like melted butter, oozes from the broken stems.

'Oh, but I didn't mean it seriously,' the old lady protests. 'A little bunch of your pyrethrum maybe, if you could spare some, but not your poppies. Poppies are so fragile, you know, they never last once they're cut.'

Ashley looks at the glossy herbaceous border, a mass of complacent colour. Beyond it the monotonous green of the rolling County Down countryside. She cannot identify the pyrethrum. She sits down with the poppies in her lap, unwilling to offer them again but not wanting to lay them on the grass and watch the petals droop and scatter like shreds of orange tissue paper, emphasising her foolishness. A bee blunders onto the flowers and she twitches them, hoping to dislodge it without annoying it. The pauses in the conversation grow longer.

'It's so green here compared to Belfast,' Geraldine offers.

The aunt agrees. She turns to Ashley. 'How you must love it here, the peace and quiet, after all those years in a town flat with no garden.'

'We had a window box,' Ashley says. 'We wouldn't have had time for a garden.'

Geraldine looks at her watch, rises with a show of alarm, saying it's a good hour to Belfast and her baby minder's supposed to go at half-four. As they walk down the sloping lawn to the gate she says, 'You'll have to come and see me really soon, Ashley.'

'I did come. Adam had a meeting in Belfast, he brought me up. You were out. I walked up and down outside the school I'd taught in, looking in through the railings. I felt like one of those P1 parents who deliver their four-year-old darlings up to The System and then mooch about outside the gates, looking forlorn, feeling they haven't got a role any more.'

'Oh, but you'll have a great rest now,' the aunt says. 'You can potter in the garden and look after your flowers. You'll need to get that bindweed out of the hedge, you know, and deadhead your rambling roses as soon as they start to turn brown.'

She is still offering advice as Geraldine starts the car. She rolls down the passenger window and continues to point at shrubs and flowers until engine noise and distance drown her voice. Ashley walks slowly up to the house again. It is set on a ridge and the garden seems to have too much sky over it; there is sky sloping off to both sides as well as above her. Walking up the lawn, she feels like an insect crawling on an open hillside. She carries the tea things into the kitchen, nibbles at the piece of cake Geraldine left on her plate. It is too sweet, cloyingly sweet.

'How you must love it here, after all those years in a town flat with a delicatessen just round the corner,' she says aloud.

She stacks the plates beside the tiny, elegant sink. In the space left for a dishwasher – which they can no longer afford with only one salary – she has stuffed cardboard boxes, and as each new box is unpacked she flattens it and crushes it into the hole. She did the last one this morning. Now she goes to her desk, bristling with books and papers, a rampart she has erected against the overwhelming greenness outside. She opens a file, begins to write: 'I am interested in this post because . . .' There are so many forms to fill in, some of them not even for teaching jobs, but she tells herself this is her opportunity to branch out, try something new, get out of the rut she's been sinking into for five years. 'Branch out' makes her think of the honeysuckle along the back fence, a thin, straggly plant she dislikes, looping out across the pergola and through a sickening drop of air, trying to find a new foothold.

When Adam comes home he finds her stirring things in a wok. She has added chopped walnuts and the colour has gone into everything: onion and carrot and mushroom slices all steeped in a curious purple dye.

'Is it meant to be that colour?' he asks.

'It was fine ten minutes ago,' she snaps, and then she makes

80

herself smile, why should she reproach him when he has to stay later, his new job gives him so much more administrating to do.

'Sorry,' he says. 'I got talking to the fella at the garage when I was filling up the car. Amazing guy. Couldn't get him stopped. Knows all his customers, where they live, knows all about them.'

'You'd never get that in Belfast,' Ashley says. 'Nobody would have the time.' She tips frozen peas into the unappetising mixture, trying to do something about the colour. Adam knows her too well to miss her annoyance.

'Sorry, sweetheart, I meant to come back earlier.'

'Oh all right, it doesn't matter, don't keep apologising.' She jerks round and most of the frozen peas go on the floor. 'Oh God.' She stops Adam as he starts to bend down. 'Don't pick those up, the floor's filthy.'

'I'll wash them,' he says. 'All right, all right' – as he sees the look on her face – 'I'll put them in the bin.' He scrapes a brush across the floor and the frozen peas rattle into the dustpan. Stray peas roll into corners or crunch under his shoes. His brush scurries round after them.

Ashley begins to laugh. 'Adam, this is ridiculous, we can't eat this, it looks like death warmed up.'

He hugs her. 'Let's go out.'

'Can we afford it?'

'A burger in the pub.'

'You're on.'

In the pub she tells him about her aunt, exaggerating her twitchiness, her refined accent: 'My dear, I'd simply love to steal some of your flowers.'

'You'll have to watch her,' he says. 'She'll be nipping down from Belfast with all her mates to pick over the garden.'

'I wish more people would. It's so deadly quiet out there, all those obscure shrubs and flowers staring at me, hundreds of flowers and never any people.'

'People are more trouble than gardens,' Adam says. 'Always

81

changing positions and getting tangled up. Flowers are so relaxing, they stay where you put them. Maybe I should administrate flowers for a bit.'

He never goes out into the garden, Ashley thinks. He still scrupulously does his share of the housework but he has abandoned the garden to her. She doesn't want to start an argument now, it's too late in the evening. She buys them each another pint of cider, they can't really afford it but it makes her sleepy, she is determined to sleep better tonight.

At dawn the birds wake her. Their bedroom window faces south and the curtains are too thin, slabs of sunshine lie on the carpet and the pillows, she twists about trying to nuzzle her face into a patch of shade. Adam is sleeping with his back to her, he has burrowed in under the quilt, she runs a finger over his hair and he stirs slightly and grunts, snores for a minute or two, then his breathing settles and becomes regular and deep. He has a long day ahead of him.

Ashley eases herself out of bed, careful not to wake him, goes to the window, pushes the net curtain to one side. The field beyond the garden is a lurid chemical green, pulsating with energy that has come from a plastic sack of fertiliser. The cows, sleek and self-assured, are already cropping the grass. There is no one in the field. There is never anyone in the field, but Ashley pictures people watching her as she lies sunning herself on the patio or sits under the magnolia tree reading. Watching her and saying, 'Isn't it well for some!' Along each side of the garden are trees Ashley doesn't know the names of, elegant, coppery things and greyish, willowy things, making a dense screen no one could look through, but Ashley imagines the trees themselves watching her reproachfully, itching unbearably with weeds about their roots. She gets back into bed and huddles under the quilt, turns her face away from the window, stretches, yawns. At last she is feeling sleepy.

When she wakes it is after eleven and she is alone. The house is heavy with stillness. Each window she passes is enormous, full of leaves reflecting the light on their shiny surfaces like tiny, naked light bulbs. In the kitchen the sight of toast crumbs on Adam's plate is reassuring; she nibbles some and they taste of company, of supper by the fire on winter evenings. She turns the radio up loud, sits by the phone, dials numbers without giving herself time to think.

'Can I speak to the principal?'

'He's at a meeting. May I have your name? . . . Oh. No, he isn't seeing any of the applicants. We've had over forty phone calls. He feels it would be too disruptive. Only the applicants called for interview will be shown round the school . . . No I couldn't say. If you're shortlisted you'll be notified.'

Ashley's coffee is cold. She eats her cereal, keeping close to the radio as if it were a heater. She turns it louder, opens the door wide, crosses the patio and goes down the steps to the lawn. She can hear Downtown giving out the weather report: 'Set fair across the province . . .' The flowerbeds make her eyes ache with their spiky geometric shapes and sharp colours. Lupins, roses, aggressively bright marigolds, red-hot pokers most assertive of all. When she crouches down to look closely at them she sees they are not really red but a deep orange at the top of each spike, shading down to yellow, and they already seem to be dying, at the bottom of each spike there are straggly brown dried-up bits, like the wings of dead insects.

Over the sound of the radio a bell rings. For a moment Ashley things it's the phone, the woman from Newtownards Central is ringing back, they've somehow miraculously shortlisted in the last hour and they're calling to say they want to interview her tomorrow and will she come and see the principal today, and how is she going to get the car when Adam probably won't be back till after five?

The doorbell rings again. When Ashley appears round the side of the house the woman from the next-door bungalow swings round, startled, her irritated expression softening when she sees Ashley. She is holding a shopping bag awkwardly in front of her.

'Now, I know you won't mind, dear. I have my daughter over today and she's trying to get the baby to sleep.'

'What?'

'Your music, dear, we can hear it even with the windows shut. Not very restful, is it?' She unclips the top of her shopping bag and brings out a white plastic carton. 'Now, I brought you these, just so you won't think all I ever do is complain.'

Ashley takes the carton of strawberries. There are more than she and Adam can possibly eat.

'Sure, I'll turn the radio off, no problem, would you like a cup of tea?'

'Oh no, I haven't time to stop, I have to get back to mind the baby while my daughter goes down to the shops. Grannies are so useful, aren't they? I suppose you'll be starting a family yourself soon?'

'Well, we're not in any hurry.'

The woman snaps her bag shut and her mouth tightens with disapproval – or is it disappointment? – as she turns towards the gate. Why didn't I tell her to get lost, Ashley thinks, why didn't I tell her I'm only twenty-eight, we can't afford it yet, we want to get settled? As she goes back indoors she imagines a pram in the hallway, the house filled with breathing, fretful cries calling her in from the garden. She sees herself rising from her knees and going to wash the earth from her fingers and shaking a plastic rattle to amuse the baby. The thought horrifies her. She would be in all the time, unless she went out with the pram, there would always be the pram to take about with her like a neurotic yapping dog that couldn't be left for a minute, there would be no application forms, no ringing up head teachers for the chance of a day or two's subbing and Adam giving her a lift and herself smoothing her 'good skirt' over her knees and reading the directions off her lap – 'First left – No, past the big chestnut tree – This must be it, it looks old, sort of shabby, I hope it's a friendly place –'

She goes to her desk, checks the list of jobs again. Ballyveigh, a bit far away but maybe worth a try. Hanwood Park, Lower Creagh, Somerton Memorial. All little worlds she is excluded from. It makes her feel dizzy to be excluded from so many worlds at once.

When she has posted off three application forms she feels better. She puts on shorts and a white halter-neck top and squats at the edge of the herbaceous border with a trowel and a card-board box. She's careful this time, she doesn't attempt to break the stems of the poppies; their glossiness annoys her until she turns her back on them. The lavender bush is already flowering in this hot June, a faint mist of blue, refreshing against the op-pressive scarlets and sharp greens of the border. The stems have the texture and brittleness of a well-worn emery board – they snap off easily. But surely they should smell sweet? Maybe the relentless sunshine has already drawn all the scent out of them. The flowers on the bush are like knots of ribbon for bridesmaids' hair, but when she has them in her hand they look dull and faded, a characterless blue like the cover of an old school jotter, already turning brown at the edges. She throws them into the cardboard box with the weeds. She pulls up yellowing, strag-gly grass with increasing exasperation, now that she's looking closely she sees more and more of it along the border, she hates the straw-coloured tufts and the sticky globs of earth round the roots that cling to her fingers. As she pulls the grass away it reveals the underneath of the lavender bush, covered with dry fawn bark that peels off under her fingernails, like cardboard. She feels her own skin itching, imagines it peeling off, littering the lawn. Everywhere she looks there are dry, brown, cracking twigs, everything is parched and crying out for water, she sees the whole garden withering slowly but nobody noticing because it is still falsely smiling with its inane red and purple and yellow blossoms.

For two days she keeps to the house with the windows shut and her music turned up loud. She curls up under the quilt and reads, she talks to her friends on the phone, fends off anxious enquiries from her mother, finds excuses to ring up Adam at work. On the third day the weather breaks at last. She stands at the window watching rain blur the efficient outlines of the garden and feels nothing but relief. Now she will be able to light a fire and draw the curtains. Adam comes in, grumbling.

'God, dreadful, isn't it? Usually they wait till the last day of term before they start chucking it down. Still, at least this'll settle the kids. I couldn't stick three more weeks of what they've been like this week.'

'Were they bad today?'

'No. Cheeky. There's not a bad one among them but they can be very, very wearing. I don't know which is worse, doing the admin or keeping the kids quiet. Anything good on TV tonight?'

'Not sure,' Ashley says casually. (She has already read today's programme guide three times.)

'I'm not doing any more marking tonight,' he says. 'I just had them doing basketwork today.'

'Basketwork?'

'Did you never hear of it? Get them to fill up as much paper as possible, then as soon as they're out of the room you tip the whole lot in the basket.'

'Ha ha.'

He looks surprised. She realises she hasn't smiled, though she'd intended to. She sags against him and he puts his arms round her.

'Sorry, Adam, I'm just so tired.' (Why am I apologising for not smiling?)

'Never mind. We'll have a quiet evening in.'

He falls asleep watching the *Nine O'clock News*. His arm is round Ashley's shoulders; she doesn't like to disturb him to go and pull the curtains. Her eyes are constantly drawn to the French windows. Long, sinuous shoots of rambling rose have begun to inch across the glass. The white blossoms glitter against the damp grey sky, the thousands of tiny green leaves are unnaturally still, but every time she looks away she imagines that they are moving.

Another night of lying awake, trying to ignore the luminous figures on the alarm clock – one o'clock, one-thirty, two o'clock. The heavy swishing of the rain comforts her. Nobody could expect her to be out in this weather, nobody could expect her to do anything but shut herself in the house, it's only reasonable. She can sleep on till past lunchtime, lie in bed with a book, the garden will be blotted out by curtains of rain. When she falls asleep at last she dreams she is searching for something at the roots of the grass but she cannot dig through to the earth because the stems keep twisting over her hands, holding her back, she goes all along each flower border and round all the shrubs and trees and the pergola with its snaky creepers, but it is the same every-where. When she wakes she can distinctly see a cross-hatching of stems, an after-image. In a couple of minutes it fades.

It is after three. It has stopped raining but the hall is already so dark that she has to switch the light on. On the mat are three envelopes: one addressed in her mother's writing, the other two typed. She senses it isn't good news, they aren't giving off the right vibes, she makes herself drink a cup of coffee and nibble some toast before she opens them. Rejections. Of course she's bound to have some rejections, everyone knows how difficult it is to get permanent jobs, the first one is from Mountstockart and she knows she did a very bad interview, it's understandable, of course they weren't going to offer her the job. The second one is from Newtownards Central. But they said they hadn't shortlisted yet. How can they have filled the post so soon? How can they have held interviews already? She must be remembering it all wrong, the woman must have said . . . What did it matter what the woman said, they didn't call her for interview and that's that, maybe they wanted a local person, or a man, or someone older, or someone fresh from college. That's it, it wasn't that they didn't want *her*, it was just that they already had someone in mind. It couldn't have been anything she did. Like filling in the form badly, missing out something vital, not sounding keen enough. She wishes she could remember what she wrote. Maybe she'll keep copies next time.

They are over there on her desk, the last batch; there'll be no more jobs advertised now till autumn. She'll be careful with these, extra careful. She won't start them till she's feeling up to it, really wide awake, maybe she'll get up earlier tomorrow morning. There must be other things she can do this afternoon. Ring someone up. Ring Geraldine. Geraldine had said something about going swimming at Helen's Bay. Anything. Even a coffee morning. Even a trip to the shops with Geraldine's noisy kids. Anything would be better than this.

'Ashley . . . Oh, hello . . . No, I was just feeding the baby . . . How're you doing? . . . Me? Oh, hectic. We're off on holiday next week, thank goodness . . . No, just a caravan in Fermanagh this year, going abroad is too much trouble with all my brood. Are you going abroad?'

'One salary now. We can't afford it.'

'Oh, no luck on the jobs front then?'

'No. Geraldine, it's awful, I just got a rejection without even an interview. Five years' experience and they don't even want to interview me. I know I shouldn't let it get me down –'

'Probably fifty or sixty applicants. Cheer up, remember we were both unemployed for months after college. At least you have a home and a husband now, not like the squalor we used to live in.'

Ashley says nothing. She hears the baby wailing in the background. Geraldine makes little clucking noises. She says in a pull-yourself-together voice, 'Besides, it's better than having Adam unemployed, isn't it? It's so much worse for a man.'

'Got to go.' Ashley puts the phone down. The noise that sounds like Adam's key in the lock turns out to be only the rattle of the *Telegraph* lurching through the letter box. Soon he'll be home. She thinks of Adam, unemployed, attacking the garden with zest, planting French beans and potatoes instead of the useless flowers and sagging honeysuckle, leaning over the gate talking to the old men cycling past and the postman. 'So much worse for a man.' Geraldine never used to be like that.

Outside the French windows the lawn is strewn with white petals. The heavy rain has defeated the rambling rose, even the heads still on the bush have begun to turn brown, rotten. Ashley hunts for the secateurs, they aren't in any of the cupboards, maybe Adam will know. She can't understand why he still isn't back. She goes into the kitchen, butters herself a scone. On the calendar above the bread bin June twelfth proclaims in her own careful writing: 'Adam – parents' meeting.' He will be eating sandwiches in the staff room; he probably won't be back till ten. How could she have forgotten? Her brain isn't functioning any more. It's choked, grown over with weeds, long stems of creeper looping over her, leaves and petals folding across her face with their oozing greenness, suffocating her.

She goes to her desk for comfort. She flicks her letters and papers, random phrases rise up at her, meaningless: 'State why you feel you would be suitable for this post . . .' 'Please give the names and addresses of three people who know you in a profes- sional capacity . . .' 'Your aunt seems to be doing so much better on the new pills . . .' 'I hope you're eating properly, Ashley, hav- ing lunch on your own every day . . .' Basketwork, she thinks. She begins to tear up the papers, tearing again and again till they are reduced to tiny shreds, her throat and her eyes are hot with the tears that will not flow.

Something white is fluttering outside the window. When she

opens the door she sees a white plastic bag trapped in the branches of the magnolia tree, like a bloated bird, flapping uselessly as the wind rises. She stands at the foot of the tree, puts a hand on the trunk, hating it; the gracious, scented magnolia that had been in bloom when they first saw the house now seems grotesque, its greyish-green bark is lumpy and twisted like a ridiculous elephant with deformed legs. She tries to pull herself up to reach the white thing, it is too high up the left-hand fork that sways when she attempts to put her weight on it, she feels dizzy, slithers down, scratching the palms of her hands, the inside of her thumb is bleeding, she hammers on the trunk with her fists, scraping her knuckles, pulls one of the spiky branches down further and further, afraid it will snap back in her face, but at last it breaks. She grasps it in both hands and beats and beats at the shaking leaves. All the flowers round her are mocking her, their white and purple moon faces serene and wax-like in the gathering dusk, she kicks at the thick stems of the lupins, tries to tear the laurel leaves but they are too tough for her, the creepers are thinner and she hacks at them with the branch, their dangling tendrils crumple to the ground, she stamps on the twitching honeysuckle blossoms, thrashes about among the poppies, flattening their feathery leaves, crushing the last of their petals under her feet.

When she stops, gasping, she is in front of a willow tree with half its lower branches torn away and the naked whiteness under the bark exposed. She wonders if anyone could have heard her. The garden is silent, huge. She crawls away from it, in under the laurel bushes where nothing grows and the shed brown leaves are like a rug under her as she curls up, hugging her knees.

When she wakes she looks at her watch; she has slept for two hours. Her throat and her eyes are no longer aching. The twigs and flowers scattered on the grass in front of her are pathetic broken things – there will be no more dreams of plants twining across her face and suffocating her. She looks into the space they have left and sees two tiny figures, their faces pale as the crushed petals: her aunt, always so fragile, twitching, unable to hold down a job because of her 'nerves'; her mother, weary from years of child-rearing, filling the emptiness by writing endless letters to the ones who got away.

She looks at the sky, deep blue, almost midnight-blue, arching above a garden drained of colour. The leaves rustle, blank as paper, they have no colour of their own, only what she chooses to give them. She says aloud the words for green. Emerald. Jade. Lime. Peacock. Avocado. Apple. Moss. Grass. A field in the sunshine. A vast expanse, sparkling. Beyond it her house, dark.

The lights in the windows go on, one by one. She waits for a moment, thinking of Adam's anxiety, savouring it. Then she begins to walk across the grass towards the house.

BALLOONS

Jim McCarthy

Usually when Noel remembered the time Karen became pregnant he also remembered how the winter cold forced them to get central heating installed. And because the plumbing in their house was faulty, they hired a couple of plumbers for the two jobs. As a result there was so much dust in the house that Noel sometimes imagined that he and Karen had dragged the baby from its dust-laden entrails. He felt that their shared life together had reached an apex then – together they had seized a dream.

It felt so strange living with her during those first weeks of pregnancy. It was only the changes creeping over her body that nailed dream to fact for him. But these changes both confirmed and nibbled at his dream. He began to think how static his own body was compared to hers. Her nausea made him uneasy, but he ignored his unease and tried to enter her woman's world. He brought her blocks of cheese and blocks of ice cream when she developed cravings, and feeling he was part of her conspiracy, kept his sense of sharing alive.

When the plumbers finally finished, the house looked as if it had been vandalised. Noel refused to pay them until they had righted the chaos. The disagreement went on for weeks and late one Thursday, while he lay with Karen, the plumbers drove across from the southside, fuelled by alcohol. Their kicks drew mute screams from the door, drew sharp screams from Karen's throat. The very walls appeared to cower before the violence.

'I'm really glad we left the car in for servicing,' she whispered.

'I'll go down and sort them out,' he said.

'No. For me – and the baby – don't.'

He remained where he was but they were anxious until they heard the drift of neighbours' voices and the life-stirrings of a car engine. Soon it was as though peace was pouring from walls that had known tumult mere moments before. But although the peace flowed all about Noel, it didn't enter him, for the bad feeling caused by the plumbers had struck him like a premonition.

'Good God, this mess will never be fixed up,' she said. 'And there's so much more to be done on the house before the baby's born.'

'I'll do the lot myself. Can't trust these chancers pretending to be experts.'

'You've enough to be doing.'

'No matter, I'll enjoy myself. Every pint of sweat lost is a pint of stout earned.'

Karen took a half-day off work to attend hospital and on coming home, she announced: 'The doctor spoke of the baby in centimetres.'

Apart from some small talk, that was all she said. Noel thought how formal it sounded and his eyes stayed on her as she walked from the sitting room to the bathroom. He kept spacing centimetres with his fingers, trying to relate such measurements to his world.

'Are you OK?' she asked when she returned.

It was all right for her, he brooded. *She* had control over the baby's growth. He was excluded by his body from this most ordinary, most miraculous of processes. He feared he was destined by his nature to be part of the other world, a world parading as might that measured things by size and barely knew this world of unassuming miracle, where mere fractions could be all of a life. He was growing apart from her and wondered what was happening to all their sharing.

A rash of burglaries erupted in their neighbourhood and the

country seemed to be slipping beyond control. He was less and less certain that they were right to bring a baby into it. Could they really shoulder responsibility for another life? And what if the child wasn't normal? Could he and Karen love it enough? But these were usual fears, they could be discussed. How could he discuss what was really bothering him?

He looked for good omens in the March weather. It was like reading a malevolent Ouija board. Made miserable by a vicious day, he sought around him for relief. He searched desperately for its signs in the glazed eyes of concrete buildings, in the unfeeling metal of vehicles. As though some perverse god had answered him, hailstones lashed his face and he had to shelter in a newsagent's doorway. The papers were displaying their prize headlines, but Noel saw only his own headlines: 'Wombless Things – Concrete, Metal, Men – Take Over Dublin Today.'

It was at this stage that he began to dwell on the plumbers' violence.

The hours he worked ate at his body. By day he put in time at the builders' providers, where business was clearly slackening. In the warm summer evenings he laboured at home, where tasks increased inexplicably. He was often fatigued, but on one of those evenings the depths of *her* tiredness surprised him.

'Talk about bad days at the office,' she said. 'And to top it all, there's no ointment in the house for this damn blister on my foot.'

Without hesitation he went to the little all-purpose shop at the edge of their estate. On his way back he took a short cut through a laneway and was met by a gang of youths. One of them challenged Noel, cider dripping from his lips.

'Wanna drink? . . . What bleedin' right have you to spy here? . . . Put this bottle to your mouth. You won't catch the pox from it.'

Noel couldn't stop staring at the cidered face.

'What ya lookin' at, smart boy? I'll sort out that bleedin' mush of yours.'

The bottle smashing off a wall sent urgency through Noel's blood. He took to his heels because the odds were stacked against him. Later he realised that there was another reason why he fled. The encounter had attracted him – it drew him like a half-remembered smell from childhood.

Noel's parents had moved to the Wicklow countryside some years earlier. They spent their time amongst animals and plants, away from the sores of the city. His father drove into Dublin with a terrier for Karen.

'The dog will hold your mind,' he said, 'give the nerves a ballast when things get out of hand.'

'I'm sure he will,' she answered, shaping her words towards a joke. 'I'll treat him like a baby. Until the real one arrives, of course.'

But the terrier caught a disease and died. His death affected her like that of a close friend, yet made her all the more aware of the life inside her. They brought the remains out to Wicklow and Noel and his father dug a grave. During that long, sad, autumn weekend in Wicklow Noel somehow distilled the emotion and frustration of months into the one pure fact of the terrier's death. It infected him, the infection showing clearly the night they returned to Dublin, blackness spread thickly over their house.

'There's something not right in here,' she said as she closed the front door.

'That's the same thought I had.'

'God, we're really living on our nerves. I can still hear the echo of the front door being closed.'

'Yeah, funny how – Wait, that's not an echo off the front door.'

'Noel! Christ, be careful,' she shouted, watching him run into the kitchen with the coal shovel in his right hand. The back door was open and he flicked on the garden light switch before he went through. He saw cider-face and two more youths that he recognised from the laneway. The others were already along the boundary wall, but he caught the scrambling legs of cider-face and they both tilted groundwards. As he lowered the shovel Noel saw the fear shrinking this enemy who had once threatened him with a cider bottle, heard the cry when blade struck testicles, intuited the blood prior to his hands tattooing the face.

Karen stood close by. While the light mixed their shadows into hers, she saw how her husband relished his power to hurt.

'Yes,' she said to herself, 'Aunt Jenny's house *is* nearer the hospital than this place.' And she cried quietly, the tears dropping towards her unborn child. They told of its father leaving. *Leaving them for the other world; a world that paraded as might, but actually kept cracking its body into fragments. Scratched each fragment for scab, something to pick at.*

Left on his own in the house, Noel missed her. Sleep kept its distance from him and he saw her face rise and sink in the dark bedroom among memories of his savagery. Each time her face rose before him he asked it questions. Questions he quickly answered himself: 'What do *you* know about such things? . . . A man has to defend his family and home.'

Having at last reached sleep one Friday night, he felt a baby curl along his groin. A shout freed itself from his lips and he awoke thinking his body was composed of glue cells. He stabbed the light switch with his right middle finger and looked at the semen on his thigh. He wondered what such wan drops had to do with a blood-filled baby. His reverie was cut short by a din from the road and he switched off the light. When he separated the curtains he saw a mob on the corner, gutting a stolen car. Flames and empty bellies of smoke were spewed at the sky. He opened the window and inhaled a smell of rubber, a smell of rancid incense.

Late next afternoon he rang her aunt's house. A voice answered: 'Karen is gone to the hospital. The pains came on her earlier.'

His mind now an oversensitive receiver, Noel drove towards the hospital. He had arranged to be at the birth and here he was in a limbo of his own making. What was happening? The red traffic lights that halted him had no answer. He could almost touch the area of fear suffocating him, the red lights radiating a stasis that clotted the flow. Strapped in his seat, he looked across at a woman in a Renault, with music blaring from it. She was done up to the nines. He could hear the song words so clearly: '. . . where peaceful waters flow . . .' What was this crap about peaceful waters? Other people chanced on music to suit their needs. Why couldn't *he* hear something that reflected the upheaval inside him? He muttered a string of words.

'Jesus, when you start looking for relevance in pop music! Take it easy, Noelly boy, or you'll be spitting piss and pissing spit.'

Rapidly his thoughts shifted back to the woman. He envied her her luxury of a vacant gaze, a bored air. He guessed she was on her Saturday night out, an outing similar to those of other Saturday nights. He wished they could swop places. Yet he knew, by the angles of her body and by the inattention of her fingers on the wheel, that she was glutted with this routine, knew she longed for the unique occurrence that would change her life. He had something unique to attend, and here he was, totally uncertain. The thought of a child on its final journey to them thrilled him. But he wished he could be centre stage in the drama. Also, would Karen even want him there in a bit part after what had happened? A sliver of shame prodded the fear. The red light had abdicated in favour of the more urgent green and the Renault had nosed ahead. He urged his car to more life.

He entered the hospital foyer and when he saw that all those waiting there were women, he felt he was intruding. He went to the enquiries desk, wondering why he kept looking at the public phone booth alongside. He was told to wait a while and he sat down, staring at different products of wood – the bench he sat on, the statue of Mother and Child mounted on marble, a crucifix hung on the wall. He wished he had reason to use the toilet in the corridor.

The porter at the enquiries desk called him over. 'Your missus left the reception room a short time ago. They'll have more info for you soon. But if you like you can go upstairs to the husbands' waiting room.'

Noel went to the lift shaft and stood before its fixed folding gate. He took in the lift's slow descent, the black metal bars of its trellised door so outwardly like the fixed gate, its potential so naturally different. The lift was roomy and smelt strongly of disinfectant.

'Where to?' The lift porter's practised tone came across.

'Second floor . . . Or is it the third? . . . The husbands' waiting room.'

'Don't be so nervous, son. The husbands' room is a lot better than prison. At least there's more chances for suicide if it gets to you.'

They passed a picture of the Nativity shedding its humbleness and dominance over the first floor. Uncharacteristic gestures betrayed Noel's anxiety. A hesitance in those gestures betrayed his intimidation by the hospital scenes flashing through his mind, every scene leaving a sharp imprint of system and efficiency. However, he sensed thin pencil lines of mystery still clinging faintly to each scene.

The lift porter wished him well and Noel walked away, not grasping the directions he'd been given. He came to a door marked 'reception room' and decided to knock. Since there was no reply he went into the room – following in Karen's footsteps. He counted six trolleys containing files. He stared at them, but experienced less their actuality than the way they complemented the matter-of-factness he had met in the hospital. His eyes shifted to a painting of a small boy flying his yellow kite in a meadow. And around the room, in vases, was a flourish of meadow grass, which appeared to have been delivered from the inanimate two dimensions of the painting and have had an extra dimension of life breathed into it.

He didn't hear the nurse come in. 'What are you doing here?'

'I . . . I'm Karen O'Neill's husband.'

'Well, Mr O'Neill, you should be down in the husbands' room. You know how to get there?'

He nodded.

'Good. At the moment Karen is –'

'At the moment she is part of the efficiency . . . Or part of the mystery?'

'Sorry, what's that?'

'Nothing. I'll be off.'

'Right then. Oh, Mr O'Neill, one little thing.' She went to an inner room and brought out a green plastic bag. 'Your wife's clothes are in this.'

His fingers held the plastic shell, his eyes examining their surname scribbled across this container of now-redundant objects.

He passed time in the husbands' waiting room. For imagined eternities he waited there, alone with pictures of trees, the corner television, and a notice stating that floor toilets were solely for staff and patients. He puzzled over the television's role. Was it being put to its customary use, a flavouring sprinkled on boredom? Or was it meant to be more – an attempt to divert the unknown, to hold back fear?

The door sounded and in the corridor he picked among the words of another nurse.

'Your wife is doing fine. You can join her in a while.'

Floundering in a scramble of impressions, he threw some irrelevant query to her. She paid him no heed, just continued fixedly.

'It should take three to four hours. At the moment she's getting an enema and later she'll have her waters broken.'

Some image springing from that phrase *her waters* slapped him – an image evoking tides and wombs, an image exclusively woman. A wave of helplessness broke over him.

There was still no one else in the husbands' room. He went to the window and raised the sash. The murky night, lying in wait, confronted him, its body cut open by two bright lamps fastened to a brick gable. He jerked towards the opening door behind him and was met by a man with the green bag of brotherhood. The newcomer's name was Christy and he came from Tallaght. Though he was only thirty, anxiety had written extra years across his face. But unexpectedly, a natural giddiness seemed to prolong adolescence in his body.

Noel was summoned to the delivery area. He saw Karen, her face red, a nurse there with her. *Her face red, similar to the blood she would sweat.* The nurse's voice was Welsh and soft, the bruise on her arm, traceless and hard. He must have been heeding it, for she was moved to comment, 'I was at a party . . . But I don't know how I got the likes of that.'

I know how, you lying bitch, he thought.

'Take deep breaths now, Karen,' she said. 'Slower . . . slower.'

Though Noel tried to hold her hand, his wife found it difficult through her pain. It was an effort to think of her as his wife. He couldn't think she had a first name or ever had – this sufferer, here fronting his eyes, of pain he could never hope to endure. Twice, beads of vomit came from her mouth, twice, the nurse fed her a silver dish. There was a lull and the nurse listened through the hard plastic of a small black cone, small channel to the baby heartbeats. She filled in a progress chart. Then the sufferer wanted to push.

'I'll get sister for breaking the waters,' the Welsh nurse said. 'And you'll have to leave, Mr O'Neill.'

He sought the husbands' room but distracted by thoughts of deep breaths and pain, he ended up on the stairway. Christy was sitting on a landing.

'I couldn't stick it inside any longer,' he said.

Noel ignored him.

'I was reared on a farm,' Christy went on, 'so I'm used to births. But attending the birth of your first child – that's something else. This is one of the biggest moments for us men as well, you know.'

'It's really got little to do with us men, *you know*,' Noel mimicked before his tone changed. 'They've good stuff in their bodies, they can grow things there. There's only gas inside us. We're like balloons.'

Christy looked at Noel and a certain part of that look provoked him beyond endurance. Next moment he was on top of Christy, grabbing him by the hair. But he stopped. This time hitting someone didn't seem the answer. And almost as soon as it had sprung to life his rage died.

'What's the use?' He pulled himself off Christy and hurried away.

There were two strangers in the husbands' room when he got back. They both looked at him, silently inviting him to drop words into their confusion. He kept his eyes averted, afraid they'd see something not quite right about him. Finally Christy returned, showing no sign of what had happened. The four of them sat in isolation, each man a displaced link, no conversation to chain them together. The room air became a pool fed by the experience-streams of all who'd undergone this before and into which all four slipped easily, each drawing out what thoughts he could to fit his particular case.

Mute televised images drifted about Noel's brain. From fragments of Irish country music and all-Ireland football violence he retrieved what the Welsh nurse had said: 'The labour is speeding along.' Over and over he probed her remark, in vain hope of latching onto some part of it, of easing his separateness. Again he was summoned to the corridor, was told things.

'Your wife is panting . . . A mask over her face to help her

101

breathing . . . She doesn't want you in just yet . . . But she knows you're still here, anyway.'

He thought those last few sounds he heard offered no grasp of the inadequacies of being a man, the pain of exile from the centre of life. Yet when he considered it, he rejected this exclusion and when he went back inside, the real drama began. He felt the pains rack him and he fell to the ground. They propped him on armchairs and Christy was leaning across.

'Push,' he said. 'Breathe and push.'

But Noel couldn't. The breathing had left him, had gone out there to the unknown.

'Push,' they all shouted, 'Push, push.'

And though his face was burning, he couldn't. Though his face was such, it had sucked in all the room colours. They gripped his legs, they held his hands – it was no use. The pallid room was draped around him, accusing him through its bloodlessness. He hadn't a name – how could he ever have had a first name? They were filling in progress charts – how could they chart the pain deep inside him, the pain he couldn't expel, that wasn't a proper pain?

He had been waiting a long time in the husbands' room when he was harassed by the need to urinate. He was so sure something would happen soon that he tried to resist the need. He failed to do so and had to rush out. Unsure of the direction of the lift, he had to go down the stairs to the toilet. Still, he had the presence of mind to fix landmarks for his return. After using the toilet he started back. The corridor was empty, the hospital quiet to his senses. He was powerful, a master who strode majestically in a building that whispered his might. Then he fretted lest he would miss the birth and he scampered up the stairs.

Christy was at the top. 'Hurry, the delivery area. They're looking for you.'

Reaching the delivery area, Noel was faced by a scene stripped to its core. A midwife and a curl-haired nurse were supporting Karen's legs; blood and womb-water covered the sheet she lay on. Here the system and efficiency had been skinned, meat-raw. A mass of red showed at the vagina opening and she was panting – faster than running, harder than sex, pure panting that had taken on a life of its own. He wondered if it was some foreknowledge of all this pain that caused Karen to be so unimpressed with the world's force.

The miracle of the head happened, hopes and fears appearing as form. While he tried hard to understand, the baby was helped from its first home. Someone said – he heard it through the bells beating at his head – 'It's a girl.'

Karen squeezed his hand and he felt a great love for her.

The umbilical cord twisted like some blue and white earthworm between the outside of the baby's body and the inside of its mother's, briefly joining the two worlds. Then the baby was cut free of her last link with the wombdarkness, her cry now another detail of the world Noel belonged to. They weighed her: 'Seven pounds, fourteen ounces', quantities and limits now attached to what had been unknown and indefinite. They put the child in a green wraparound and Noel recalled green, the old people saying it was *his* colour. He was allowed to hold her, this small wonder, as he watched them banish the afterbirth – it reminded him of an uncooked slab of liver.

For the moment his torment was fully replaced by joy. But he knew it would return once this initial euphoria was over. He just hoped for the courage to face up to it honestly.

He had to leave once more while Karen was being sutured. Christy came into the husbands' room shortly after him, just the two of them there again. Like Karen, he seemed to have forgotten Noel's earlier violence.

'My wife had a girl, a lovely little thing,' he babbled. As if *his* girl was the only one. 'I was there.'

Noel answered him this time round. 'I was there too. It . . . it makes you feel like nothing at all.'

Both men knew a bond, as though they had shared in a war or a death. Noel was touched by these unsoiled moments – free as newborn – that whatever came after couldn't stick to or mar. Christy took up his green bag of brotherhood and they embraced. Noel kissed him on the cheek, giver and receiver showing affection as clearly as close sisters.

COUNTERPOINT

Gerardine Meaney

The old man's voice rose and fell, rose again slow, melodious dripping of long ago and far from this into the cool, sour, clean place where he now sat, rocking, slow forth and back and back again. The old man's voice was hoarse, sometimes seeming stuck in an ever tightening chamber where sounds, when one is young, reverberate and flow. What the old man spoke, no one could know.

'Nonsense, yes.' It seemed to satisfy the plump physician. 'Totally withdrawn. It must have been precipitated by whatever stroke or accident brought him in here thirty years ago or so. Perhaps he was mad already.'

'Any family?'

'No one ever claimed him, poor old devil. He's no trouble at all, muttering away to himself. But there's nowhere to send him, you know, so he must stay with us.'

Giggling noises and a peal of little rasped-out chuckles followed the slight and somewhat disturbed young student and her instructor out of the ward.

Next day the old man seemed livelier. The laugh like little chiming bells greeted his observers. He babbled then, politely, with the air of a man returning to their puzzled or amused comments, urbane and civil comments of his own. When they stopped he stopped too. All looked at each other and the old man uttered a single sound as they turned and were gone.

All night the student tossed and wondered why that sound reverberated in her brain. It rang there, a call and a cipher. It sounded as the call to prayer might sound, high and alien and clear to one who has never slept before in the vicinity of a mosque.

Early, before the duty rounds, when the nurses were busy elsewhere, she went and stood before the old man. She said it. There now. He answered her. There could be no doubt, for he nodded and smiled with what seemed to her the gratitude of a fellow countryman met, lost and alone, among strangers. He spoke further, earnestly, and now it was her turn to smile and nod, grateful but helpless.

Later, on the rounds again, she asked her senior colleague if there was any possibility that the old man spoke a real but little-known language, perhaps one that had died out altogether. A frown of interest, then he dismissed it as not feasible, not now.

'A century ago, even half a century. Have you ever looked up old case histories for misdiagnosis on those grounds?'

Half a century ago. Not so long as that. She addressed the old man with a word for farewell she had learned as a child. He replied, adding a few courteous phrases beyond her repertoire.

'Don't mock the poor fellow.' The older doctor was stern, shocked.

'It's the old speech of my people, I'm not sure what people really.' Embarrassed, she was gazing beyond the old man. 'My grandparents remembered some stories. And some words. My grandmother taught me bits of the language, whatever she could remember. It is her language he is speaking.'

Not fifty, not even twenty years. 'And do you want an apple now? And how do you say "I want" in Granny's tongue?' Grandmother had coaxed and bribed and bullied what her daughter called 'that nonsense' into the child's head. The old woman regretted volubly that she had not known what she had to give her own children when she had remembered more.

'Are you sure?'

She had gone far away and the old man and the doctor were

looking straight at her. Could she be sure after so many years from fables and childhood and even family? The woman who taught her this lost language was remembered only as a large lap that had smelt warm and nurturing, that had turned sour in that last year or so, dying.

'I can't be positive. I was only a toddler when my grandmother died. I haven't heard this dialect, or whatever it is, since then. Even she seemed to have only words and a few phrases.' She felt curiously bereft.

'Why didn't you tell me this the first day we came in here?' Had this stammering little know-all been making a fool of him? Making a fool of the poor old man too, pretending not to understand. Cruel.

'I didn't know. I told you I'm still not sure, but I thought I heard him bid us farewell. Yesterday. So this morning I greeted him – I can remember that much – and he understood and answered me.'

'You said the word first, gave him a cue, as you did just now?'

'Yes, yes, I suppose so.'

'Perhaps we had better talk this over.'

The voice rose and fell and fell again, dropped to a murmur, crooning and rasping, scrub – vicious and thorned – singing in the thrush's warble. The old patient's eyes were sympathetic and tolerant as a hand on her shoulder.

'Better jumping to conclusions than with no imagination in this game, after all.' No need for the senior man to be too hard on her. 'All young once and so on. Cramming for exams, are we?'

The old man breathed in and out; breathily he chirped her farewell.

When she said she wanted to research a paper on language loss, as he had suggested, the doctor took it, as she had intended, as a compliment. He had talked her out of that lost language nonsense, shown her the scientific basis. Couldn't remember suggesting a paper though.

'Trauma and loss of linguistic capacity,' he suggested now. 'Very good, very good. Plenty of material here, you know, plenty of case studies.'

She studied only one. He was surprised to see her back. Recording his old voice proved easy. He spoke ceaselessly, smiling at her, occasionally and incomprehensibly admonishing.

In the beginning he had babbled good-humouredly on. One day his voice rose, booming sonorous and solemn, washing the sterile ward with waves of sound. The old man had an innate grasp of acoustics, she had learned. He stopped himself now, forcibly, and looked at her. She had during the previous evening's 'research' recognised or seemed to recognise some handful of words. Using what she remembered and what he reminded her, she communicated haltingly with him, having recourse time and again to sign language. The old man appreciated her efforts, rewarding them with the song of his punctuated warbling.

Now she was missing some signal: he wanted something from her. She sat waiting and he sat opposite her, waiting also. *What* was still beyond her vocabulary. You want? She wasn't sure if she had said *you want* or *I want* or simply *want*. But relieved, delighted, he echoed her word and again began the long flow of his speech, ending not in sleep, as on other evenings, but interrupted when the night nurse asked her to leave.

On the following evening he was looking out for her, anxious. She was still setting up her recording equipment when he began, excitedly, impatient. She understood little. His tone, however, she recognised as different: gesturing, agitated at first, then slowing to a dirge-like strain, more dismal than she had heard it before. The pace speeded up a little, lilting along in a half-humorous, half-sad tone, his flow interrupted here and there by little intimate chuckling asides to her that ended in a sigh. Love. He was speaking of love, as the old speak of love to the young. Not rambling, not any longer. Or had he ever? She would have to listen again to the earlier tapes. Now, hour after hour, she heard the cadences, the rhythms and ornaments, the varying paces and tones of anger, adventure, danger, love and death. My old friend is a storyteller. He told and kept on telling until long after she should have left. A slow crescendo to the final coda and then the old man began to snore, grumbling through his nose. She called a nurse and left him sleeping in his chair.

Now when she arrived he awaited her word. Repeating it, he began his story. Using up her meagre store, she offered him words of his own, for he needed a start, a challenge. Perhaps this was some old storytelling game and he the champion. Whatever the word, the same themes, or rather the same tones and moods, shadows and light on the voice, recurred. He learned over weeks to mould his art to the times of the hospital regimen. The flickering electronic numbers on the opposite wall were no match for his inventiveness. Mutating ever the sequence and particular quality of each of his timeless preoccupations, he cheated the timepiece that she had feared would come to measure the sensuous whisper of the grey and deathly skin still hugging its bones in the chair.

No repetition of her leading words was possible. She had once or twice attempted to offer a word used weeks before for a second tale and his reaction had been that of a man who has caught a dear friend cheating him at cards. He recoiled, he was silent; disappointed, he sulked. Presents or her faltering attempts at apology only insulted him further. Starved for her tale, her gift, she had learned to reproduce, slowly, sounds from her tapes, searching for the combination in which he would find sense and from which he could begin. Soon she could control this, choosing the potential words from moods in previous stories that matched her own moods. When he realised this he reached and put his hands on her head, as priests once conferred blessing.

She offered him one night a word, a sound from a mood that,

unlike the others, surfaced only occasionally and in what she recognised as the most demanding tales for the teller and for herself. It was a guess, chance; she had begun to attempt to isolate syllables from those words she was sure were words. These two 'syllables' seemed to recur, though never in immediate juxtaposition, in the mood that matched her own as she sought a tale from the old man and thought her training here was nearly over. She uttered two sounds that seemed in any case to overlap. He gasped or sighed, not in pain, and his eyes were unbearably steady on and in hers. She wouldn't move. Recollecting all of herself to the present, she concentrated on the sound she had made, trying to connect it with what his eyes, telling more than he had told in all these months, told now. He held her thus in his gaze and gazing into the word for only a moment, as long as she could bear it. Then he was content. He was content. He nodded, raised his hand and closed his eyes. The tale was over for tonight.

Next day the nurses told her he had died in the early morning. No pain, just exhausted and old. 'We all thought you were marvellous, giving him all that attention, all he wanted really.'

The old man's voice rose and fell, fell again, melodies dripping of long ago and far from this, dropping to a whisper filling her room in the night. His flowing lilt was interrupted as it commenced, a whirr as she rewound her recording to repeat itself.

She sat at a wide table, papers flying. She thought she had an alphabet now and the patterns of sound had wider patterns, not sentences perhaps. Sometimes it all broke down to lovers and dangers and death and the tales, it seemed, were telling themselves.

Sometimes she could distinguish no patterns, no figures, no words, not even individual sounds. Then there were two high, clear notes that seemed to overlap and a crooning, murmuring, rasping counterpoint.

THE PASS

Patrick Semple

I hadn't heard from Joe for a long time. He left a message for me to phone back as soon as I came in. As usual I had to hang on until he got a minute to come to the phone. All he said was 'Can you come on Thursday, after lunch?'

'Yes,' I said.

'OK, see you then', and he put down the phone.

As I approached the town along the estuary road I passed the spot where I first met Joe on a summer day some years before. He had a puncture and flagged me down to borrow a wheel brace. He was fiftyish, his face was round with a serious expression. He was heavy but tall enough to carry it well. He wore a collar and tie, a cardigan over a pair of baggy grey flannels, and sandals. He spoke slowly and with a great economy of words. I'd have bet he was a schoolmaster.

'If you have time when you're in town I'd like you to have a drink.' He gave me the name of a pub, The Barrack. I thanked him and made a noncommittal reply.

I didn't take him up on his offer. In fact I forgot all about it but some months later I was back in town again and with time to spend. By chance I came upon The Barrack and remembered the puncture. The pub was on a corner with the door set back three or four feet, the overhang supported by a pillar. It was mainly bar with a small snug partitioned off at the far end. It hadn't seen a coat of paint for at least twenty years. There were two customers in the bar: one sitting at a table reading a paper and one sitting sideways-on at the bar, gazing out over his pint into the middle distance. Neither of them was Joe. As I stood up to the counter, from the snug I heard the slow, deep voice that had invited me here in the first place. I tapped the counter and out from the snug behind the bar came Joe. He was wearing the barman's old-fashioned white apron. He greeted me warmly, glad of the opportunity to repay the debt.

Since that first visit we soon discovered common ground. I always called when I was in the area and from time to time he would phone, as he had done on this occasion. Joe became my best contact in the south of the county. If he didn't know about it, it didn't happen. He never greeted me by name, but apart from that treated me like any other customer. I always sat up at the bar, if possible at one end or the other, and as soon as he wasn't busy we would talk. First the pleasantries, then a summary of bits and pieces of interest. No matter how important a piece of information he had to give, he would start with the trivia. He didn't enthuse lest my evaluation of his intelligence didn't coincide with his own. In fact his judgement was as good if not better than mine and when he sent for me it was always worth the journey. Our conversation was usually interrupted and he spoke so softly and cryptically I had to concentrate very hard not to lose some vital detail.

I arrived at The Barrack. There were six or eight people in the bar. Joe took my order, gave me my change and I set in to listen. Normally when he gave me directions I could follow them quite easily but this time the spot was so remote I would need someone with local knowledge. With a barely perceptible movement of his head, like a dealer at an auction, he called up my guide and introduced us.

Jim was about sixty, small, average build, with grey hair showing under a mature cap. He wore a wide American-style tie with a white shirt and a double-breasted blue suit-jacket over a shabby pair of brown corduroys. He had thick glasses with tortoiseshell frames, held together at both hinges by sticking plaster. One lens was even thicker than the other. He perked his head to one side as if to look through the better lens and with a reticent smile said, 'Pleased to meet you.' I knew immediately we were going to get on.

The Twin Rock was about fourteen miles away. Jim would bring me as far as the turn to the old quarry where there was a small country pub, and I would leave him there and pick him up on the way back. We finished our drinks and left.

It was half-day and shops were closed. We walked towards the quay, where I had parked the car. It was May and a clear blue sky. Despite an onshore breeze there was warmth in the air. A screech of gulls was crying like banshees over a trawler where crew were dumping offal. A little further out a tern was sitting on the breeze, dipping from time to time to the ruffled surface of the water. The car was like an oven; we opened the windows and set off.

I knew my way until we turned off the main road nine or ten miles out, so I didn't need the help of my guide at first, but the conversation was slow to get going.

'What do you work at?' I asked.

'Nothin' much these days, the auld sight is gone.' Pause. 'I'm tryin' to get the blind pension.'

'Don't you need to be totally blind to get that?'

'Well I nearly am, so I thought I'd get most of it; but the bloody auld TDs round here are no good. I'm after bein' to more doctors and medicals; I nearly know the charts off be heart.'

Jim would only talk if I started first. After a long silence I said, 'You're not married?' – sure in my mind that he wasn't.

'I am,' he said.

'Have you family?'

'Twelve livin', but there's only three left in the country. The rest is all in England or America. I have one in Australia.' And after a pause, 'God, isn't the country in a shockin' state. The last two to go went to England after Christmas. I do have to laugh when I hear our crowd condemnin' Thatcher when she can provide the jobs and they can't. They can't even afford to give me the blind pension let alone jobs for me children.'

'Times are hard, right enough. But I think things are looking up,' I said, trying to lift the conversation a bit.

'They are, but aren't the young people gone to the divil with drink and drugs and all this sex?'

'You're right,' I said tersely, not wanting to get into that particular area.

We turned off the main road and Jim directed me through a maze of tiny roads; despite his poor sight his navigation was faultless. We climbed steadily on a narrow road that only had room for one car. The may was coming into bloom. Primroses dotted the ditches on both sides in nature's inimitable asymmetry. The signs of spring were well established.

I dropped Jim at the pub and gave him a few pounds to punch in the time. I turned up towards the quarry and arrived at a clearing on the right-hand side of the road. I left the car and walked quietly up the road past the quarry gate, as Joe had told me, to a high bank on the left. I climbed the bank and lay on my stomach, surveying the scene. I had a bird's-eye view of the derelict quarry. From cracks in the long-abandoned quarry face to my left sprouted grasses, gorse and an occasional small tree. The moorland stretching to my right had worked its way back to the bottom of the rock face.

There was absolute stillness. I noted roughly the point on the ground in tall vegetation beyond the quarry face that Joe had described to me. I lifted my binoculars and searched the sky all round. There was no sign of anything. I lay on my back and waited, scouring the bright, clear sky from time to time. At last, after about an hour and many false alarms, I saw the male harrier coming towards the quarry from my right. At first it was little more than a spot; then a recognisable flight pattern.

I slid back down the bank eight or ten feet to the cover of some low gorse and sat back on my haunches. I was aware of my pulse. Keeping my glasses trained on the approaching male, I glanced at the spot on the ground. Too soon. I looked to the incoming bird. I could now see the blue-grey colour and the black wing tips. I glanced to my left again. Still no move.

As the cock came closer, his steady wing beat slowed. He began to lose height and I could see the prey locked in his powerful talons. Before he was above the mouth of the quarry he started to glide. I turned to look at the spot, tingling with expectancy. There she was, the hen rising from her concealed nesting site towards the cock. With the cock slightly above and ahead she rolled on her back, showing her pure white rump, relief from her overall brown. He dropped the prey. She caught it in a flash in her outstretched talons. It was magic. In a split second the pass was complete and the birds parted.

At that instant the crack of a rifle shot shattered the stillness. I saw a sprinkling of feathers come from the cock. The birds flew in opposite directions but I could see from his flight that he was not injured. In seconds both birds dropped and disappeared into the vegetation beyond the quarry face.

I didn't move for what seemed an age. My heart pounded. I became aware that both my knees pained and one of my legs locked in cramp. I slumped down and sat on the bank. It took some time for the pain to abate. I was thrilled and stunned. My first sight of one of the most spectacular happenings in the bird world, the food pass of the hen harrier, had nearly ended in tragedy.

I crept slowly back up the bank and peered out over the top. Everything was as still as when I arrived. I lay quietly for a long time. There was no sound and no sign of anyone. I went back to the car and sat thinking about what to do. There was nothing for me to do except to tell Joe when I got back. I turned the car, and switching off the engine, freewheeled slowly down the lane towards the pub. I thought I might come on the sniper and was half glad that I didn't.

Jim was waiting. He wanted to buy me a drink but I declined.

He finished his pint and we left the pub and got into the car. I hadn't told him the purpose of my mission and I assumed Joe hadn't either. I didn't know if, from Joe's point of view, it was all right for him to know but I couldn't keep it in. Jim listened carefully and when I finished he perked his head to one side, looked up at me and said, 'The gobshites.'

OPPRESSION

Aisling Maguire

In that filthy coat is the weight of Alice's trouble. She lifts it off the floor and stretches it on the counter. Dawn tires against the window. She begins to pick at a lump of dirt on the sleeve. Cascading chains of the first skip to leave the dump commence the day. Her head flinches over her shoulder. The door remains shut. Her fingernails continue to lever the scab of dirt. She could call him again. She goes to the door, listens, returns to the counter. Silence means he is awake. The once-beige, second- or third-hand camel hair is now clogged with dirt. Her hand smooths the back until it jolts the canister of hairspray he swilled last night. At the rattle of the ball bearings in the empty tin she twitches again, her two hands attempting to muffle the noise. The pale lining is stained in such a way that the liquids it has absorbed – alcohol, urine, vomit and worse – have spread lakes that meld in varying dark shades, their dried edges magnifying the weft of the fabric. The Crombie label is obliterated.

He fancied himself glam after finding it on a bench; swaggered although it was too big for him. From one pocket he drew a half-tube of mints which, with large gestures, he distributed among the children, making them giggle and call it a 'Santa Claus coat'. Alice had smiled. Through her mind was running the fear that he had stolen the coat, that a knock would come to the door and he would be accused. Her smile remained although she knew that he looked foolish in the dress of a prosperous middle-aged man. He flared the coat at his rump and stalked a circle. He buttoned it and minced to the wall and back. He laughed at her and said she was jealous.

117

'No I'm not.' She went on smiling. His fist smacked her brow all the same.

Her hand, still stroking the lining, knocks the canister again and the ball bearings jiggle. Gently, she turns the coat over. Absolute silence is required. Then he will get up. She knows he shouldn't be late. But if she calls him again he will chastise her for nagging. Another skip rolls out of the dump. Her head swivels and returns to the coat which the smear of sun has seen fit to bless. Only now does the smell assail her: a faecal stink that clutches her stomach and gobs her throat. How had she not noticed it before? Her eye scans the front panel, seeing the bulge of the frayed pocket, seeing the congealed cuffs, the burst stitches under the arms and the split-collar grin. Her finger prods the stale garment. She is inane with fear, fighting to hold peace. Revulsion chides her. She disgusts herself for having so long tolerated this smell. God above. No hum could be worse. And it must be on her too. On the children. The way they are all locked together in a solitary room. For the kitchen doesn't count. It's a cupboard.

Here is Alice's hope. If she is quiet; if he can wake peacefully and take his coat (even though the day will be warm, she can feel that already in the milkish light); if he can go out that door without hitting her – she will breathe again, she will love the children, she will deal out the slices of bread, she might even regret not having offered him a sandwich. All right then, bread and butter, but it would have been something . . . and something's better . . . These dreams are better checked.

Her jaw is tense. If she prepares in her mind, maybe the blow won't feel so bad. Why is she such a coward? She wills herself numb in expectation of the pain that would, for an instant, stun her, then rough-house her bones and present itself in blue and yellow stains. If it wasn't for that, she thinks, I might chance running away again.

How come she doesn't hate him? That's the thing foxes her. How come she doesn't go into the chemist and buy a drop of arsenic? Or to the butcher for a knife? She doesn't love him. She wriggled out of that tender trap years ago. Before her the big coat yawns. Its angles match the set of his body. Yet its colour and shape put her in mind of a desert. He looks strange in it. Maybe there's the point. She doesn't know him any more. If ever she did. She knew he made her laugh. When they were no more than children and getting married was a game.

Her hand ruffles the coat, avoiding the hairspray canister. She always does her best not to scream. At least she can say that for herself. The children don't see her pain. She knows she is being stupid. She should run away. Anywhere. But she won't.

Once, she ran. Gathered her trinklets in a plastic bag and shut the door. Let him look after the kids, she thought, and that time there were only three. Merciful hour, here she is now with treble the number. No dodging that brood. By the time she reached the end of the street the voices were at her to go back. They continued even while the boat breasted the channel. Not a wink did she sleep all night but sat with the plastic bag rolled on her knee. Reflected light spanned the dark water. People wambled from the bar to heave over the railing. The beer, or the sea, or both, getting the better of them. Anyway, she was finished with all that business, so she thought.

A tall woman bobbed into the seat alongside her. Puffing, the woman put a hand to her hair, then patted her face. Dim cabin lights showed the sweat standing off it like pimples. Her hands came to rest on her stomach as if she bore a child.

'Oh, missis. You've no idea of the pain,' the stranger said, twisting this way and that way. Her husband had run her through with the carving knife, missed the colon by that (her thumb and forefinger pinched the air). Three months they were married. 'Never again. Oh never again, missis.'

119

She had brought him his lunch to the factory, just as usual. The first of June. Light-hearted, in her sunny white dress she crossed the waste ground, admiring the bosomy poppies, counting time blown off the dandelion clocks. There he was, against the wire mesh. Oh, even the axle grease on his face gave him a fine strong look. After eating, they shared a cigarette. That was when the foreman, walking by, tipped her a wink and she winked back. Finished she was then. Her husband stubbed the cigarette and left with ne'er a touch nor a word. She had no lightness in her homeward step. Every shadow hurt her skin. She tried singing but that was no help. One time she was a real singer. Had she said? Name a song, she knew it: 'My Way'; 'Starlight Serenade'; 'Paper Moon'. Where was she? At home. Waiting. In on the door he come and straight to the kitchen for the carving knife. Dead jealous. To get her out of public eyes, he married her. He pulled the knife clear and she hit the kitchen floor, seeing blood swill around as if it belonged to someone else, redness expanding over the sunny dress.

'Missis, I was lucky I survived.' Her salvation, a neighbour chancing in to use the phone. Six weeks in the hospital and still she felt the gap in her gut. 'You could have blown a pea clean through from front to back,' her laugh guggled. 'I need a drink now, missis.'

The impression of the stranger's voice soaked down to silence. Unlike that woman, Alice could not name the start of her worry. With the children she was always tired. He hated their noise. He expected her to drop them and feed him as soon as he stepped through the door. She could barely laugh any more. There was no space for peace. The children slept in drawers pulled from the closet, and the baba between herself and himself in the bed. That never stopped him. Small as he was, he could flatten the breath out of her. Pain stabbed her milking breasts. Her body stiffened like a plank.

She turned to the window. The wash curled off the ship's

keel like wood shavings. Where was she going? Her hands tightened on the plastic bag. Was she going out of bad into worse? Straight off the ship, she would look for a boarding house. Then a job. In the bag was a picture of the home she wanted. She had found it poking from a bin where the sun shimmered its foil surface. Cutting away the grocer's legend and the month of December, she laid it on the table while feeding. The baba and herself swayed away to the grove of trees and the garden sweet with roses and lilies where the stone house warmed in the sun, its thatch trim as a new broom. With the gentle sensation of the baba's suck, happiness had grown inside her.

About to take the picture from her bag, she stopped when the tall woman returned swinging a vodka bottle by the neck, her other hand wrapping the hand of a man. Reseated, her escort settled across the aisle, the woman began her story again, pausing for the man's commiserations. She clamped the bag shut and looked through her own face to the dark. Would she end up disrespectable as this woman? For no matter what, the woman was still the knife-man's wife. Alice could never spill her grief to any and everyone. She scarcely drank and never conversed with strangers. Here she was, twenty-one years of age, and she had two ways of considering life: either she had lived more than plenty already and there was nothing left, or else, long new days ribboned ahead of her, waiting for her to find them.

She had put her thoughts on the future until he frogmarched her home. The picture vanished. He walloped her as no proper mother, no proper wife. The priest agreed. She was here to serve God, her husband and her children.

'And who serves me?' she brazened.

'Consider yourself blessed to have the one true faith,' he chided. 'Reflect on the darkness swamping the heathens. Five Hail Marys, five Our Fathers. Now, I confess . . .' His voice trickled Latin under her contrition.

The prayers stuck in her craw. Blessed. He gave the word a foreign sound. Yet when she knelt before the Mother of Good Counsel, peace settled on her heart.

Although she gets no answers, she never lets up pleading. Her life is shrivelled to the size of the dingy coat. She folds back the sleeves like wings, cautious of the hairspray canister. In fact, she is not stupid. Only tired. When the kids are bigger, when she doesn't have to be lifting them and telling them off, then she will be able to sit down and figure things out: one, how she came to accept being trapped by this stink; two, how she is going to get rid of it.

Yet she can no more credit such prospects than she can the buildings she cleans at night. Walking into those places is like going to the moon. King Kong plants reach out of white boxes. Machines natter like birds in a cage. The view from the high windows sickens her. All she can see is lights. No people. No cars. No houses. Not even a cat or a dog. If this is flying, she wouldn't thank you for a ticket to Bali Hi.

Even while her mind runs on this way, every inch of her is alert for sounds that might come from the room. Her fingers knead the clot of dirt. What is it? Black. Tar? It could be. Or blood? Not that. He showed no sign of bleeding. Unless it came from someone else. But he never got into fights. Which was the odd thing. What then, if not blood, if not tar? Better not to think. Say chewing gum. She goes on picking the way a brat worries its nose.

Whenever she hears 'My Way' or the other songs riding out of shops or car windows, she recollects the tall woman on the boat.

'My larrings is bollocks'd' – the woman swallowed her vodka. 'He might as well of taken a knife to my throat. I'll never forgive him that.'

Her hand cups the stain. She is worse off than that woman. No one has made a keyhole of her guts: true. She never had much of a voice: true too. It's not that she can't sing. She lives like a person walking blindfold down a railway track. He has snatched the world from under her. Every waking minute she is on the watch for his foot or his fist. This ruggy coat is a skin stretched over her and the children. Her own skin is lost, and all as she feels any more is grief.

The banging catapults Alice's heart out of her chest. Sweat scalds her joints. She can't move. Her hands blot the coat. Again the ferocious knock. She eases around, terror bolting her limbs. Both doors are shut. She opens before the next knock. Two men step in. They fill the kitchen, their charcoal suits stopping the light.

Her finger goes to her lips. 'My husband,' she admonishes, 'he's sleeping.'

'It's him we want,' one says, pinching his nose back from the smell.

'He'll be up soon,' she whispers.

'Get him out of that bed now.'

'No, no,' she pleads. 'No.'

Her hand flies to the coat. Could it be? No. That was years ago. Although how many she could not say. But the spot? Her terror blinks at the men.

'We're bailiffs,' says the second. At least he has a gentle voice. A sheet of paper unfolds from his hand. She shakes her head.

'You're being evicted,' the loud one speaks.

She shakes again. If they keep quiet, they will all be safe. Her shaking quickens. Then stops. He is standing in the doorway. Three of the children gawk around him. Slim, a little stooped, his pale face offset by spongy hair, he waits for the story. Blood-webbed eyes search her, then the men. The white page is held before him.

'You can't evict me,' he asserts. 'I bought this place.'

Alice nods.

'You've defaulted on your repayments,' the loud one says.

'Yeah. But that's only temporary. I'm looking for work. All there is going now is part-time. Odd jobs.'

She nods again. Inside, her mind exults. This might be the way to escape and she would be blameless. Not that that ever made a difference. She is a coward. Otherwise she would step out in front of these men. Ignoring his blows, she would say: 'It's true. He's bought this place. And he can't find proper work. When he does he drinks the money. I have a job but that only goes to feed the kids.'

Oh yes, she could go on. If she wasn't so afraid. She's been hit before and look at her now, standing on her own legs. It would be worth it. Even if he did kick her all the way down the stairs. 'Go on,' she would continue, 'throw us out. I'll sleep on the streets. Anywhere. Not to be obliged to him. Tear us apart.'

Yet and all her nodding defends her husband's indignation. She knows what he's thinking: these fellows only want to put the squeeze on him because he's down. That's their kick. Making little men feel like worms. Then they can be big fellows. Exploitation. Often and often he's seen the heels of their boots. He's been on this earth long enough to know a bruiser when he meets one. He is right. Her hand clutches the coat. What would they care if she tossed herself on the ground before them? Nothing. Only politely step over her, the way they would avoid a dead thing on the road. Why don't they leave? Why did they come and disturb the bit of peace she was having? She'd like to shove them out the door. Then she could apologise to him and peace would maybe return.

The kids look unnatural. Blank, afraid, as she, of their father. They are sickly, dirty. They came so close together she hardly knows which is the eldest. Now she sees them as if they were a stranger's children. The way they appear to the two men whose faces are clenched against the stink. How long have my children been so dirty? she wonders. How did I not check the grubbiness creeping over their little skins? Their hair looks as if it never met a comb. It dawns on her to consider, too, what way she looks. One of the bailiffs probes his tooth with a match. Letting her husband take his own time. Alice knows they are seeing a family so lost for self-awareness as to be incapable of defending itself.

She allows her smile to withdraw. She glances down at the coat to find she has been unstitching loose thread from a buttonhole. Her fingers straighten and cover the destruction. What these men are watching, she feels, is a group of people so inert that there is no cause for upset whether they live or die. Although, pressed to it, anyone would say die was better. Already they reek of the grave. How far is death? When the blows whack and her insides curdle she believes she can see it: a mild slope, bare, save for grass and a solitary tree, rises before her. She is going to lie down there and shut her eyes beside the daisies. The calm sweetens her expression.

'We'll be back,' says the loud man.

She shivers. Her eyes start wide. Where has she been? Affinity for her husband rises like vomit in her throat. She knows the way being hit makes you want to stay down. She might help him dig but she does not want to carry his pain.

Her glance commiserates.

He scowls.

She knows that as soon as the men have echoed down the concrete stairs, his fist will bolt her jaw. Her tongue will burst with the iron taste of blood. The agony will blind her before the next blow comes at her ribs or her abdomen.

She turns away from the men and neatly folds the coat for her husband to wear stepping out.

IT'S THE LIVING THAT KILLS YOU

Monica Tracey

'Will you see your ex-wife?' the sister in the Royal Victoria asked him. Standing at the threshold of the ward, I could feel my face burning with shame. You don't get ex-wives in Belfast, only in places like Hollywood or England. He would be glad to see me, for we always got on very well together – except when we were fighting. But I understood that she might be frightened in case I had come to bully him or beat him up. When one of his brothers phoned the previous evening to say it was only a matter of days, there was no question but take the first plane to Belfast.

He choked a welcome, though the words locked in his throat. His eyes were covered by a thick film but I could tell he was pleased I was there. It was a couple of years since I last saw him and my memories were a muddle of what he had been like then and of the man I knew a long time ago. Of course he would have changed but I was not prepared for the wasted figure, skin stretched tight over his skull, one hand clutching the bars of his cot, the other burning in mine. The pain and the passion we had known together! Who would ever believe it? For we had laughed and loved so hard that when he first left, it was as if he took the sunlight with him. Time passes and memories blur. Sitting there in the narrow curtained space, talking to him and listening to him, what I felt was impersonal – pity for what he was suffering and for what lay ahead of him.

In the days after we left Ireland we had both strayed from the religion that told us what to think and what to believe. Day in, day out, through childhood and most of our adult life, we had prayed the words 'Now and at the hour of our death', 'Assist me now and in my last agony.' We had liked to think of ourselves as civilised people who did not try to influence each other, but that was a lifetime ago. Now, like it or not, he was getting the prayers for the dying. Anyhow, he was in no position to argue. There had been too many rehearsals for him to miss the real thing.

'May I breathe forth my soul in peace with You', his nod of acknowledgement of his certain death, the pressure of his hand in mine, the first tears I ever saw him shed in all the years I knew him and my own tears, splashing onto the sheets, crashed through the barriers we had built between us and shattered the pride, hurt and arrogance that had turned us into strangers.

Two of our daughters arrived from London in the afternoon. They had suffered the stigma of a broken home, living as we do in a Catholic ghetto in the north of England. They used to pretend that their father worked abroad and their infrequent meetings with him had been marked by embarrassment and unease on both sides, but their immediate reaction was to be with him. As he lapsed in and out of consciousness during the days we were with him, they talked to him about their lives and their plans. The only voluntary movement he made was to sit up suddenly, reach out his arms to the younger girl and hold her close to him. Her infancy and young life had passed us both by almost unnoticed, so intent were we on waging our war of attrition; yet his face was transformed with pure joy as he said her name over and over again and stroked her face.

Some of the wards of the hospital open onto a veranda that overlooks the tennis courts, where patients can stroll or sit on deckchairs. It had a touch of the country club about it – drinks in the evening sun, warm and glowing in the May heat – patients supporting each other and sympathising with us: 'Give that wee girl a fag. Keep the whole packet, luv.' 'He's niver yer da, ach sure I thought he was yer granda.' Cups of tea were handed out, life histories exchanged: 'I lost my son with cancer last year and my daughter two year ago. I went a bit stupid, started drinkin' an' all. Then I said to myself, "Catch yerself on. Other people has worse troubles." '

And they all smoked – patients with lung cancer, liver cancer and heart conditions – they smoked as if there was no tomorrow. Somebody had even stuck a cigarette in Queen Victoria's mouth, where she stood at the entrance to the hospital, staring stonily. It's a great thing to be with your own people at a time like this. For we may maim each other and kill each other because we fly different flags and attend different schools and churches, but all of us from Northern Ireland have been hacked out of the same rough earth, speak a language whose nuances are understood only by us and share a sense of humour that is uniquely our own.

Next day our eldest daughter arrived from Budapest. She was the only one who had ever really known him and she had memories of a happy childhood spent a few miles from the hospital. My friend Minnie, who minded the children when I went to work, said it was the happiest home she ever knew. Years later when she was widowed and I divorced she summed up our respective lives: 'You get over death. It's the living that kills you.' However you interpret her words, allowing for the liberties that are taken with the English language, I think there is a world of wisdom in what she said.

How we tended him! When he opened his eyes we forced ourselves into his line of vision. We poured liquid, unasked, down his throat. When he mouthed the word 'bottle', in our ignorance we uncorked more juice, more Lucozade, and we left him to steep in his urine. His only escape from our grieving and praying was to drift into sleep. All his life he had needed so much to be on his own, or with company of his choosing, that he had put oceans, and more recently the Irish Sea, between us. 'Don't smother me,' he used to say. We gave him no peace. We killed him with kindness.

About three o'clock on the morning of the day he died the effects of the drugs wore off and through the agony of his consciousness he told us how much he had always cared for us, and then said goodbye. I remember an unreal three-way conversation between my son from the other side of the world, myself, and my own voice boomeranging back over the telephone. It was too late for him to come but we would give his father his love.

They had intended to move him to a hospice for the dying, but as somebody said, the journey would have killed him. I don't think he could have died in a kinder place than the Royal Victoria. We will never forget the solicitude of the consultant who brought us tea and told us what to expect, or the staff who saw their job as looking after us, since there was so little that could be done for him. The sister told us that the sense of hearing becomes very acute before death, so we talked to him about the good times we had known together and we recited to him the poems we could remember – Yeats, Wordsworth, Hopkins – applying our own censorship. One of the girls said she only knew 'The Charge of the Light Brigade', but in the absence of the other five hundred and ninety-nine we ruled that one out. Strange the things we said to him as he struggled: 'It won't be long now', 'You're nearly there.' Another push. The same sort of encouragement a woman in labour hears; the same urgings at both ends of existence.

Just before he died two of his neighbours came to see him. Their relationship with him had been close. They had helped and supported each other over the last few years and it was, in some ways, more appropriate for them to be there than us. But the immediacy of their sorrow and the unrestrained outpourings of grief at the loss of someone whose life had touched theirs each day was disturbing and incongruous to us, his family. 'Fancy him having all them big girls! We never knew he had any family. Where do you live, luv? . . . Lewisham. I've got a cousin lives in Lewisham. No, wait a wee minute. I think she lives in Clapham and works in Lewisham.' We started saying the rosary and that put an end to the questions.

I felt his pulse throb steadily till it slowed and stopped and life seeped from the man who had given life to my five children.

'Till death us do part.' Many years ago, when we left the divorce court together and sat for hours in the pub, stunned and relieved by what had just happened, we knew we had settled something but that neither of us could ever completely cut whatever it was that had tied us together. Death had, once and for all, put an end to our misgivings, longings and recriminations.

My brother shook hands with me: 'Well, you're a widow now. You're free to get married again.'

I had always been reminded on previous visits that in the eyes of God I was still married, in case I had any other notion. I didn't know if he was congratulating me or giving me permission.

There was no mistaking the meaning of my ninety-year-old mother: 'One man is enough for any woman, so now that he's gone don't you go making a fool of yourself at your time of life.'

I had shed the shame of the divorcée and assumed the tragic dignity of widowhood and was fit to be reinstated and openly acknowledged as a respectable member of the family.

I left Ireland the following day, glad to get away from the crowds and emotions. My daughters looked forlorn when I left but I needed to tell my youngest child about her father rather than telephone her. She was the product of our last and otherwise fruitless period of reconciliation. She had stayed in England because she had A-level orals, and anyway, she never really knew him. It was good to be back in my own home. Peace and quiet, all that behind me, done and dusted. I had seen it through, done the decent thing and had had enough of finding out if old wounds had healed.

How could I be so wrong? Didn't I know that no one is really dead in Ireland until after the funeral? My place was there with his family and my family and there was no way I could stay away. So next morning the two of us took the plane back to Belfast.

He had a great sendoff. He wasn't brought home for the night because the bleak dwelling where he had spent the last few years had been home to none of us. The wake was packed – plenty to eat and drink, chats with friends from the past, stories about him, stories he used to tell. The church for the funeral Mass was full too. The priest spoke of him as 'a quiet, friendly man, one who always kept a certain distance between you and him'. We could go along with that. Each of my daughters read a lesson or a psalm, their Geordie voices judged posh among plainer Belfast accents. An Irish funeral is a powerful institution. There's the warmth and solidarity; concern for the living and respect for the dead. Hatchets are buried, however temporarily. News travels fast and people come from far and near, maybe just to say 'Sorry for your trouble' or to be there for the wake and the funeral. Above all there's time to get used to the fact that someone is gone for ever.

Kneeling in the church, I remembered my father's wake, where his two brothers, big Donegal fishermen, downed a bottle of brandy without a drop touching the sides of their throats, and thinking, it's a terrible pity my da is not here, for he would have enjoyed this. They had arrived wearing coarse jackets and hobnail boots. They appeared in the church in their dead brother's suits, shirts and shoes. My father in duplicate, at his own funeral. Then there was the day my Uncle Joe came back from his holidays in Scotland in a coffin. A taxi came from Donegal to the Belfast docks. The coffin was strapped to the roof and we proceeded along the twisty, thirsty road to The Rosses. When we all went into the first pub someone asked, 'What about Joe?', to get the reply, 'Joe will be all right up there. Sure the dacent man won't be going anywhere.'

After the Mass the five of us were put in the chief mourners' limousine. It was a bit like a scene from *The Godfather* – five dark women all playing a part and playing it well. We weren't chief mourners. His brothers who had supported him during the bad years should have been there and his sister, just back from holiday that morning, her tanned face stricken. Or the young man who told my daughters how their father had helped him get his life together. He said he didn't know how he could go on without his guidance.

The journey to the graveyard was even slower than you might expect, because we got caught up in the Belfast Marathon and were separated from the hearse by groups of runners who paid their respects as we glided alongside them. When we arrived at the graveyard it was alive with soldiers, running along hedges, lying flat on their bellies, rifles at the ready, crouching down between the gravestones. Nobody paid any attention because that's what it's like in Belfast. In other circumstances my spot would have been booked beside him and a space left for my name on the headstone, but there would be no room for me there beside his mother and father.

It was said by veterans of such events that the get-together after the funeral was better crack than manys a wedding, not just the food and drink but the chat and meetings with old friends after so many years. I was sorry I had to leave in the middle of it and glad my daughters were staying. On the plane I had time to think over the events of the past week and rightly to anticipate the embarrassed silence of my colleagues when I would return to work the next day. Most of them made no reference to what, no doubt, seemed an irrational jaunt – and I never did let on about the second trip. Somebody explained it with, 'But you're Irish!' Only my boss, another sort of Celt, said she would have done the same thing.

It's a fact; dying is something we do well in Ireland. But then we've had a lot of practice at it.

AT ARROMANCHES

Harriet O'Carroll

At Arromanches the sun was shining. The warm tide slid quickly up the hot beige beach. Out in the blue water, like large remembrances, the square grey cassions stood. Frivolous wavelets mocked their dour solemnity, nudging vainly at the slow-to-crumble concrete. In the village square the heat leapt up from the pavements and the parking area. At the top of the steps to the beach there was a wide space where a gypsy kept her fleet of hobbyhorses, pedal cars and buggies for hire. Indeed the square was the village and it ceased quickly as the streets marched up into the gentle hills behind. All around that square the perquisites and merchandise of a seaside village fluttered in the wind – inflated boats and windmills, spades and buckets, small plastic rakes, brilliant in synthetic colours. Postcard stands and centime-sucking machines stood in mute invitation. The Second World War had once rolled through and demolished this village, but now it was good for business. People came and bought the local ceramics. They drank their coffee or their wine or their cider in the sun. They ate the local patisseries and they went home with ship-in-bottle souvenirs.

A minibus drove up and disgorged a group of English teenagers, who competed with each other to be the first to hand their francs to the gypsy for the pleasure of a ride on a pedal car. A small crowd hovered outside the war museum. It was closed, like almost everything else in France, for lunch.

'I don't know how they do it,' said Bill Altmind. 'How can a country get as prosperous as this by sleeping half the day?'

Lily Altmind was writing postcards. She had sat for a while in the sun, enjoying it yet feeling slightly guilty, as if she should be doing something for someone. Then she remembered with relief that this would be a good opportunity to get her postcards written. She walked across the square and picked out three, one for each of her children. She wrote, not what she felt but what was expected: 'Best wishes. We are having a marvellous time. You should see your father, he sure enjoys that *vin du pays*. We are going to Paris next week.' Similar messages to all three, love to the two married ones, Robert and Susan, love and encouragement to her baby, Christopher, who was about to graduate from law school. She sat beside her husband, looking what she was, a neat American woman who had chosen to go blond rather than grey. In the silence of the first holiday in years alone with her husband she was wondering what it was they usually spoke about.

'You're being crabby, Bill,' she said. 'I guess they work late instead.'

He was not to be cheated of his irritability. 'Oh go on, Lily, you'd try to think of excuses for Hitler.'

It was true, though of course it would be ridiculous to admit it. At one time she had privately tried to think of excuses for Hitler. In the years before she had left England, when she was young and reaching for optimism in a world dissolving, she had tried to believe that there could not exist such a monster as he appeared to be. She had forgotten about that for years now. Planning their holiday in France, she had not thought about the war. She had fallen for the brochure notion of *joie de vivre*, for the image of a country old in civilisation and in history. She had pictured walled towns and ancient streets, the echoes of splendour from vanished courts, the richness of a past that stood guard over the present. All these promises were fulfilled, but also there was their own past, the war.

It had started in Cherbourg. They climbed up to the war

museum, crossed the rickety wooden footbridge and paced around the exhibits. It had been Bill's idea.

'Why don't you want to forget?' Lily had groaned. 'To you men it's all just a great game.'

Bill's war had been in the Far East. He did not talk about it much, nor had he kept in touch with old buddies from those days. None the less she felt excluded, a spectator, like the child who doesn't enjoy football and wishes that no one else did either. She had had, she supposed, as much chance as anyone of dying in that war. She had been born in England and had not departed for America until after the last victory torch had burnt out. But she had not willed her participation, she herself had not gone out to kill or die.

She passed with disinterest the uniforms of generals, the boxes of medals for courage and achievement, the regalia of honour of the survivors. The weapons, too, she passed, thinking only that the energy that created them could have been put to better use. She stopped before the great wall maps, looked at the black arrows fanning out from Normandy. Finally, the fact of a Europe under siege became a truth for her. She studied the coloured areas on the map, the areas of objective, the areas of achievement, the sheer immensity and impossibility of the task, flicked at, teased and caught her imagination. There had been, after all, a design behind the endless destruction of those days. In her memory it had been a recurrence of people leaving. Here she was being offered an explanation of sorts.

Unexpectedly interested, they had driven down small country roads in the rented Peugeot and sat in the square at Arromanches. They watched the paddlers and the sand-diggers and the teenagers on their buggy rides. They waited with the others for the war museum to open.

'*Votre chemise, monsieur,*' said the uniformed attendant to the teenager with the golden tan on his exposed chest.

'Like the Vatican,' said Lily while Bill muttered about the price of the tickets. It was not that he was mean, exactly, but being abroad, he was constantly wary. He liked to get value.

The museum was small and people churned around and tried to sort out the explanations in their own languages. In perspex cases, models re-created the invasion of Normandy. Tiny troop carriers swayed on fake waves, armoured vehicles stood on ramps, model soldiers carried model guns onto the beach. The back wall of the museum was all window, where you could look from the stormy model to the sunny present. The grey cassions stood; built to endure three months, they were there immobile after thirty years. It did not seem possible that all those years ago they had been built in England, towed across the channel and sunk to provide a five-mile harbour for the invaders.

'I can see why they make such a fuss about it,' said Lily. 'It must have been some surprise for the Germans.'

Bill Altmind was enthralled. He owned a light-engineering business and was fascinated by the technology and logistics of the operation. Mine clearing, he thought, ah yes, flail tanks. But a Sherman duplex drive in front, then coming behind the bridge for the anti-tank ditch, that would do it.

'Son of a bitch,' he said to himself, then to Lily, 'What a damned great enterprise. Imagine getting your teeth into that one.'

Lily immediately felt hostile. It wasn't a game, she didn't say, they really died.

They trooped around the exhibition, listened to an account of the invasion from the viewpoint of a British pilot. On a lighted screen ghostly parachutes floated down. Bombardment clamoured, searchlights split the fake sky, boats waited, tied by the worst storm in years. The voice of the commentary went inexorably on, in accents of hope and victory, the accent of the time and the accent of hindsight. When the lights went on in the small auditorium Lily could see tears in eyes that must have first looked on the world after it was all over.

It was a sober group that went up to the cinema to see a spliced-together film taken from the newsreels of the time. It seemed a hundred years ago to Lily since she had heard that note of breezy optimism, the voice of the Pathé news. It spoke only of success, bringing the same innocent energy to news of Princess Elizabeth visiting a hospital, or the chaps sailing away to put a spoke in Hitler's wheel. The world was one world then, with all right-thinking people knowing what to think. On the screen the images were black and white, the ships were berated by the storm, the houses were demolished, a young chap dived onto a wintry beach, and was still. She closed her eyes. It was all over. She had survived, and her children had not been to Vietnam. By her grandchildren's time men might have got sense. The flags of the victors were waving outside the museum and she was numbered among the victorious.

They drove through the French countryside that afternoon. Bill struggled with the unfamiliar gears of the small Peugeot. Flat sandy soil, unhedged, intensely cultivated, brimmed with summer grass. They looked at the stone farmhouses, their shutters flung open to the sun, and admired the small slates on curving roofs. They felt that the countryside was extremely cosy and inhabited. Even the trees were subjected to man's will, pruned into acceptable shapes. Thin fingerposts allotted a name to every area: Le Vieux Chêne, Les Jumelles. They stopped beside a field of flax, luminous blue in the sunlight.

'How about the tapestry?' said Bill. 'Shall we go back to Bayeux?'

'One war a day will do me,' said Lily. 'Why don't we give it a miss? We could go tomorrow.'

'Whatever you like.'

'Let's walk a bit.'

'I'd better park in the shade, otherwise the car will be stifling.'

They drove for a while before he found a clump of trees. The sun had that special pleasantness of being new and fresh, the land was not dried up, the leaves were green and soft, it had that particular felicity of sunshine that is neither habitual nor reliable. They walked separately, side by side. It was a quiet road; there was no traffic to disturb their silence.

'If you could bottle peace,' said Lily, 'it would feel something like this.'

'Glad you came?'

'Yes. And you?'

She knew the answer. It had been her idea to come to Europe, she had talked about it and planned it and wondered about budgets. Then at the last moment, overawed by the responsibility of organising their enjoyment, she had been ready to back out. By then Bill had become committed to the idea. He was enjoying their holiday, having decided that he would. On this fourth day he was relaxed, he had begun to forget the habit of pressure, to discard the urgency of timetables, the specifications and limitations of his business.

'Shall we look for a restaurant, then?' asked Bill.

Their footsteps were soft on the sandy road as they walked back to the car. Sparrows shuffled in the dust, shook themselves like puppies, then bubbed along. The quiet was sufficiently profound to reveal the undetected noises of summer, the stir of leaf on leaf, the rasp of a grasshopper. A woodpigeon called and was still. Bill reached for Lily's hand and they walked together. As they walked they remembered unconsciously the accretion of good will that accompanied their years of marriage, the irritations forgiven, the misunderstandings understood, the limitations respected. Without fear of irritation each from the other they changed their minds about going back to Bayeux. They found a relish in changing their minds. They were on holiday, they said to each other, free even from the constraints of their own decisions. They would eat where they chose, on impulse, without consulting the guidebook. If the meal was expensive or unusual, they agreed, it would not be the end of the world, they would take their chances.

They stopped at a restaurant set in a small garden. Young people in jeans and T-shirts with messages sat under parasols and drank wine. 'Fight poverty, marry a millionaire,' read Lily.

The table linen was pink, the restaurant was busy and the small waitress was demented. She had her own notions about what people should eat, and did not like to understand departures from the accepted menu or order of courses. The young people were ordering single courses in English and Dutch, but not, they noticed, in German. The waitress would accept only French and became irate at attempts to point to the menu.

'*Vous voulez les moules*?' she snarled. Lily watched a young woman abandon her efforts to order a *côte de veau* and obediently consume a bowl of mussels.

Bill and Lily were given a large bottle of red wine, then the waitress disappeared into the kitchen without waiting for their order. They poured out some wine and forgot her. They started to talk about Christopher. It was, after all, something satisfactory to have reached a point in time at which one's youngest child was equipped for life. He had been, they admitted, only to each other, their most rewarding child. It was not perhaps any virtue of his own, it was more through his luck in having been born into easier times for them. He had been all that they could have hoped. They had made a success of their marriage, an undertaking upon which they had embarked with so much optimism. They had remained faithful without extraordinary effort. They had been reasonably secure. All their fears had been unrealised, childhood measles had not become encephalitis, adolescent disturbances had not lasted. Their children, in so far as they were aware, had not taken drugs, parented illegitimate children, or become involved in strange religions. It was, perhaps, extremely dull but they would not have chosen otherwise.

The small waitress reappeared. '*Monsieur*?'

It seemed advisable to select the *plat du jour*, which was *rôti du porc froid à la mayonnaise*. Bill filled their glasses again.

'Oh dear,' said Lily, 'I'll be drunk before we get anything to eat.'

'Do you good,' said Bill. 'I like you when you're drunk. You should do it more often.'

'I don't get the chance,' she said. 'Somehow the atmosphere has to be right. It's no fun being tight in the wrong ambience. And then you need the pangs of hunger.'

'It's good for the pangs of hunger,' said Bill. 'You barely notice them.'

'I would make a very cheap alcoholic. Such a little booze puts me on top of the world. Do you think anyone would notice if I started to giggle?'

Their order was served. It was a grilled pork chop and was quite delicious.

'I feel like one of those travellers in the desert,' said Lily, 'explorers, or pilgrims, travelling across infinite monotonous sand dunes. Then night falls and hunger bites and quite fortuitously my pilgrim comes across an encampment of nomads. There on a spit, over a glowing fire, roasted to the precise point of excellence, is the carcass of a young lamb. These nomads share with the pilgrim and I feel as if I have never eaten, or tasted food, or savoured flavour, until this moment. That is how I feel about this pork chop.'

Under the influence of the food Lily felt quite warm and wonderful. She watched a young woman at the next table steal a snail from her companion's plate. He protested, feigning anger. She smiled, persisted: 'I'll take another one, give it to me, do.'

As they argued, it seemed to Lily that their eyes spoke to each other of love. As she watched she thought how universal was the phenomenon and how varied its manifestations. How inevitable, she thought, the magic recurs, people who look at each other as if they have just been re-created. She wondered about the young couple. Had they just met? Was it a holiday romance? Would they marry? She put her hand on Bill's hand. How lucky she had been, she thought, to have found fidelity. She had forgotten the silences of the morning when they had nothing to say to each other.

'Have another glass,' said Bill.

They talked about the exhibition they had seen. Bill explained to her the advantages of the Sherman duplex. It had a seventy-five-millimetre M3 gun, he told her, and two MGs. The twin propellers were linked to the tank's track. In calm weather it could attain a speed of three knots. The propellers could get damaged on land, that was their major problem. More recent amphibians used the principle of jet propulsion. Lily listened, sharing his interest.

'It was a five-man tank,' said Bill. 'They had a collapsible canvas screen supported by a series of rubber tubes to maintain buoyancy.'

They took their coffee out under the umbrellas, where the swallows were beginning to dart in the dying light. The colours had all become shapes, the red salvias were triangles, the trees shivered in the devious evening chill. The young people had gone back to their camp site, giggling and singing.

'It was a lovely evening,' said Lily.

'Despite the mad waitress. I wonder what happened to the cold roast pork.'

'She probably gave it to someone who ordered mussels. Doesn't it get cold suddenly?'

The sun had died abruptly, sliding behind a low cloud. The swallows swooped like bats. Lily drew her coat around her and wept.

'What is it now?' asked Bill.

'Oh dear, oh dear. It's nothing, nothing at all, it will soon pass. Pay no attention.'

'But what?'

'I have nothing to weep for at all. I know that. We have so much, look at our life. An ordinary successful life. We've had the money we needed, we've had children, friends, health. It was just that you reminded me . . . It was just a memory that I thought long-buried.'

Lily took a deep breath. 'There was a boy I knew in England in 1943. We used to go around together, cycling on bicycles and leaning on gates. Talking together about life. I don't suppose we were in love, but we were fond of one another . . . companions. I was seventeen and he was twenty-three. He wasn't much older than Christopher is now. He went away to die, maybe on that beach today, maybe on another. All these years have passed while we have lived and he has known . . . nothing. Half the people who mourned him must be dead by now. The last shadows of his life are fading, he has no child, no place, no independent memory to leave behind. He is one alone among the dispossessed. They lie in thousands under their crosses, dispossessed of their lives. They did not question the need to die. They all went hoping, hoping that death would come to some other mother's son, to some other girl's fellow.'

'Just as well we did,' said Bill. 'It was a war that had to be won. Don't weep for all the world, Lily.'

'I know, I know. It will be over in a moment. Even for a million dead, one cannot mourn for long.'

'Be thankful we survived, at any rate.'

'And that we met.' She found a tissue for her eyes.

They drove slowly back to their hotel. The lime trees by the side of the road flickered into amber life under the headlights, then sighed into the darkness behind them. Lily thought of Bill's enthusiasm for the nuts and bolts of war, the flail tanks and the Sherman duplex, the trajectory of bullets and the traverse of gun turrets, and of how it had reminded her of the boy whose optimism and excitement had been extinguished in death. The war was past now, both for herself and for the boy she had known. Even the dead were at peace. She was, as Bill had said, thankful they survived at any rate.

CHINCHILLA

Harriet O'Carroll

I once had, or thought I had, a great love for an older man. I was reminded of him the other day when I discovered a gift he had given me. It was abandoned in the back of a drawer of socks. That time of grief, intensity and hope came back to me through a haze. In contrast with my present mode of life it was an era of luxury, independence, and a pleasant sort of irresponsibility. I was, of course, raw out of school, well-stocked with theory and innocent of practice, full of boundless confidence in the powers of wishing. If I hope hard enough, I used to think, if I hope and hold on and only have faith, he will see me and that will be a start.

What precisely would start, I did not wish to foresee. At the beginning it was enough to be noticed, to be recognised, to catch at small facts and slowly unfold the nature of the beloved. What rubbish all my aspirations were was obvious to me much later. I would have been better off conferring my adoration on a picture on the wall, a safely distant image, than on a man of flesh and blood pacing the lecture podium in stylish shoes.

It is amusing to realise for how long we had both schemed to achieve roughly similar aims. I cannot remember what particular occasion focused my interest in him – it was certainly not his brilliance as a lecturer. Quite early in term it just seemed as if my happiness depended on hearing his hesitant voice enumerating various basic economic theories. Missing a lecture seemed a disaster of quite terrible proportions. Life seemed to compress to exclude the trivial and allot the status of importance only to that hour, ten to eleven o'clock, first-year economics, his brown bony cheekbones, his smart shoes.

I did not have the courage to attempt to attract him in any direct fashion, but I imagined that carefully applied eye shadow and fresh mascara shouted to him to look at me, as indeed they did. It was helpful that there were not many girls in the class, so competition was not severe, at least in terms of numbers. There was my friend and flatmate Sarah, whose fair good looks contrasted well with my darkness. She was so firmly and so obviously attached to her boyfriend that I felt she was removed from the field.

His gift to me, as I looked at it, was so typical of him in many ways. Smart, decorative and luxurious, it was a model of a chinchilla brought back from a conference in the Andes. It was in real fur with shiny, beady eyes. It reminded him of me, he said, dark, sharp and shy. It reminded me of him. It has always been a source of some conflict in me, being the only one of his presents that has not worn out, or been used up, like perfume. I have a reluctance to give it to the children because of its expense and value, and an equal unwillingness to display it on the mantelpiece because of its echoes, while my parsimonious streak prevents me from giving it away. So I thrust it into odd drawers, put it away for winter with the summer clothes, and it continues to emerge, releasing always the same whiff of memories.

It is hard to believe, though I know it is true, that it was actually he who engineered our first meeting. I had expended so much concentration on him. I had taken to arriving for class just two minutes late so as to enter the room immediately after he did. My seat, the same every day, was in the front row through a trick of the alphabet. I always delayed after the lecture so that I would be the last to leave – with what vain hopes I do not know; because he was always the first to leave. Sarah had a regular date with her Michael in the canteen for coffee. I had no

144

other particular friend in the class and my delay went unnoticed. One day when I reached the Great Hall he was still there. I waited, and stared at uninteresting announcements about college societies, and wondered would I ever have the courage to speak to him. Better to live in hope than to make one's cast and fail, I told myself. I believed that then; there seemed to be so much time, days and hours to be spent in wishing. I did not seem to be aware of the options life offered and of the way in which the choice of one excluded the others. I took life as it came and submitted to my fate.

'Excuse me, Anne Barrett? You are Anne Barrett? Am I right in thinking that you're a niece of Francis Barrett the historian?'

I did not dare believe he was speaking to me. I blessed Uncle Frank, the brains of the family, writing obscure books in New York, of all places. I felt a sudden sense of sadness, as you do when you wake out of a pleasant dream, before realising that the morning is not necessarily cold. All these thoughts I had. The moment stands in my mind, bright and sharp. I stood and stared a long time, until I thought he must think me stupid, and said, 'Why yes, Uncle Frank, he's in New York', and stopped and looked at him.

'He was a great friend of mine. We still correspond occasionally. Frank was a great character. I thought you must be connected. Do you keep in touch with him?'

'He was over here two years ago,' I offered, though if they were friends he must know. Uncle Frank was a fairly shadowy figure to me, I had not paid much attention to him during his visit, once the novelty of having an American uncle had worn off.

'Yes, I met him then. He's quite a card, your Uncle Frank. It's a pity you don't see more of him.'

'He said one of us should go out to stay with him some summer.'

'You should do that. You should take him at his word. Tell me,' he said, 'are you free this evening?'

'Yes.'

'Well, why not have a meal with me? We can talk in peace. I'll pick you up. That's decided.'

'Yes, all right.'

'Eight o'clock, then. What's your address?'

I told him. He didn't write it down, just listened, nodded and walked away.

Afterwards he told me that he had planned the conversation for some time, but had been foiled by my practice of leaving late.

'If I hadn't left last I wouldn't have been alone,' I said.

'Ah, so you too had thoughts. But it wouldn't have mattered, I would have detached you, gently but firmly.'

In such silly conversations a great deal of the joy of our relationship was expressed.

That evening I did not believe he would come. Sarah had gone off to the library and I fretted in comfort over what I would wear and what I would say. I told myself he would not come. When I was completely ready, down to the last eyelash, I turned the clock to the wall and set myself to read a critical study of *King Lear*. I heard his car draw up. I heard his footsteps approach the door. I stopped myself from rushing downstairs before he had even rung the bell.

That evening went like a charm. It flowed smooth as honey as few first occasions do. It was probably the most enjoyable evening of my life up to that date and I attributed my enchantment solely to the effects of love. With hindsight I realise that other factors were not without their influence. I was impressed by the restaurant where we dined. Had I been more sophisticated I would have been even more impressed, for it was one of the few, maybe only the second of two, restaurants in Dublin at that time famous for the excellence of the fare. As it was, I was simply pleased by a profusion of white linen and flattering service. I was pleased with myself, too, and with my poise in coping with the event. I was glad that experience at a relative's

146

wedding enabled me to express a preference when asked about red or white wine. In fact I did not think I liked either very much, but I knew I could at least simulate an appreciation of white and I would have chosen to die there and then rather than admit that my tastes were in any way out of step with my company. I was surprised when the wine arrived to find it so palatable and to discover the sense of power and confidence that accompanied the disappearance of the first glass. I instantly understood all these boys who rolled up to dance halls at eleven-thirty, cheerful with Dutch courage, for didn't one need every ally in the game of love and did not alcohol seem a formidable ally?

Ciaran's conversation, too, seemed to me to be delightful, so remarkably free from references to sport. He chatted on about his work, his holiday in Vienna, he told me little anecdotes about his friends, all in a way that made my contribution to the conversation minimal but at the same time made me feel that my reactions and my approval were of no small importance. We spoke very little of my Uncle Frank. I remembered we disposed of him even before the soup was finished. In the following weeks Uncle Frank became a sort of motif for us – the more we mentioned him, the more unreal he became. It was as if we were reminding ourselves that he had been a pretext, that our coming together was based on attraction.

After dinner we drove up into the mountains behind the city and sat in the car and stared at the lights below and the lightship winking far out on the water. There was some repetitive foreign music on the car radio and the smell of pine needles in the dark air. It was a truly wonderful moment, the mood quite perfect and invulnerable.

Eventually he started the car and drove down into the nighttime city through the small lawns and semi-detached houses of the suburbs, until we came to the tall, decrepit building that housed my flat. I fled from the car, muttering thanks, clutching to myself the perfection of the evening. As I went up the stairs I said triumphantly to myself that this was worth waiting for, this was worth hours of longing, days of grief hereafter. Why I should have thought then of grief, I do not know. Maybe it was some commercial feeling that every joy has its price, every pleasure had to be paid for sooner or later with sorrow.

The next fortnight was a brilliant, glowing time. It remains in my brain, illuminated and fixed, like a series of slides on a screen. When I think of any fourteen days in my present life – uneventful, busy days, days spent in ferrying children to school, shopping, cooking, chatting – these days swirl and dim into each other, uniform and indistinguishable. It is amazing that such a short time could retain such clarity and dazzle. Ciaran means nothing to me now, but memories of him persist. He saw me practically every day for that time and I did not question it. I was so happy that I presumed his pleasure was of the same nature as my own, that his desire to see me sprang from the same roots. We drove through the Dublin mountains, along quiet, coniferous roadways. We sat in the car by the pier at Howth and listened to the wooden knock of boats against each other. We ate and drank at various places so that all the city seemed haunted by our contagion. In unhappier times, when I wanted to forget him, everywhere I went was rotten with memories.

The moment when I realised that our idyll was not quite what I had presumed it to be was unexpected and, of course, contrived. He had picked me up in his car as we had planned an expedition to Wicklow. I loved these trips and it seemed he was equally happy to drive where the fancy took us.

Just as he started the engine he said, 'We'll have to stop off for a few minutes. I've to take my wife's fur coat out of storage. She's coming back at the weekend, you know.'

I stared at the dashboard for a long sixty seconds. I inspected the trickles of rain on the windscreen. Shoals of small drops were swept down by the steady arc of the wipers. One, two, three, they went, four, five, six. What do I say?

'Where do you have to call?'

'The place is in Grafton Street. It won't take a minute. Parking will be a bit of a problem. What about Harry Street?'

Of course I should have known he had a wife. What man of his age did not? Was it fair of him to assume I knew he was married? – as it seems he did. Had I studiously avoided discovering such a fact? I wondered did Sarah know – she would surely have enlightened my ignorance. Now that I did know, what would I do about it? That problem I did not wish to consider. I watched him return to the car with a large box and told myself that he was mine for the rest of the day at least. I would worry about the future in the future.

As it happened, I did nothing. He saw me less frequently in the following weeks, always without notice, usually at odd times. I lived with this and made myself happy with residual romance. I tried to wrest each occasion into the shape of my feelings. I suffered no great pangs of guilt. By this time anything I was stealing seemed so slight and sometimes so totally in my own mind that I did not think anyone could grudge me it. I had the consolation of my morning lectures. They gave me the illusion that he was accessible. They hid the extent of my dependence.

The winter deepened through the term. I dreaded the Christmas holidays because of the geographical separation involved. The separation was much greater than I had anticipated, for it was then he departed to the Andes.

The days had a fog-like feeling without him. I kept to myself and studied, and thought about his wife. Was she missing him too? Or did she care for him at all? Had he ever mentioned me? Since he had mentioned his wife I had lived in dread that he would some day say, 'You must meet my family', and thereby domesticate me into some sort of harmless acquaintance. I did not know what he felt about me. All my previous assumptions had been so wildly incorrect. All I was sure about was that there were strands of affection and strands of sex in the ties that connected us. If the former did not preclude introductions to wives, surely the latter did. That our relationship had no long future did not upset me, anything more distant than three months ahead seemed too remote to worry about. I suppose all I really wanted was to be allowed to admire and partake, however remotely, in his life. It was such a slight aspiration and yet it loomed so large. Its very triviality isolated me from sympathy. Sarah had by now concluded that my interest in the association was chiefly a liking for expensive meals and comfortable car drives.

It was thus that Ciaran found me when he came back from the Andes, unchanged but unhopeful, pleased with his gift, and disproportionately pleased with what he could afford to give me of his time and attention. I was always ready when he wanted to see me. I cut lectures, missed sleep, broke appointments and cancelled weekends at home merely on the hope that he might see me. Each time we met I had the same elusive certainty that he was totally mine and that he, like me, lived only for those dishonest meetings. Strangely, the affair did no harm to my prospects of passing my exams as I spent more time waiting than not, and to distract my mind, I studied. When I consider my present relationship with my husband, which contains quite as much take as give, I find it hard to understand how I could have been so pliant and patient. I did what he wished, I was what he wanted. I gave him as much rope as he wanted and fortunately for me he hanged himself.

The way in which our love came to an end bothers me to this day. It happened with a suddenness for which I was quite unprepared. It was an evening exactly like most of our evenings. We were eating and drinking our way through an extravagant bill of fare. I was slowly sipping through a Nuits-Saint-Georges, my palate having become more sophisticated as the months passed. He had commenced one of the anecdotes that had so delighted me. Then I realised with horror that he was repeating a story he had told before. It was not so much the story, but that every turn of phrase, every inflection was identical. As the well-chosen words flowed round me my brain raced. I was reminded of commercial travellers in my father's shop: 'As I said to him', 'As he said to me'. Salesmen's jokes repeated mechanically. Professional patter processed and polished. I looked at Ciaran's brown hand cradling the wine glass and thought, that tan must need a sun lamp to maintain it. All that extraordinary beauty and wit that I had adored as a natural phenomenon was really the result of effort and artifice. For the first time I tried to put a figure on his age. Could he be as old as fifty? It seemed a great age to me then. Fifty was too old for creating a good impression, fifty was for being one's unadorned self. I couldn't wait to be home. I couldn't wait to be alone.

I had always imagined that when a love affair ended the one who had fallen out of love escaped scot-free. It was not so. I knew that night I would not see him alone again, and I did not. I always managed to remain with a group in college and Sarah's presence at the flat deterred him from appearing there for explanations. I was slightly consoled by his persistence in writing and telephoning. It appeared to indicate that I had meant something more than an admiring audience. I did not see any hope for either of us in embarking on communication. I did not want him and I did not want anyone else either. It was as if the death of love between us meant that love could not exist, and time stretched ahead, mundane and purposeless. The season passed into spring and warmer days gave a promise of hope I did not want to accept. To hope again meant to suffer again. Eventually, of course, I got over it, for what else is there to do?

There was an epilogue to the affair that did throw a little light on his actions. Years after I had qualified I worked for a short time with a woman who had been at the same college as me. She had been there two years later and we whiled away a boring half-hour in the staff room by trying to find common acquaintances.

We were not doing very well, when she said, 'And what about Ciaran Hyde, the economics lecturer? I bet he went after you.'

I was so surprised that I asked her how she could possibly know.

'For one thing,' she said, 'you have the right sort of colouring. He always did go for the raven-haired types.'

It was an aspect of things I had not considered at all. 'Did he really?' I asked. 'Did he go for many raven-haired types?'

'There was always someone. As far as I knew. Mostly first-year students. He was quite a creep, if the truth be known.'

The bell rang for class and she got up to go. I looked at her black hair and dark eyes and thought how much we could tell each other if we were friends. Strange, how one can play about round the tip of an iceberg and then float away, while the icy crags and chasms beneath remain forever impenetrable.

THE BRIDGE

Emma Cooke

The three children – Laura, Catherine and the baby, whose name was Elsie – came so often to the same part of the river that they felt as if it belonged to them. The deep indentation in the river bank and the sandy ground at the water's edge made it a place for sand castles. Out in mid-stream a big stone in the water served as a jumping-off point or a den for chasing-games. The low ridge of grassy hills that stood between the river bank and the fields the girls crossed on their journey from home had a small convenient gap where the bigger two could pitch camp and leave the baby safely tumbling on her rug while they played. About fifty yards up from the cove the river was spanned by the red iron railway bridge and whenever Laura and Catherine heard the whistle of a train in the distance they would race back to Elsie, and whoever got there first would hold the infant in her arms while the three of them gazed at the metal monster rattling across the bridge and Laura and Catherine would argue about whether it was going to Dublin where auntie lived or to Tipperary where Granny lived or to 'somewhere else'.

Laura – who had been to Dublin once to visit Santa Claus and Toyland – claimed superior knowledge. The Dublin trains were the ones heading towards the chimneys of the electricity power station. She had seen them out of the carriage window on that magical morning, gleaming like some giant's castle through the raindrops slithering down the glass. And coming home in the evening – tired out, sticky, a damp patch on her new coat where she had dropped some ice cream in a big, bright parlour with loud music and shiny, coloured tables and millions of people she had never seen before in her life – the chimneys had welcomed her back with her present for Catherine, whose turn it would be next year, and the game of Ludo that Santa Claus in Snow White's Palace had pulled out of a big cardboard drum and a new elephant brooch bought in Woolworths pinned onto her stripy jumper.

Catherine, a year younger, only arguing for the sake of arguing, covering her distress – because she hated the noise and Laura did not – by shouting 'Tipperary! Tipperary!' no matter which direction the train was travelling in, would lapse into silence after it was out of earshot, her heart settling down again under her skinny ribs like a little startled bird finding its nest.

Catherine never did go to Dublin after all. It should have been her turn before last Christmas. When the time came, and she should have been roaring away with Mummy in the big train, the money from her money-box safe in her Sunday shoulder bag, waving goodbye to Laura left on the station platform, they got baby Elsie instead, and Mummy said she was sorry, but no one from their house would be going anywhere for a long, long time.

Not that it really mattered. Baby Elsie was nicer than Santa Claus or Snow White's Palace. Nicer even than Rosabelle, the doll who could sleep and drink and wet her nappy. Elsie's blue eyes stared up at the grassy hills – which were not even proper hills, only small mounds – as if they were the biggest mountains in the world. Her pink face crumpled and silvery tears sailed down her cheeks like little fishes when a butterfly with orange-tipped wings landed on her nose. Lots of things surprised her. A blade of grass stroked under her fat chin made her legs wave in the air and her mouth open so that you could see her two new teeth. A cardigan dropped on her face for a second or two made her go all silent, and watching the pupils of her eyes contract when you lifted it up again reminded Catherine of the way her own night-time dreams vanished when she woke up and it was a school day.

And there were some good games they could play with her using the pram: racetrack – down the bank, round the next gap in the hills and back through the cowslip field. They took turns, Laura or Catherine sitting on the edge of the bank counting 'one-a-pecker . . . two-a-pecker', the way you did between lightning flashes and thunderclaps, while the other one galloped the pram around the route and Elsie bumped about on her pillows, fists waving and her solemn eyes encouraging the pusher to clippety-clop as fast as she possibly could.

All the multitude of things about the river bank flitted around baby Elsie on moths' wings. The smell of the grass mixed in with her own smell. Little breezes rubbed her cheeks. She gurgled and cooed at the clouds and the thistledown that glanced against her forehead and sometimes everything except the faces of her two big sisters swirled and swooped, appeared, vanished, came back. The roar that was the train meant nothing special to her, just noise rushing through a dark cave. A void. Brightness again but different all the time.

Then things began to be the same as other things. The same faces were joined by the same colours, and fixed shapes came out of the whirlpool, a patch of whiteness that she wanted. The same obstacle pushed her back – push, back – push, back – push, push – and another blackness and a new brightness and the same swirling and swooping and the faces, and she gurgled because the world was unwrapping her and she was able to roll over onto her tummy.

The baby's progressions sprang on Laura and Catherine like hidden traps. At the beginning of the summer she had been a soft, heavy bundle that flapped around like a mollusk robbed of its shell when she was dumped on her rug. By August she had turned into a creature with her own dynamism. A creature that needed watching. A creature that rolled towards a stinging nettle while they were diving off the big stone. A creature that laughed when she was sung to and turned bright red and bellowed when her legs were smacked for being a nuisance. But how it had happened they could not remember. Baby Elsie's chubby fingers closed over a pebble hidden in a tuft of grass and she pushed it into her mouth while they watched her. Laura grabbed her by the heels, Catherine screamed. The baby yelled as her head bumped against the ground and the pebble popped out. Laura and Catherine shouted in hysterical relief, strapped Elsie into her pram and tried not to notice her cries too much while they had their swim.

But baby Elsie's bottles and the occasional rain showers that kept them at home during that hot summer were just ripples on the even surface of the days that stretched in a glittering procession, week in, week out. The passing trains and a gang of dirty children who sometimes appeared on the opposite bank with lumps of soap and raggedy towels and who splashed around rowdily and clumsily while Laura and Catherine stayed moored like two tiny skiffs in their special cove were the only reminders of the outside world.

Laura and Catherine always ignored the dirty children, even when they shouted and catcalled in their direction. None of them was able to swim well enough to breast the deep water in the centre of the river and so the girls knew that they were safe. Unless . . . Once, Laura felt her eyes drawn towards the bridge basking in the heat. Waiting. The gang on the opposite bank were playing football, kicking around a bundle of paper tied with twine. The paper ball flew up in the air and disappeared over the fence that wired off the slope up to the railway tracks. Laura riveted her eyes on her cotton skirt. The voices hummed like a swarm of angry bees. They got louder. Someone shouted. She waited for the clatter of feet on metal and then the voices faded away. The children disappeared in the direction of the cottages and she could see the makeshift ball lying abandoned near the top of the embankment.

June, July, August, melted into September. Cowslip balls withered in their memories. Daisy chains had to be replaced by buttercup garlands. It was too dry for mushrooms. They brought old newspapers in Elsie's pram, folded paper boats and watched them sail tremblingly downstream towards the town. It was so quiet that even the birds seemed to have grown accustomed to their presence and only sang their coolest notes.

Catherine had grown that summer. When she and Laura measured themselves against each other it was plain that she was catching up. Because of this, Laura claimed the right to be in charge of Elsie. They put her down on the grass to see which one of them she would crawl towards. She started towards Catherine and then suddenly changed direction and headed for the side of a hill. Laura grabbed her and put her in the pram. Her red face winked up at them, as secretive as a dead planet. When Laura held out a forefinger Elsie grabbed it and pulled herself into a sitting position for the first time. So Laura was in charge.

For Ada Wilson, the children's mother, the days of that summer had become just one long, languid stream. Ever since the baby's birth she had inhabited a realm of ghosts and whispers. She travelled through it on feet that always hurt a little, with eyes that seemed fixed on some nebulous target, and a dull ache somewhere in her spine. She spoke in sentences that floated away like feathers. A myriad of difficulties danced like midges around her head. She ignored them as best she could. Things piled up. Soiled nappies. Old newspapers. Her hands shook as she cleared the tea table, and the china jug, part of her life with its rosy flowers and golden stems, lay splintered on the dusty carpet.

Then there were the children to be cared for. She sat staring at them. Their dinner plates revolved like cartwheels. She crumbled a water biscuit between her fingers. Food. Washing. Cleaning. And she only had the energy of a snail. The girls sent secret messages across the table to each other. They were as untidy as a pair of little tramps, but their faces were brown and shiny – and their long, stick legs and their bony arms. Catherine, with her tousled, sun-bleached mop, put an arm around her mother's neck and kissed her cheek. It made a shaft of pain shoot across Ada's left eyebrow. They were off again. She peered after them through the net curtains as they turned down the side lane, pushing the pram between them. She remembered all the fairytales of her childhood. And the magic words. Abracadabra. Open Sesame. What had she forgotten?

And yet there was nothing much wrong. Her confidence would return if she was patient. The real Ada was gathering herself behind this pale, frightened mask that stared so oddly from the hall mirror. A late baby was hard on the mother, her neighbours soothed her, kindly misunderstanding her tired remoteness. But she saw some things more clearly than she had ever seen them before. The baby burnt as brightly as a little flame in the centre of all the muddle, encouraging her to go on. Before its conception everything had been growing cold and lonely, and then her husband came home unexpectedly and found her nostalgic and vulnerable, brooding – although he did not know this – over a false admirer. A horrible man. The baby had saved her – them – the marriage. She believed that the future would vindicate her folly.

Her husband, surprised at her late fruitfulness in what he had come to think of as a barren desert, allowed his gnawing doubts to be assuaged by her protestations of wellbeing. She would come out of purdah when she was ready. Her vagaries, although intense, always ended happily. And the children thrived like sand boys.

There came a morning when Ada Wilson pinned a row of nappies onto the clothesline. They looked like pennants flapping

158

encouragement to wayward wives. She permitted herself a smile. One day soon, she promised herself, she would face the question of where she was going and answer it adequately in a way that would include all of them. She walked back to the kitchen and found she was looking forward to winter and dark evenings. A trip to Dublin. Lighted windows packed with colour. Catherine this time, that was a promise. And as a token, she would make a queen of puddings for the dinner.

When Laura and Catherine arrived home they saw that their mother had grown better, although they had never thought of her as sick until they returned to find her energetically sweeping the doorstep and later ate their dinner under a barrage of questions from her about which of them could swim the longest under water. And where had they spent the morning? And what were their plans for the afternoon? They both chattered like magpies and their voices were not a bit too loud. Afterwards, waiting in the front hall while Elsie was fixed up for the afternoon, they grinned foolishly at each other, as if they had both just escaped the dentist's drill because they had brushed their teeth so well.

In her bedroom Ada Wilson, putting her palm against the baby's hot cheeks, wondered if it was wise to send her off again with the bigger girls. And then, when a bout of fractiousness stopped suddenly and the baby began to chew the sleeve of her little jacket, she sighed over all she had forgotten about babies and teething, and thought decisively of a peaceful afternoon. 'It will pass,' she said to Laura and Catherine when the baby began to grizzle as she was put down in her carriage. As if to prove how right she was, Elsie stopped and gave them a seraphic grin.

But it was only a temporary lull. Baby Elsie did not share her older sisters' euphoria. Instead she glowered from her pillows the whole way to the river bank, and when Laura and Catherine left her parked where she could watch them give vent to their

159

animal spirits with a splashing match, she howled vigorously until they came back to joggle the pram and talk to her.

For Laura and Catherine something ended that afternoon. The little cove on the river bank stopped being a special place. The sandy patch seemed to have shrunk to a straw's breadth. They shifted to a spot further down the bank. It was worse. They came back and peered into the water, trying to see something more interesting than the minnows that always died so quickly and floated with their bellies flip side in the jam jars hidden in the pantry. Baby Elsie roared furiously in her pram. In desperation they unstrapped her, climbed through the fence and up across the railway line to the hedges on the far side to see if the black-berries had ripened yet. They had not. They chewed leaves off a bread-and-cheese bush and pretended to enjoy the taste. The Angelus bell rang at last and released them from their ennui. They bundled the baby up and hurried her home.

The next day a letter came from Tipperary. Out of the double-Dutch conversation that ensued at the breakfast table Laura managed to gather that Granny was sick. Another of her turns, the letter said.

Ada Wilson debated aloud as to what she should do. Should she rush down at once? Should she wait and see how bad it was? 'Oh Lord!' she cried. 'Why does a blow always fall just as things are beginning to go right?' She reached for her husband's hand and Laura slipped away from the table and her mother's lamentations that she was going off her rocker.

That afternoon Ada kissed her daughters goodbye. 'Granny will outlive us all, you'll see.' She tweaked Laura's hair.

'What will we do with Elsie?' Catherine asked in a small voice, not wanting to think of creepy things like coffins or ghosts.

Her mother sighed. 'Just don't get in Mrs Moloney's way.'

Only the thought of Mrs Moloney's sharp tongue kept them out of the house for the rest of the day. Baby Elsie, another tooth poking through her gum, dribbled contentedly and made hardly any claims on their attention. But Laura and Catherine could not raise the inclination to do anything except crouch on the grass, nibbling rusks purloined from the baby's carton. Sheer habit had brought them down to the little cove. When they sat up and waved at a passing train they both found they had pins and needles from sitting too long in cramped positions. Because of Granny, neither of them liked to mention the train's destination. When it was out of earshot a hush crept over everything. You could nearly hear the grass growing.

'Let's play,' Laura said. She ran over, climbed through the fence and went up through the bracken to the railway line. She tripped across the red iron bridge on flying feet, turned round and came back again. 'How long did I take?' she called.

Catherine did not know. She repeated the journey and Catherine stood on top of the grassy hills shouting 'one-a-pecker . . . two-a-pecker' with all her might.

Their mother was expected back on Saturday evening so that Mrs Moloney could stay at home to cook her own family's Sunday dinner. But instead a telegram arrived saying that Granny seemed to be sinking. Their father announced that in the circumstances he had better take the car down to Tipperary. It would be needed for collecting the relations. Mrs Moloney saw him off with assurances that she would take care of everything. Her old man wouldn't miss her one bit. It was all the same to her whether she slept here or in her own house. She was only glad that she was able to do the favour and she hoped the old woman wouldn't be gone before he got there, although she knew it would be a blessed release for the poor soul.

When he left she transmuted her rage at missing her regular Saturday night in the pub into a furious harangue about untidiness, boldness and brassiness that lasted until dinner time the next day when, full to the gills of glaucous stew, Laura and Catherine were pushed out of doors with Elsie and told not to come back before six because Mrs Moloney had jobs to do in her own house as well and she couldn't be in two places at once, could she? And she knew the mess they would get the house into if they were left by themselves for two minutes flat.

They hurried towards the lane as if they were fleeing a sepulchre. The whole town was indoors, mooning over Sunday dinner. An ancient dog snuffled as they passed him. Down at the cove they spread pram blankets on the ground and sat Elsie in the middle. They were sick of the place, of her, of each other. Catherine went to the edge of the water. She dipped a toe. It was freezing. Summer was gone. She came back and threw herself on the ground, thinking of all the things she would like to do. She stared at a crow hopping along the red iron parapet. Slate-grey clouds drifted along the horizon.

'What will we do if it rains?' she asked.

Laura shrugged, arms wound round her knees. How nice it would be when school opened. A water rat scuttered across the footpath and vanished down the bank, unremarked.

Which of them suggested the game? It was impossible to say.

'Bags be first.' Catherine danced across the bridge and leaned between the balustrade halfway, crying, 'Hello, Laura, Elsie!'

Laura went further. 'Goodbye, Elsie,' she cooed from the far bank on which no rough children gathered that day. 'Goodbye, Elsie, goodbye Catherine.'

Catherine dashed across the bridge to join her and they both giggled on the opposite bank as the baby turned her head and tried to sit up.

The train thundered out of nowhere. They watched in fright as it rushed past, and the abandoned baby began to scream. They covered their eyes as she heaved herself up. What if she reached the edge of the bank and tumbled in before they could reach her? They laughed in relief at her wails as she remained floundering on her rugs. When they got back she refused to be cajoled. They carried her along the bank and back again. They climbed up onto the railway track and rooted in the chippings between the sleepers for a piece of marble or something precious. They helped the baby to clap hands. Time crept by. They carried her out to the middle of the red iron bridge to look down into the water. The railway tracks stretched away from them on either side – to Dublin, to Tipperary, to everywhere. A grasshopper ticked in the weeds.

Catherine felt a drop of rain on her hand as she gripped the balustrade. They had forgotten to put the blankets into the pram. Lashed by the thought of Mrs Moloney's tongue, she hurried down to gather them up before the shower. Laura picked up the heavy lump that was Elsie. In the distance smoke puffed from the chimneys of the power station. Would she ever go rattling past them again? Laura lifted her face to the sky to see if the rain was going to come down. Behind her back, in the distance, a signal dropped. She wondered about Granny, about why Mrs Moloney wore an orange hairnet when her hair was grey, and if people brought presents back from funerals.

Catherine folded the blankets and put them into the pram. She stuck her head under the hood. It smelt sweetish and milky in there – like Elsie. She was never going to have a baby. Never! Never! When she took her head out again she looked up at Laura standing on the bridge with Elsie in her arms. She did not notice the sound right away; the reverberating seemed to come up from inside her skull. One minute – silence; then – noise everywhere. As if the whole familiar scene was just a cloak concealing a monster. And as it gathered momentum she felt herself and Laura and Elsie being pulled into its maw. Laura turned round slowly, a clockwork girl on a pivot. There was a sharp sound – the whistle of a train or a scream? Catherine did not know. Laura was walking through the tumult on slow-motion feet, Elsie clasped against her stomach with pink heels kicking the air.

'Laura! Elsie!' Her shrill cries sounded as faint as the squeaks of a cat-cornered mouse, her eardrums were exploding. 'Laura!

Elsie!' And she was running, not towards the fence but away down to the cowslip field, and even there the earth rocked and cracked, throwing up cascades of noise. She fell, burrowing her face into the grass, moaning, 'Laura! Elsie!' And then, 'Oh, Mummy!' The noise rolled away into the distance, leaving behind it an eerie silence. Catherine pressed herself against the baked earth. Tipperary. Tipperary. They were playing hide-and-seek and she must stay there, in the blackness, until they found her.

It was given to a Christian Brother out for a Sunday stroll to gather the fragments. Because of the oncoming rain he had decided to take a short cut back by the river. He heard the cries of the child. Then, as he paused on the top of a wooden stile some way distant from the bridge, he saw the bundle lying on the tracks. He walked warily towards it, and when he got close enough to see what it meant, he felt the whole afternoon congeal into a scene he would never forget. When he had overcome an appalling dizziness he managed to walk towards the gory mess, deprecating his sick horror as he covered it with his raincoat. Then he turned thankfully towards the cries and hurried down to where Catherine lay wailing senselessly in the now steady drizzle. He was an unseasoned young man and had not yet learned to make full use of the words 'the will of God'. He picked her up, whispering endearments he had not used since he left his family. She turned and grabbed him convulsively, the way she had last seen baby Elsie clutching onto Laura. The crumpled damp heat of her was like a poultice on his spirit. Her hair was full of pieces of dried grass that tickled his nose. He put his arms awkwardly around her and wondered what on earth he was supposed to do next.

ELDERBERRY WAKE

Edward Power

The public bench was vandalproof, made from gun-barrel metal and cold to sit on even in the April sunshine, so the kids from the housing estate used it most. This morning there was the usual litter of chewing-gum wrappers, empty beer cans and cigarette packets, and one lone figure looking lost for something to do. Connie. There was something different about him: a sense of aloneness, and the way the light never caught the colour of his eyes, only the tint of nicotine on unwashed teeth. He got up and scuffed around, went down the street a bit, loitered, and came back again. He might have been waiting for the midday bus, but when the bus did come to a halt he didn't seem to notice it nor the few old ladies with free passes in one hand and shopping bags in the other. His head didn't turn and his eyes were hidden somewhere under shadowy eyebrows. When the bus pulled off again and took its shadow off him there was a lighted cigarette in his hand and threads of smoke coming from his nostrils.

Across from him the church looked like a gothic store that did no business on weekdays. He thought of the emptiness inside it, the locked tabernacle, the Body of Christ guarded by statues and nuns from the adjoining convent chapel. But if he went in there now, it would be to the crying-room to spill his dark mood on the floor in a pool of tears and release one long, anguished howl against the perfect white walls.

The cigarette burnt down and singed his fingers but it took a long moment for the pain to register. 'Fuck ya!' he snarled, and ground it under his heel.

The sunshine increased but now even the dull glint of teeth was gone and a thick-lipped scowl animated him. He looked toward the school-end of the street. The new building, full of desks and boys, threw its shadow across the road and he watched the traffic rushing over it. When the shadow got to the broken white line it always began its retreat back to the wicket gates on the verge of the concrete playground. Once, he broke a window and got inside. He didn't mean to do any harm, just go in and see what it felt like. The ghosts of his classmates sat in the empty desks, his own ghost among them sitting next to the third-cleverest boy in class with whom he'd exchanged sandwiches. Then it got scary and he felt light-headed. All the sounds of the classroom somehow got inside his head and he panicked, kicked over a lockerful of learning aids and jotters, and made a blizzard with fistfuls of red merit-stars. When the room was in chaos his head became quiet again and he sat down, crying onto the knees of his trousers. When he left there was vomit on the floor and a wash-hand basin overflowing.

The road between the corner shop and the church went by the new cemetery and stopped at the river, two miles down. There was a song about the river but it said nothing about drownings or about the poison that flowed into it. Some of those old-time songs were a bloody laugh. 'Flow on lovely river,' his father sang sometimes when things were going his way. Jesus, Connie thought, it's a sewer. That's how the people on telly pronounce it too, and they don't know how right they are. He went and swam there once and got a rash. Sometimes he blamed the river for everything, as if it had somehow got inside him and poisoned him with the strange feelings that drew his eyes to the schoolhouse and everything.

It was play-hour and the school yard was loud with children. He got up, crossed the street, and sat waiting outside the corner shop, watching them file in and out, some with money for sweets, others hoping for a share-out. He frowned as the small groups came and went.

'Hey,' he called.

'Wanna sweet?' a boy said.

Connie shook his head and grinned crookedly. 'Where's Des today?'

'Dunno. He's not in school. Why?'

'No why!'

'His mother sent in a note to the teacher,' another boy said.

'Sure you don't want one?' The first boy held out a packet of fruit pastilles.

'Nah.'

The shadowy eyes rested somewhere between his boots and he hardly noticed the boys drifting back again toward the school yard. A handbell rang and he looked up at a tall figure in the doorway in the distance. He couldn't see the face from where he sat, but he knew every line and every mood on it. The eyebrows were always either arched way up or way down and never settled like you expected normal eyebrows to do. What he remembered most about his school days were the teacher's eyebrows. If someone asked him in twenty years' time, he'd say: eyebrows. 'Lanky bastard,' he muttered, as the figure herded the boys back indoors.

He tried not to think about the note, but it played on his mind. The boy's mother writing it. The teacher reading it. Were the eyebrows up or down? That first time in the tree house the boy was scared – but that was mostly because that creep Hogan spied on them. Hogan got his kicks that way. Connie gave him every coin he had in his pocket. Sixty-eight pence. The last of his dole money. After that Hogan contented himself with a knowing grin and went back to crouching under windowsills. No one else saw them. You could pass by underneath the tree house and not know there was anyone up there. He built it when he was fourteen, made it from bits of finished wood and galvanised sheeting. It was still cosy and exciting but none of his friends had any interest in it. 'Kids' stuff,' they said. They had other things on their minds – like hanging around the amusement arcade in town and getting into fights. They got clapped-out motorbikes, patched them up, and revved them up and down the waste ground behind the estate. Something about the bikes and the riders excited him, yet somehow kept him apart from their world.

Cars drove through very fast, as if there was no speed limit. He had terrible visions of a car ploughing into a bunch of kids from the school. They usually came out in groups of five or six. High spirits and high jinks. He knew the feeling as if he'd just finished school yesterday and not three years ago. The bench hadn't been there then, just a patch of waste ground near a gable end. He could still see the scar of a smaller house on the gable end and tried to imagine himself inside it.

'Jesus!' The screech of car brakes startled him. For a wild moment he saw Des and the others fly up in the air like rag dolls. But it was the Nolans' cat. He went up to where it lay, but it was squashed like a brindle rug and he felt like flinging a stone after the car as it sped into the bottleneck of road between the garda station and the parochial house. You never saw a guard around for things like that, he thought. The only time he saw one was when he signed on for the dole on Tuesdays or when the phone box was wrecked.

'What this place needs,' someone said, 'is a zebra crossing.'

'Or a lollipop man,' someone else said.

The idea appealed to Connie. He'd like to be a lollipop man, right here at the school. Then sitting on the bench all day would make sense and the boys would look up to him. Especially Des. He smiled, and for a moment his blue eyes appeared out of their shadowy recess.

Yesterday there was a funeral. Not a big one – it was for the posh old lady who lived in a lodge down by the river. They said

168

she didn't have two pennies to rub together, but she always looked as if she was better off than anyone else around. He didn't like funerals but he went to hers and knelt in the pew just inside the door. She had relations overseas but no one got around to telling them anything.

Instead of praying, he felt bitter and angry. Why was she less than the rest? Jesus, he thought, they crossed hurleys over most coffins and then spent the rest of the day drinking and talking about it in the pub. But they buried the posh old lady who hardly ever spoke to anyone; they buried her in a dirty, weedy corner of the old graveyard – in the end paid for out of parish funds. He stood a little apart from the small group and once caught the priest giving him a sharp look. Or maybe a puzzled one. But it made that end of the graveyard even more forbidding than before.

The priest spoke very quickly and the grave diggers wasted no time in filling in the clay. Connie listened to the muffled sounds and felt like an only mourner. The sprinkling of holy water was no substitute for real tears and his eyes brimmed at the injustice of it all: not just death but the things that didn't seem fair about life. An only mourner. The posh old lady had never even spoken to him. Her head had been in the clouds, but the clouds had no silver left.

He walked to her lodge house later and stood outside the rusty gate. The windows were dull and sad, briars climbed up the trellis and the garden was even wilder than the corner of the graveyard. Empty, the lodge was suddenly small and miserable to look at. It looked like the end of the world right there and he wanted to run from it but couldn't resist the urge to peer in one of the windows. He knew she made her own jam and wine but all he could see was a dirty white curtain and beyond that a vague, dingy, disturbing interior. Everyone knew about the jam and the wine. The cider-boys would check it out sooner or later, he thought. At least they'd drink to her, in their own way, and maybe he'd join them. She deserved something of a sendoff. The prospect made him strangely happy.

After the burial and visit to the lodge he sat on the public bench, smiling to himself and thinking of an elderberry wake.

'If the council don't let out those houses soon,' a woman said across her neighbour's wall, 'there won't be any houses left worth giving out.'

There was meaning in her voice and he shifted uneasily in his seat. She knew he was sitting there but he wasn't the only one to squat around in the untenanted houses. They were taken over at night by courting couples and by the cider-boys, who got so daring about it that they lit fires in the grates and used anything they could get for fuel. The first time he joined them he drank half a flagon of cider and got sick. He was new to it and gulped it down like apple juice. Next time, he told himself, it'd be different.

'It's a disgrace,' the second woman said. 'And my daughter living in a dirty caravan.'

'And those hooligans with the run of the place,' the first woman said, with real venom. 'And half of them not even shaving and the other half not going to Mass.'

'Nosy bitches,' he muttered, scowling as he walked past them to loiter deliberately near the untenanted houses. Their voices dropped behind cupped hands and their eyes glinted in his direction.

He felt uneasy again and thought of the note sent to the teacher. He was sitting on the tarmac but remembering sitting behind a desk at school. The two women were replaced by the teacher and those up-or-down eyebrows. And the snapping voice – 'Connors! Take your hands from under the desk.' The accusation in the voice was worse than anything else. He wasn't doing anything but he blushed anyway. Those eyebrows were up full and the class grinned mockingly. Lanky Bastard got a kick out of it all – the jeers and whispers. Was that what those two old bitches were doing – whispering about him? He looked up but they'd both gone indoors. When he passed by it felt like they were watching him from the windows.

Sometimes he felt he was alone on a stage or something, and eyes drilled into him so much he felt a kind of pain cutting through him. Lanky Bastard didn't just look at you, he thought. His eyes turned on you and you felt foolish and sort of half grinned because the way he looked at you, it was either that or burst out crying. So you grinned like an imbecile and then Lanky Bastard made out you were showing contempt and the eyebrows went up and down so fast they looked like a pair of black hairy-mollys crossing a street at rush hour. The idea brought a slight grin to his lips and again the blue eyes flashed out of hiding for a moment.

A woman clacked by in high heels, gave him a strange look, then shook her head and compressed her lips. He blushed, re-alising he'd grinned aloud. She either thought he was laughing at her or else thought he wasn't the full shilling. That was the favourite description for anyone who didn't go about things the same way everyone else did – not the full shilling.

There were cracks about sixty-eight pence too. Once, when he joined in with the cider-boys, they played cards for money or half-empty flagons. He had a good hand and bet twenty pence. Aces and kings were worth that, he thought. Three of them saw him and he lay down his winners with a grin.

'Jesus, Connie,' Hogan said, 'that hand was worth at least sixty-eight pence.'

Hogan loved that. He had an audience and they loved it too. Hogan wasn't his real name. No one had a real name here – everyone was nicknamed in a crazy, off-the-wall way. Hogan was a big fan of an Australian comedian. That was a joke. He was small and weedy and nothing like the original. Jesus, Connie thought, he'd run a mile from a crocodile handbag. He glared at Hogan but said nothing, and tried to ignore the grinning faces.

171

He felt like leaving but you couldn't just up and go after winning a pool of money. That was one of the rules. These guys had more rules than they knew what to do with. He felt like jumping up and kicking the cards and the money up in the air like used lottery tickets. Instead he shuffled the deck and slowly dealt the next hand.

The nicknames were like labels – they stuck to you whether they made sense or not. The kid who passed by on a bicycle just now, whistling above the racket made by a loose chain, called across at him. Wild, but good-natured. Connie couldn't figure out why they called him Slightly. Slightly what? Slightly who? Slightly didn't seem to care one way or the other. He grinned when Connie shouted after him, took his mind off the road and almost ran onto a kerb.

'Feck ya, Connie!' he yelled, fighting to control the bike but still grinning.

Connie liked him. Not as much as Des, but he liked him enough. He liked the way the dark eyes shone and danced, like foreign ones, almost. Slightly could easily be on some of those adverts on telly, he thought. Always slightly grimy and always on that old boneshaker his father had cobbled together for him. It probably had no brakes but that'd be the last thing on Slightly's mind when he got going – not sitting on the saddle, though he could reach it now, but pumping the pedals like a Tour de France rider.

Once or twice he slowed and chatted; you could never say that Slightly actually stopped – just slowed for a bit. Long enough for a drag on a cigarette. He didn't smoke much and his smile was still clean and friendly and the cracked, uneven front teeth made him even nicer in Connie's eyes. He couldn't explain to himself what he meant by that except that the more he thought about Slightly's front teeth, the more he hated braces. Some kids wore braces for hardly no reason at all. Maybe they wanted *perfect*, sugary little smiles like some of their mothers. Jesus, the place was full of Grecian 2000 and kids with braces who were learning the hard way to be snobs. He was glad about Slightly's teeth. And he was about the only one who didn't make those cracks about sixty-eight pence. He felt so much good will toward the kid that it took him over and made a lump in his throat.

He stretched out full-length on the bench and closed his eyes. But his eyes weren't relaxed closed and he felt every inch of the bench getting colder and harder. He tried to think of Slightly, and the bike, and the beautiful, cracked, uneven front teeth, but instead he thought of Lanky Bastard and the note and Des. Everything – the bench, the day, the passing traffic, the church, the school – seemed to abandon him. He sat bolt upright and stared at the ground, shivering. He didn't feel comfortable but he grasped the edge of the seat until his knuckles showed white and he felt he couldn't move from there, as though he were fixed to the public bench as much as it was fixed to the flagstones. He thought he was going to die or something. The river's poison, maybe, but he didn't.

After a few moments everything felt like it always did and he eased his grip on the edge of the seat. He looked toward the school. Lanky Bastard shook his head and a bell rang. Two eyebrows crossed his mind like black hairy-mollys. The car roared by and killed Nolans' cat again. And again, and again. When it all stopped happening he took a deep breath and ex-haled, as though he were blowing smoke from a cigarette. He sat there and felt like he was stuck at both ends of eternity.

FORCE

Simon Korner

It was winter in the playground. Crystals of ice coated the tarmac, which sparkled whenever the sun shone and looked as if a bridal veil had been laid over it. I was waiting in a queue for one of the small slides – as befitted my age – and watching the older boys dashing down the longest run-up and turning their huge feet skillfully to the side, like surfers over the ice. That year, in the space of one Christmas holiday, I'd gone up from Mrs Reed's class to Mrs Wall's, where all at once I found myself surrounded by children a year older than me. I felt I'd lost my balance.

Every morning in our prefab the heavy milk crate would be placed next to the radiator so that the milk could thaw. At break, when we drank it, the classroom would be filled with a sickly smell. I could feel the milk inside me now as I waited my turn. I ran up the scuffed runway and my cautious slide took me no more than a yard along the ice and left me feeling foolish. Some of the milk came up into my mouth and I winced.

'Line!' came the shout, and I turned to see a horde of the big ones bearing down on me. I joined onto one end and ran with it. My friend David Dunkel was there among the bigger boys. I saw a mad glint in his eyes behind his glasses. And then, facing us, a rival line had formed, and we were two armies.

'Charge!' David shouted strangely, and he – of all people! – led the line forward, his arm in the air and a bubble in one of his nostrils.

'What are we doing?' I asked him, running by his side, appealing to him as the friend with whom I spent hours at home

174

poring over a draughts board in silence. But he only yelled 'Charge!' again. Then the whistle went and the armies dispersed under Mrs Wall's gaze.

Mrs Wall was a great oak of a woman who roared at us in a deep voice. We were doing pounds, shillings and pence. Her wide back moved across the blackboard, uncovering yet another sum. I knew hundreds, tens and units very well. I remembered with longing the speed with which I'd been able to process them. But that had been in Mrs Reed's.

Beyond Mrs Wall's back there now lay a terrifying calligraphy, figures and signs so complex that I couldn't believe we were meant to decipher them. And yet here was Jan next to me, humming to himself over his exercise book. I peered over his shoulder. He noticed me and moved his forearm over his work, and I blushed and turned back to the blackboard. Mrs Wall was making her way slowly from table to table. My brand-new exercise book lay untouched before me. Jan began rubbing something out vigorously, his attention distracted. I turned my head very slowly, forcing my eyes to the limit of their muscles, so that they ached. At last they reached his page and searched feverishly for a meaning. But the precise figures seemed to be scattered across the sheet at random. In desperation I made an approximate copy of what I saw, only, with my eyes straining to focus on Jan's page, they couldn't supervise what my hand was doing on my own page. Crude grey shapes began to appear out of the corner of my eye and then terrible smudges spread out like clouds of smoke under my fist. There was one figure of Jan's I couldn't work out at all – a loop, as if a loose cotton thread had fallen off his sleeve onto the paper. It was repeated several times, exactly the same perplexing shape. It was disastrous to copy it, I knew, yet I couldn't ask him to explain.

I felt a sudden uprush in my head and became unbearably hot. Mrs Wall was bent over the next table and I stared into her tartan skirt-folds. I tasted sour milk in my mouth. I felt I had entered a dream in which I was rising from my seat and piping in a faraway voice, 'I feel sick', and gliding to the door.

'Richard, go with him and make sure he's all right,' said Mrs Wall.

Cold air rinsed my face as I floated across the icy playground, my feet slipping on the empty slides. In spite of the cold my face was burning up. The next moment I was in the boys' cloakroom, pushing open a toilet door and tearing down my shorts and pants. Foul-smelling liquid gushed out of me. Another spasm twisted through me and the sour milky smell rose into the air. Everything went quiet, and I gazed at the chipped floor with its puddles of disinfectant. I rested my head in my hands and sighed thankfully.

Then the door banged open – I hadn't had time to lock it – and there stood Richard Strang, grinning under his fringe of orange hair. His white skin made his teeth look very yellow. He laughed, bent double.

'I've had diarrhoea,' I grunted.

He banged the door several times and each time it swung open to reveal his grin and his finger pointing at me.

It was that term also when Slaves swept the school. I was Timmy's slave, along with David Dunkel and another boy. I felt possessed by a powerful allegiance to Timmy which was exhilarating. And yet for much of the time I remained a spectator. Every break Richard's knees pinned my biceps to the grass in an unbreakable lock. I didn't know why he chose me. I would swing my legs up and try to kick him in the back, knowing it was futile; he was simply stronger than I was. Apart from the occasional burst of struggle, we would remain still, locked in position like two crabs compelled to grapple with one another.

With my arms aching, I stared at the upside-down trees and watched the other children playing Slaves, wishing the time would pass quickly so that Richard would release me and I could get up. The playground was alive with running, screaming forms; in groups of four, three younger boys harnessed like a team of dogs to an older one who gave commands. The slaves did whatever the master said, which was mostly careering round the playground in chariot races.

It had been this way for half a term. Richard would seek me out and after a while I didn't bother to run away. I knew he would catch me and I couldn't stand the suspense before he did. Now, as he approached, I would already be letting myself down onto the frosty grass. Once, I waited there for minutes without any sign of him. I became more and more anxious and in the end I had to go looking for him myself. My daily surrender to him put me out of action for the first half of every break and was accepted by the other children, like a duty as milk monitor. I came to know his face well, with its freckly nose and yellow teeth, and a perpetual triumphant smile distorting it. And in the air between us hung a sour, milky smell that always brought back the memory of our first encounter.

Jan, a year older than me, was a frail, giggly boy. He spoke English with a Swedish lilt that gave him an unworldly air. We became great friends at home, taking turns at riding his bike, but the friendship did not transfer to school. Although we shared a desk in Mrs Wall's class and I no longer needed to copy his work – it soon became the other way round – there was a tacit agreement that we ignored each other the rest of the time. Secretly I knew this was my doing and it filled me with an uncomfortable sensation whenever I thought about it. I'd left him out of Slaves at the start of the craze; he was hovering beside Timmy and me and I didn't suggest him.

At break Jan stayed by the climbing frame, which was a kind of lepers' colony inhabited by children who found themselves unacceptable in the mainstream. No one else went near it, and I felt especially wary. But one day, after Richard had released me with his customary punch in the chest to go and harness up his own slaves, Timmy and another master drove their slaves straight towards the climbing frame – I don't know why – and started to swing themselves along the high crossbar. Jan and the other climbing-frame children hung back in silence, gawping. We stayed there till the whistle and from then on the area became a favourite haunt. The older boys would do tricks on the top bars and I made my mark when I discovered I could hang upside down from the lower bars.

Soon, teasing of the original inhabitants began. I laughed as comical nicknames were coined. I even joined in when someone made up a spiteful rhyme about Jan. 'Jan, Jan, the frying pan,' we sang as we swung on the bars.

He ignored us at first and then retorted hotly: 'I'm not! I'm not a frying pan.' I'd never seen him angry before. He went bright red in the face and charged at his tormentors like an angry young bull.

Day after day at the climbing frame I watched Jan's long pale face harden with rage, turn scarlet, then lilac at the temples, as he shouted at the jeering circle, until the moment the crowd was waiting for. Then he would suddenly seem to explode inside and lunge in a mad fit of hatred at whoever stood nearest him. Sometimes he would reach them but more often the circle would break open, children scattering in all directions, and Jan would pursue hopelessly, first one, then another and another squealing figure.

'Jan, Jan, the frying pan,' went the endless chant. I hung upside down in my special position, knees hooked over the bar, chanting with the others, laughing uproariously when Jan made his move, but all the time unsettled. At home we still played together as if nothing was happening, still took it in turns to ride his two-wheeler bike shakily up and down the cul-de-sac. We still went to school together in his father's queer-shaped Volvo and shared a desk in Mrs Wall's.

Spring was arriving and with it snowdrops under the trees, rain, wind. The grass felt soft and moist beneath my head when

Richard pressed me down against it. My shorts got smeared with mud. The playground was full of long, light blue puddles, the colour of the gusty blue sky above. In Mrs Wall's we had windows open. The bottles of morning milk were cool and fresh-tasting. I tried to make amends to Jan by helping him during the lessons. Jan's strange loop turned out to be a two and it seemed appropriate that he should do it in this slightly exotic way.

One Sunday, Jan's birthday, the whole family went next door to tea. That evening my father called me into his study and heaved me onto his lap. Then he asked me if I knew that Jan was very unhappy at school. I answered no. I was surprised at the suggestion until my thoughts settled, almost by chance, it seemed, on the climbing frame. I could see one of its green bars close-up, with raindrops hanging in a row, and I realised what he meant.

'Miserable?' I said. I feared he was going to tell me off.

'He's being bullied.' The disgusted way he said that word made me shiver. 'You must help him – he's your friend.'

I felt as though I had known this all along. I nodded in a kind of despair and wanted to go to sleep.

'It's cruel,' he continued. 'Jan's parents are worried about him.'

'But what can I *do*?'

He shrugged. 'Well,' he hesitated, 'you could stand up for him.'

'How?'

'Be on Jan's side. Tell them to stop.'

'Oh.' My heart beat faster. I saw the logic clearly and a gust of dread and relief blew through me.

As I approached the climbing frame the next morning – late as always – the chanting had already begun. Jan was throwing back retorts. This time I didn't go and hang upside down. I stood in the circle, slowly filling up with the injustice of it. I could see the agony on Jan's features. They were cruel. Bullies! I could hear my father's voice saying that word.

'He's not a frying pan,' I muttered, but nobody heard and I didn't say it again. With deep shame I waited in the circle, longing for the whistle to blow. The voices brayed all around me. A sour, milky taste in my mouth made me nauseous. I felt myself to be a formless being, without substance, only at my centre a pain burning fiercely, and no self other than it. It was with a start – of horror almost – that I found myself sauntering back after the whistle amidst a group of the bullies.

The following day the wind was blowing hard through the playground. Miniature waves scurried across the puddles, girls' hair swung about wildly, skirts tossed. The children ran about boisterously, flinging their voices into the wind. As I neared the climbing frame I could feel the wetness at my elbows and my bottom seeping through my clothes. Jan's agony had hardly started and he stood with his hands in his pockets. I felt removed; I felt nothing for him or against the crowd. I felt none of the burning pain of the day before. I had become detached from where I was and had returned to my father's study at home. I was arming myself there, fitting helmet, breastplate, sword, before my parents' gaze. Then I was setting out. Jan's parents watched me go.

I arrived at the climbing frame as the chant started up: 'Jan, Jan, the frying pan', at which I drew my sword and stepped into the circle beside Jan. The wind carried the voices forward.

'He's not a frying pan!' I shouted in a clear, righteous voice, and silence fell. Raindrops from the bars blew into my face. The moisture felt like blood, gave me courage. 'Bullies!' I yelled.

I was surprised when the crowd came for me. It was as if I'd assumed that they would suddenly see their cruelty. Jan hadn't time to get worked up and presented no threat to them; he was looking baffled and calm.

'Bullies,' I repeated, but as the crowd began jostling us I couldn't say it with the same brave voice. It came out as a bleating noise, quavering, almost pleading.

For the remainder of that break Jan and I were chased all over the playground. Eventually we found ourselves huddled together, breathless and panting, on a narrow bench set into a recess in the wall of the building. Around us the crowd pressed in, chanting, jabbing, now and then throwing someone forward on top of us, at which moment the shout went up: 'Pile on! Pile on!' and we would be buried beneath the howling ruck of children. But from beneath the pile of arms and legs we kept up our piteous moaning: 'Bullies, bullies! It's not fair!'

It was only Mrs Wall's bellowing voice, deep as a man's, that abruptly released us.

Months passed, and now the summer holidays stretched ahead before us all. The weather was impossibly hot. On particularly boring days Jan and I would ride his bike – one standing on the pedals, the other seated – past the paddling pool and circle the school railings, peering in at the deserted playground. The sun beat down on the tarmac, scorched it; heat shimmered in waves.

It was odd, but only a week or so after my intervention and just when I had got used to the idea that making a stand was not the end of the matter – not in the least, perhaps only the beginning – the bullying died out. Or rather, it moved on to its next victim. I liked to think it was because we had shown an intention to resist. But Jan had resisted from the start, of course.

My humiliation at the hands of Richard Strang also stopped around this time. His family went to spend a term in America, so he was gone. Soon it was as if it had never been. I was suddenly older, the bullying far behind me. Jan returned to Sweden and his parents cried and thanked me for sticking up for their son. He gave me his bike. New Australian neighbours moved into the university house next door, but they had no children my age.

Alone now, and the weather still hot, I haunted the paddling pool near the school. The place was packed. My mother disliked the noise but took us when she couldn't stand our whining any longer. I was oiling my bike lovingly, crouching beside it, away from the pool in the shade of the wooden toilet wall. There was a smell of warm creosote from the wood and now and then a whiff of urine and disinfectant from inside. I was imagining riding my bike no-handed along miles of road, swerving this way and that, when someone reached down out of the sun and took hold of the handlebars. I scrabbled to my feet, squinting. It was Richard Strang, back from America, grinning his usual grin.

'Can I have a go?' he asked.

'No, I'm oiling it,' I said. I knew that things were different now.

'But I *want* to,' he insisted.

'Hard cheese!' I replied sternly.

But he had the bike all the same and was wheeling it away in spite of me. I couldn't quite believe he was doing it. He seemed not to have understood the passage of time.

'Give it back, Richard!' I shouted. 'You're getting oil every-where.' His freckly white skin annoyed me.

He took no notice and sat down heavily on the saddle. When I tried to grab him he pushed me in the chest and I lost my balance and fell onto the grass.

'It's not fair!' I roared.

Here again, after this length of time, was the unavoidable fact: he was stronger than me. I refused to accept it; I wasn't bullied any more, I'd stood up for Jan. I got to my feet and chased him but his hands warded me off time and time again.

Suddenly the world seemed an impossible and monstrous place and I was taken back to my first days in Mrs Wall's, which I couldn't imagine having survived; I pitied the self that had. I could feel my throat aching with the onset of tears.

I ran to my mother. The words 'Stolen! Richard Strang has stolen my bike!' hung on my lips, ready for outraged delivery. She was sitting on the grass with another woman, both of them laughing and smoking cigarettes. I was on the point of blurting out what had happened when I saw it was Richard's mother. I faltered and drew back in confusion. My mother seemed for that perilous instant to have changed sides.

I stumbled away, defeated, back towards the toilets. I went inside. In the gloom I sat on the seat and felt my insides move. I came out into the harsh sunlight. Richard was still riding my bike round and round the pool. He waved at me happily as he went past, inviting me to play, and it was as if he had only been joking before or as if it was really his bike and not mine.

I felt a giddiness in my head. I lay down on my back on the burning hot paving stones by the poolside. The sunlight was dazzling. The children in the pool seemed to break up before my eyes into indecipherable shapes and forms. I tried to perceive a pattern in them but there was nowhere to start. I gazed at the upside-down poplars in the distance and waited for Richard to return the bike.

YURI GAGARIN

Simon Korner

When my father told me that there was space beyond the sky and that it was black, like night-time, it made me feel rather smug, knowing that the light blue I stared at was not, after all, very far away. You could reach it quite easily, and beyond it was this permanent night, stretching on for ever. Sky became a facile concept, a kind of baby talk, space the difficult, unfathomable thing, dark, uncompromising.

It was the very hot April of 1961. I watched the moon from my bed, shining through the trees like a lantern guiding me through a forest. I felt as if I were swimming through the air towards it and yet I never got any closer. I fell asleep with the strong sensation of floating along very fast, a few feet above the ground, always just missing the branches that came at my face.

My sister Naomi was born at home amidst an atmosphere of chaotic serenity. The telephone kept ringing and my father kept going out in the car and returning with more bags. My mother cooked us pancakes while smoking a cigarette in that droopy way of hers and screwing up her eyes against the smoke.

'Do you want lemony ones?' she called from the kitchen.

We sat eating Ricicles at the dining-room table, staring at the back of the packet.

'Honey!' Rebecca shouted back, and Toby and I copied her.

My mother brought in the pancakes which we rolled up into tubes to eat. Our shy au pair girl was on her hands and knees scrubbing the kitchen floor, something I had never seen anyone doing before. My mother made her coffee, then they both sat at the kitchen table smoking. Drifts of blue smoke curled in through the doorway into the dining room.

After breakfast I didn't see much of my parents. Rebecca went swimming for the day. Toby and I stayed up in our large, airy bedroom, where we'd been sent, playing with the Lego. A deep hush fell upon the house. For hours, it seemed, the only sound was the rattling of the Lego bricks as we sifted through the pile. I longed to go upstairs and see what was happening.

It was mid-afternoon when my father came in and told us the baby had arrived. He led us up to see it in our parents' bedroom. The baby had dark hair and was yawning; a fat midwife in a rustling blue dress shook a thermometer very fast in her hand and popped it into my mother's mouth.

My mother smiled and we went up and kissed her on the cheek. 'Hello dears,' she said very quietly.

'Mummy needs to rest now,' said my father, leading us out immediately. I wanted to protest. She was already resting. On our way out the midwife held the baby down to us and we touched its dimpled feet.

My father had fine hands of a light brown colour, with well-cut nails. His towelling short-sleeved shirt was dry and warm as I pressed my cheek against it and fiddled with his hand, twisting one huge finger over another into a crab-like claw. He had Toby on his other knee and was making him writhe as he picked bogeys out of his tiny nostrils. He had taken us into his sun-filled study, which smelt of books and cigar smoke, and we were sitting in his armchair. When my turn came and I felt the sure hands round my face, pushing it this way and that, I gave in to a feeling of absolute trust.

'You must both be good boys while I'm away,' he said in a serious tone, 'and look after Mummy. You know she's very tired.'

'Why is she so tired?' I whined.

He bent closer and I could see one of his eyes magnified

through the lens of his glasses. 'That's it,' he let me go, and I sat myself up on his lap. 'Well, you see, having a baby's very exhausting. It's like running round the garden a hundred times.'

'When will you come back?'

'In a week. In time to take you to your new school.'

I was fumbling in his trouser pocket and came upon his cigar clipper, which I took out and began to snap open and shut.

Toby raised his sleepy-looking head with a frown. 'Are you going away, Daddy?' he asked.

'Yes, I'm going on an aeroplane.' He paused. 'Like the one I went on to France. Do you remember?'

We nodded. He leaned forward, opened the smaller of his cigar boxes and took out a cigar.

'Can I clip it?' I asked.

'It's a little one. It doesn't need clipping.' He showed me the cut end.

'Can I light it?'

'By all means.' He guided my hands carefully and they struck the match. 'I'm going to Moscow,' he said, 'in Russia.'

'Can we have presents?' Toby said.

'I'll see what I can do,' he replied, and smiled, so that we became excited. 'I'll be in Russia when they send a spaceman up in a rocket,' he said, as if he were beginning a bedtime story. 'Last time they sent two dogs up, but now they're sending a man. The first man in space!'

'Has he got a parachute?'

'Yes.'

'He can go to the moon,' I said.

'Not quite. This rocket goes round the earth in an orbit.'

'Does it have to?' I was disappointed.

'Well, it's a sort of experiment. I'm sure they'll put a man on the moon one day.'

'Man-in-the-moon!' Toby chimed.

'Toby, a rocket goes higher than the sky,' I explained. And I could see the silver rocket soaring through the inky blackness with a jet of flame behind. 'So it just goes round the earth,' I repeated gloomily as the thought struck me again.

'It's still in space,' my father assured me.

I was relieved, and now I saw the rocket approaching a bright crescent moon, having to avoid it, as if steering past a jagged white rock.

Doctor Silberstein arrived and went straight upstairs. On his way out he stopped to talk to my father. He cupped my cheek in his flaky hand while he spoke. I got bored and began chasing Toby in and out of my father's legs.

'Ah, children are the future,' Doctor Silberstein croaked as he inched his way out of the front door, his great protruding stomach pulling him along after it.

'How about going to play with George, while I drive the midwife home?' my father asked.

I told George the baby was born.

'What's it called?' he wanted to know.

I realised I hadn't considered it might need a name. We were drinking our Jaffa Juice in his kitchen, gulping it down fast so we could go out and play.

'*What* did you say?' said George's mother, in such a harsh voice it startled me. 'It's *here*?' She let out a piercing shriek.

I nodded meekly.

'How's Mummy?' she yelled at me.

I didn't know. 'In bed,' I replied, 'resting.'

George set down the long beaker. 'Slowcoach. Come on.'

I felt torn, sensing some duty I ought to perform.

George's mother resolved it by saying, 'Right, you two. Out! Go and play.' Then she smiled at me with extraordinary tenderness, her face radiant and her eyes clouded. 'I'm just popping over to visit Mummy.'

The house was stirring. Through the open windows of our

bedroom warm air breezed in onto my face pleasantly, lulling me, and the leaves hissed for a moment like a garden sprinkler, or like shingle dragged by the tide. I woke into this with a feeling of such delicious comfort that I lay on the bed without moving, as though I was floating on my back in the sea. I remembered that the house was full of guests. The Reddaways were here, and at the thought of it I stretched myself out even more luxuriously in the bed. The single blanket over the sheet moved easily, almost silkily, only with a perfectly satisfying weight to it. Toby was drowsing in the next bed.

The laughter from Rebecca's room grew louder. There was screeching, thudding, and I smiled to myself, wondering what they were up to – having a pillow fight, perhaps. I wanted to rush in and join them, but knew it would be inappropriate. And the days ahead would all be like that. I was too young, a bore (to them), but I didn't mind. I was happy to be near such hilarity, drawn to it irresistibly as to fireworks or a fair, completely fulfilled by association.

The morning of the little drinks party to celebrate the baby, the girls were trying on old hats of my mother's that they had rooted out from her wardrobe. Every few seconds they would poke their heads round the door to show us. My mother, guiding her fat brown nipple into the baby's mouth, sat on the rocking chair and smiled, her eyes half closed, while Liz Reddaway giggled.

Later Patrick Shine, Liz's new husband, loped through the house in white trousers and white shirt, carrying a cricket bat, stumps and bails from out of his car. 'Cricket in the garden!' he called. And while the other grown-ups milled about on the terrace with the babies, Patrick played cricket with the children, leaping after the ball.

From the new-mown lawn rose a rich, spicy smell. Piles of cut grass lay everywhere, and it was moist and warm when you picked it up to throw into the air. Midges swarmed about our heads, and we clapped our hands to kill them, and scratched our hair. I waited for the ball to come rushing towards me. But it was Nicholas, Liz's eight-year-old son, in bat and he kept sending the tennis ball flying way over our heads into the next-door garden. He was moody over the new marriage and when it came to his turn to bowl he did it as hard as he could and kept getting us out.

That strange afternoon-stillness descended on the garden. The sounds of the cricket players cheering and of the adults guffawing on the terrace seemed to have dissolved and become a single, soft, murmuring backdrop. The round-shouldered willow that leaned over from the next-door garden into ours nodded its bulk at me like a sad green elephant, and a glider hung motionless in the blue sky, unable to decide which way to turn. I felt as if the world had fallen asleep and all the colours and movements in the garden were its dreams, flickering and bright.

'... seven, six, five, four, three, two, one – zero!' the older ones shouted in chorus. Nicholas had run into the house and fetched the rocket Patrick had given him, while we waited for Toby to return with the ball through the hole in the hedge. I watched the plastic rocket reach its pinnacle and start to descend. I began to think about the numbers beyond ten. It gave me a panicky feeling. I couldn't work out when you'd stop counting.

Suddenly, from a door in the side of the rocket, a red and white parachute unfurled, and the rocket came swaying down to earth beneath it. The rocket had four fins and a very sharp point. I was speechless, fascinated by the door that let the parachute out. An intricate gadget like that made it more than a toy, and I had the idea that if you pulled the elastic band far enough, you could shoot the thing up out of sight and lose it in orbit.

Patrick's thin forearm was straining, as if he wanted to fulfil my fantasy. The parachute didn't open this time and one of the rocket's fins broke off as it hit the ground. Nicholas started to cry and the cricket was abandoned. I felt responsible for comforting him, even though he was older than me. I kept thinking of my father. As Nicholas nursed the broken fin I crouched beside him and I could feel Patrick hovering behind us. Nicholas's face crumpled inwards as he cried. And now Liz was coming down the steps of the terrace.

While Nicholas's sobs were dying away, someone said the name Yuri Gagarin, and it made me laugh because gaga was our our family word for faeces. The name immediately felt familiar to me. I could see him in my mind, no face, just a big round helmet with reflecting glass at the front, his spacesuit of cleanest white, and I was filled with joy. Everything was so new, so modern, like my father's brand-new lab which also had great sheet-glass windows like the cosmonaut's helmet. I pictured my father waving at Yuri Gagarin and Yuri Gagarin waving back out of a little porthole as he blasted off. Patrick said we should be able to see the rocket passing over the garden later.

That evening, after supper, we all went and stood on the terrace. The night air was like a silk scarf caressing our faces and our bare legs, exuding the warm scent of the daytime, as if it had been wrapped around it. The stars were out, spread in a fine white dust over the heavens; one or two of them gleamed like grains of sugar caught in sunlight. Sometimes a movement would pass through the trees like a message being whispered from one to another.

My mother suddenly told us to look up, over the quince tree, pointing her arm at the sky. I tried to follow her finger, but there was nothing there.

'Yes, I can definitely see it,' she said.

'So can I,' said Liz.

'Where? Where?' the children shouted.

'Oh yes! There. Look! Over the tree.'

'Yes!'

'Can you see it?'

'Yes, there it is.'

'Where?' I could feel myself being stranded. They could all see it but me. 'Where? Where?' I cried. I bunched up my face but still saw nothing at all.

'There, dear, look, over the quince tree.'

I lowered my gaze a fraction. A shape had materialised just above the tree. It was exactly like Nicholas's rocket, only gigantic. It stretched across the whole garden and seemed to turn slowly in the breeze like a balloon. It was jet-black, and yet I could make out its form against the blackness of the sky, as if it had been cut out of thick black felt. It had a sharp point at the front and fins at the rear and made its way horizontally over the trees, very low.

'I can see it!' I said. 'It's a real rocket!' I assumed that everyone was seeing what I saw, until my mother told me to look higher up, and that the rocket looked like a twinkling star. I did as she told me and saw nothing. I looked for my spaceship but couldn't see that either. 'Didn't you see the big one?' I said.

'What big one?' she asked.

'The rocket one. The rocket one.'

'You must have imagined it.'

'I didn't!' But even as I spoke it was dawning on me that perhaps I *had* made it up. No one else had seen that shape.

The more I thought about it, the more I thought that they were probably right and that I had made a mistake in my excitement, what with Nicholas's rocket in my mind. Nevertheless, the astonished feeling would not leave me. I didn't care if it had been real or not. It was the possibility of it that I was elated by, the fact that it had hovered over *our* garden and that I had seen it with my own eyes.

As everyone turned to go indoors I ran up to the bedroom and began tugging wildly at the toy cupboards. We had two of them, one for Toby and one for me. Having emptied out the toys, I managed to lift one up onto the other, my strength suddenly enhanced by my desire to build a spaceship and sit at the controls. The cupboards slid into place easily, the one cross-wise on top representing the fins. A chair on top of that again was the driving seat. And then I was aloft, high up in my room with a clear view out of the window in front of me. The lights from the house threw light onto the lawn below and I could see shadows moving on it as people moved about downstairs. The fins shuddered with the speed. I was riding through space, Rebecca, Toby and the baby riding behind me, balancing on the fuselage, and soon my father would come back from Moscow with presents for us all.

THE FALLEN
a novella
by
John MacKenna

*For Frank and Breege Taaffe –
from whose home the Hannons went
to join the fallen*

I wore a lavender skirt that night, a slate and brittle blouse. There is a lavender skirt thrown across the chair. A different skirt. Outside, the dark says autumn. A thick mist trembles into drops on the lead pipes. It pip pip pips the last few feet into the gutter in the yard. I turned from this same window on that night. A night in summer. I looked at what I appeared to be. I knew exactly what I was.

The road outside was just as quiet then as it is now. But that was a different quietness. That was the stillness of a summer evening as the gardens burst into a bloom of sound. The click of forks echoed, turning out the last settle of the deepest frost. A neighbour, borrowing, shouted, her voice rebounding from wall to wall along the gardens. Carts rasped in the alleyways as drivers backed and worked the loads of dung between the creaky gates. Girls with arms of precious roses hurried from place to secret place. The heels of love began to sound again. The heels of love were mine.

Here. I am here. Over here on the angle of the cobbled paths. Behind me the trains thunder. I despise the angle but I welcome the grass that is thick and long, cut once, perhaps, in eight or twelve seasons. I welcome that softness and the softness of her footsteps, unheard now by those she passes in the street. Her resolute body unseen. Her faint laughter reaching only me and my words are caught only by her. And, perhaps, by the other old soldiers grown tired in their graves. Men who still remember little things. Obscurities. The shining promise of a blade. The glisten of skin, caught, at last, after all the talk. The button blaze. The lightning smile.

Did we pay too much for the pleasures we got? The things that mattered then seem of no consequence any more.

What you want is my story.

My name is Mary Lloyd. I was born near Castledermot in the County Kildare on the seventeenth of June, 1890. I was the youngest daughter of three. My father was a farm labourer who could turn a pair of horses with a twist of his wrist and a cluck of his tongue. He cut and kept the ditches, weaving alder, sally, elder into fences every spring. He carted grain to Hannon's mill. He ploughed the acres pair by pair. We rarely saw him in the summertime, except in passing, when he'd lift us on the chestnut backs and trot us to the road. My mother was a seamstress. Her customers left their cloth in a shop in the town and we collected it after school, carrying the bundles carefully, up and down Fraughan Hill.

By the time I was ready for work my sisters were married and gone. I travelled twelve miles to find something new. From the side of Fraughan, through Castledermot on a fair day. The cattle milled on Hamilton Road, dropping their thick necks to drink from the Lerr. Farmers and jobbers and huxters pushed and jostled on the square. They glanced at me. I waited hopefully, for some remark, a whistle or a gesture. They were too busy with their money. I walked through Hallahoise, past the woods at Mullaghcreelan, by the gates to FitzGeralds' castle, on through Kilkea, Grangenolvin, to work in a bakery in Athy. I was sixteen then.

I did my work in bakery and shop. I danced. I sang. I walked with other girls on summer nights. Out past the pond at Bray and back the Castledermot Road. Board dances and house dances marked the seasons of my life. I would dream men's tongues along my breasts, their lips about my nipples. I had my share of men. They had their share of me. I was twenty.

I'd see him in the street. Him and his wife. She was young. Almost as young as me. And hard. I could hear it in her voice when she spoke in the shop. They moved from Barrack Street to a cottage on the Dublin Road, across from where I had my digs. I'd see him in his garden among the daffodils and dahlias. Everything in that garden had its place. The rows and lines reminded me of my father's garden, of his fields all ploughed and set. There were apples and cherries where the drunken bees hummed and fell. But it wasn't just a garden of lines. There were clumped and clustered flowers where you least expected them. They took you by surprise. And all the plants and slips in pots along the gravel near the door. All waiting to be sown or given out to people in the town.

I wonder where a passion like mine starts. How does it grow? Does it run in the blood or does it just get out of hand till it's beyond control? Is it like sap rising? Is it something that insists on being heard? I know it stares. It stares till the stare is returned. It flames until it burns its root and then it goes on burning. It outlasts time and place. I know all this because this passion for him carried me beyond any love I had accepted in the past.

I'd walk the roads I knew they'd be walking. I'd stay at home, miss dances with the other girls if I half thought he'd be there burning twigs or leaves in late October. I'd talk to his wife for ages in the hope that he'd arrive. I'd stand at the gate and stare across at him. I knew how foolish I must look but I didn't care. I was twenty-two.

I'm Frank Kinsella. I was born in this town on the seventh of October, 1880. I was an only son. My father was dead by the time I was born. He was never talked about and I never saw any reason to enquire.

I left school at twelve and started work for the Lord Kildare.

197

The FitzGerald of Kildare. I set my mind to like the work. I walked the six miles out and back. I did my work. I was never late and I never missed a day. I listened well to every word that I was told. I watched what the other gardeners did and I knew his garden backwards by the time I was sixteen. I knew every strain of apple; every pear along the castle wall; every breed of rose; every vine in the greenhouses. Azaleas, magnolias, hydrangea. The cypresses, the oak, the ash, the elder and the clematis. There were winter mornings at Nicholastown when the frost was as thick as cream. There were evenings when the rain was like bamboo rods across my back on the straight beyond Grangenolvin.

I'd salute Lady Nesta on the driveway. I'd stop to talk to Lady Mabel on her horse. I remember Lord Walter framed in the stable doorway with a light behind him like a golden blanket, soft and clean. It was Christmas time.

It was Christmas, too, when I met my wife. At a dance in the town hall in Athy. There she was in a crowd of girls. Her face was young and clear. It was like the light in the stable yard. And her hair was wild and brambled. She had a smile as bold as brass. We were married the following autumn. New suit, a ten-pound note and two days off. Lord Walter promised to put in a word about a cottage on the Dublin Road. He was as good as his word.

She was hard at times but so was I. I could swing a fist with the best of men on Barrack Street. But she could soften too.

If you asked me to name a time I'd go back to a summer morning. It was four or five o'clock. We'd been to a dance somewhere near Baltinglass and we were freewheeling down from Mullaghcreelan. The light was just coming up and it was a warm morning. Sometime in the end of June. We weren't even tired after all the dancing and a ten-mile cycle. We were laughing as we reached the bridge above the Griese. We stopped and I lifted her onto the parapet above the river. I climbed down to pick a water iris from the bank. The river was down to a trickle and the bank was cracked and baked. I remember my boots made an impression on the mud. I looked up. She was perched above me. And then a man rode past, dismounted, pushed open a gate into a field and wheeled his bicycle across the grass. He had a small white box tied to the carrier. We watched until he disappeared into the ruins of a church. I climbed back up and handed her the irises. She dropped them slowly in the water and we watched them sail between the rocks and out of sight. Oh, she could soften too.

She never loved me the way I was in love with her but I accepted that. I saw this as how our lives were going to be. The same as everyone I knew. She could be soft but the softness disappeared and she had a habit of denying the memories I had. I'd remind her of things and she'd pretend to remember nothing. She'd be angry if I went on about it. I never understood how she could swear the past away. And once she started that, I knew I loved her as little as she loved me. I'd think to myself that she could change as much as she liked and so would I. But she should leave the past alone.

At times she'd say she was bored. Another time it was loneliness. 'You have the garden,' she'd say. 'The garden doesn't mean the same to me.'

One of her brothers would cycle in in the mornings and they'd cycle out together. After work I'd call to her father's house and collect her. Winter and summer she'd be there, curled up like a cat beside the fire. Once or twice, when it was raining, she said she'd stay. Then more and more I'd hear that story. 'You go on,' she'd say. 'There's no sense the two of us getting wet. I'll stay the night.'

Never once was I asked to stay. She never suggested it and her father and brothers made no move. I knew they'd never have me sleeping under their roof. As far as they were concerned, she was still one of them. I'd go home and walk around the garden. I remember one wet spring evening in particular. I walked around and around the cottage, up and down every path. There was a fine rain falling and there was a yellow light from the sun over the Laois hills. Around and around I walked. Other times I'd check the potato pits or heel in cabbage plants. I'd smoke a pipe. Some nights I'd sleep there in the chair. I'd wake at two or three and toss another sod on the melted flames. In the end the winter won. The blankets burnt with a better heat. I could imagine then.

She came some Saturdays. I'd arrive and find her there. The house would smell of bread and her. The hearth would be swept. I always kept it swept but this was in a different way. More complete. The windows would be open and the washing done, flying a flag of possibilities. She'd stay till Monday. I'd begin to tell myself the past was past. And then I'd find her gone again. I'd say nothing and neither would she.

Sometimes, I think, she was on the edge of touching me. I don't mean touch. I don't mean tease or sting. She was on the edge of explaining what was there or what was missing. Or so I thought. I never could be sure.

One Wednesday, the end of April, I drove a cart into the town to collect some seed from the railway station. I saw her father and her brothers at our gate. They had her dresses and her coats across their bicycles. One of them was coming down the path, his arms spread out. He had a mirror and a picture in them. They knew I saw them and they stood like frozen cattle, watching me. I jigged the horse and carried on.

She came to see me once after that. One evening of that week. We talked about nothing. She walked the garden with me. She was full of chat about the flowers and the plants. She'd touch my sleeve. She'd sweep the hair back from her face and stare at me, a thing she hadn't done for months. She was a girl full of courting tricks again, except I knew she wasn't. There was nothing to it. She was safe. Her bits and bobs were gone by then.

She was as safe this last time as if it had been her first. And then they came to bring her home.

I'd meet her on a Sunday, safe between her brothers, on the steps after Mass. The way they carried on you'd think I was something to be afraid of. As if by then I even cared.

The whole town knew. I'd hear it in the bakery and in the shop. Every tongue had a different twist. It was because of this or that. Because he wouldn't touch her. Because he never stopped. There were always two sides at least, and every side was talked about and twisted. It wasn't that she was telling anyone. She'd still come into town but she talked as much to me as anyone and there was never a word about him or them. And he never talked. I never saw him talk to anyone. But that didn't stop the hints. By May the whole town knew.

What could I do? I was caught. Marooned. Too soon to try to make a bridge but the gap cried out for me to fill it.

Through May his garden stayed untouched, and then one evening after rain I saw him, scythe in hand, the nettles crashing from the ditch. The drops reared up and shone in every light. His sockets were still and his arms moved in them, floating rather than flapping. His head was half bent. His body was as hard as granite. I leaned across our gate and stared at him. Every now and then the blade would catch the stony wall and rasp and spark. Then it swished the wet and stinging greenery. I could hear the clean, flailing sound as clear as water. He was silent in his work, each swing was measured as he worked along the garden, never going back, the nettles laid as neat as corn across the grass.

I loved him then, by Christ I loved him then.

I wanted those arms to disentangle themselves from the work of scythes, from whatever memories of pleasure or pain that kept them straight. And I didn't care what it was that had driven them apart. Too much pain. Too much demand. I could coax or satisfy. Listen, I wanted to shout, I'm not afraid of what the people think or what the people say. I've watched until I know the flex of every sinew in those arms. I know the stoop, the stretch, the walk, the watch.

My name is Mary Lloyd. I start my day at six. I try to meet you or to see you as I leave for work. I rarely do. I carry bread from bakery to shop. I think about you. I think, she's the one that left but it's me that you ignore. I've seen you talking to her, hung there between her brothers after Mass.

Frank Kinsella, my name is Mary. Mary Lloyd.

I'd drive the four-pronged fork into the bitter earth. I'd push the tines a foot below the soil. I'd stoop, as I had stooped all day, and then I'd lift and free the prisoner of a winter I'd allowed to drag itself into the summertime. I'd speed the rhythm gradually. I'd thrust, then push, then stoop, then lift. And thrust and push and stoop and lift. And thrust, push, stoop, lift. Thrust, push, stoop, lift. I dug my way out of the past. I dug myself a shallow grave from which to breathe, in which to rest. I thrust and push and stoop and lift and then I hear this voice that frightens me because it seems to come from nowhere.

'My name is Mary Lloyd.'

'I know your name.'

'Tomorrow is my birthday. I'll be twenty-three.'

I smile, I can think of nothing to say and so I smile.

'I'd like it if you'd walk with me. If you have nothing else to do.'

I smile again. I say, 'Of course.' I have no idea why.

My name is Mary Lloyd, I say, as I walk back from work. I hurry now along the cobbled street. I am anxious to be out of these working clothes. I brush the flights of flour from my hair as I walk. I smile at people. I want to stop and tell them about the possibilities and still I do not want to stop. I want to hurry. I nod and rush on past the Railway Bar, across the bridge, out by the manse and through the yard into the house. I prepare myself. I wear a lavender skirt. My blouse is a slate and brittle grey.

We walk across the town. I don't care who looks or what they say or what it means. Neither, I'm sure, does he. I talk. It is uneasy talk but I go on talking and he laughs. Sometimes he smiles but his smile is as uneasy as my talk. Mostly he laughs. I can recall every moment of that walk.

We go on walking several nights a week. On Sundays we cycle out between high ditches. He calls for me. Comes and stands at the gate. Leaning across his bicycle, he talks to the woman of the house. He says goodnight at that gate. And sometimes, when I am early, I stand at his gate. Once he invites me in to smell the roses by the wall.

The summer passes. What do I notice? Fifty factory girls are burnt alive in England. I read about them in the newspaper. They are not me. I notice his garden. I notice how his face will cloud and clear. I notice her whenever she's about. She smiles at me in the shop.

I travel home one Saturday to see my sister's child. I travel back on Sunday afternoon. I ride in a sidecar to Kilkea and walk the rest of the way to be in time to meet him after tea. That evening we walk out past Lord's Island. We walk beyond the horse bridge, across the fields along the Carlow Road. We perch on a half-built cock of hay and gradually slide until our backs are resting on the scattered wisps. He talks and talks instead of touching me.

That night I notice the dahlias touched with rust inside his gate. Lying awake, his plant of stock outside my window, I think how I would relish sin. But he has been so rigid in his hard red boots. His collar starched and done. I wish that I could dance the seven veils. I think about how he went on talking while the possibilities narrowed and shrank with the light.

Walking back along the railway line, he'd told me. I remembered word for word.

'She never loved me the way I was in love with her but I accepted that was how our lives were going to be.'

I waited for the rest. I waited for the recognition that I knew he had to have. If he couldn't put the words in place, if he couldn't give, at least he had to recognise what I was telling him with every gesture. I waited for him to say she had never loved him the way he knew I did. I lay and smelt the stock in the blue-black night. I imagined his tongue on mine, his fingers travelling between my thighs, his lips collapsing on my skin. In the end I knew there was a depth of pleasure and I knew as well that he'd never say that kind of thing. Not this side of whatever grave he'd already dug. Was that to be our only bed?

I envied her her passion.

If she'd talked of it. If she had put some shape on it. If she had turned to touch. I talked and talked in the hope that she'd grow tired of my talk and despairing of ever kissing me, kiss me then.

I envied her her passion.

If she had skirted it. If there had been a breath. I strained and strained to say something. To move. To step out of that grave. I tried at night to put the whole thing into words. I wanted to unhook the lust from its silent pier. But then, I thought, I know nothing about that sea. What am I? A silent inland walker, scrabbling for some other words to say the words for me.

One morning I went and sat on the low wall at the road. I measured the steps that would take me to her window. I counted the possibilities. I decided on bringing her to my house. I rehearsed the possibilities. I went back inside and lay down and felt her touch in my own. I felt the possibilities seep away.

But I envied her her passion.

I thought the smell of stock must smother her in what I felt for her. Did it not tell you everything, Mary? Mary Lloyd.

I envied him his strength.

Never mind the strength to work all day and then to work on through the night. I envied him his strength to take whatever came. To let her go when she decided she was gone. And I envied him not taking what was there of me. He could have done at any time. He need never have asked. I envied him that. In spite of everything, he must have known that I was his. I envied him his strength and damned him into hell for it.

I looked at him and saw a blind and stumbling plough horse. I thought of how my father turned his horses with a twist but I couldn't turn him any way. He was too heavy to ignore. Too set to change his ways. His boots were like brown lead feathers. His eyes were set on the end of some long drills that stretched like graves and graves and graves.

I envied him his strength, but Christ, I wished that he could sense the lust, the passion trapped in every breath I drew. Could he not feel it in my fingers; hear it in my darkest gasp; smell the smell of love that frightened me with its strength? Could he not untie the harness and touch me, just this once? Could he not take some lessons from the songs he hummed or from the thoughts his body sowed in me?

I waited.

We talked about the earliest dead who had fallen in France. They were not me.

After the harvest, after apple picking, he kissed me and I eased his hands about my body. He talked about breaking from the pier. I didn't understand but urged his fingers on. He was changing, becoming another man. I thought about the curves of his body and the curves of mine. I thought of this in the early frost, hurrying to work. I thought of it in the warmth of the shop. I gave myself to it. I drew his tongue between my lips and refused to let him go. When his touch was not enough, I touched with him. I no longer cared about the smile his wife carried. I smiled myself.

Sometimes we talked about the names we'd heard. About the dead swept back on a tide of blood at Mons. About floundering sailors from the *Cresy* and the *Hogue*, sucked into the icy sea. I felt the blood pumping like water in a millrace. I felt his mouth suck my breasts between his lips. My blood drove towards one moment, all day it drove towards the moment of release.

And then he told me he was going. I asked him why. It seemed too simple to ask that question but I had the right to ask him why. I had nothing else to say. He just smiled. A wry smile. A mirror of his smiling wife? I knew then that when we'd touched we'd hardly touched at all.

Mons, Ypres, Paris. What had these to do with me?

Nothing. And nothing to do with me. They were places where things were clear. In a minute of foolishness I had told her part of what I thought. If I went, there was some chance the past would change here the way it was changing everywhere else. I had this vision of coming back and finding my wife gone, dead, something unforeseen. Something would happen that could never happen while I was here. I believed that. She looked at me when I said that. There was something of that other, brassy look. There was no anger. Just sadness.

Nothing will change unless you change. We could go and live in another place. There's nothing here that I can't live without. I'd be happy out of here. And I have no need of rings or churches or words. None. I could gladly go without them all. You've never changed. Your wife won't be gone. She won't be dead. But there

206

are other things that could die. Will die. Things are changed already. Why? I have the right to ask you why.

For once I thought that touch instead of words would stop the questioning. We were under the chestnut. It was raining. If I was to tell her why, what would I say? I had no idea why. It might be to escape. Or to evict. My fingers moved with ease, my tongue was sure. The rain dripped in a great circle from the widest branches while we lay in their umbrella. There was no escape. Her breath quickened and then became a question. Why?

There were other mouths that called me traitor from the corners of the street, from black doorways, from the market crowds. I never raised a fist. I ignored the mouths I could have bruised or broken easily. But I felt no satisfaction knowing how they longed for pain and were denied it by my fists hanging limp. If there was a betrayal, it had happened a long time ago.

I had no interest in the tunic or the buttons or the guns. They were part of a cause. I wasn't going for a cause. I wasn't going out of reason but out of hope.

What did I hope? That if I went I'd come back a different man. If nothing had changed, at least I would have changed. And coming back, I'd find the same woman.

But did I believe? I believed that she'd remain. But her question dimmed and quenched the hope.

Do you believe in everything you've said?

I believe you will remain.

What else do you believe?

I'll tell you now. I've said it often enough to myself. I'll tell you now. I believe in the beauty of your breasts, in the form of your shoulders, in the sickle of your thigh, in the ease of your hands,

207

in the power of your eyes, in the fury of your hair, in the storm of your whisper, in the passion of your thought.

Do you believe in everything you've said?

No. I don't believe in me. My past is a nightmare. I have never told you that. First there is penance. Then sleep. Then this dream.

Is that the truth?

Part of the truth. The truth has nothing to do with us. The truth has all to do with me. Everything we have done has been true. The places have always been true for me – fields, gaps in ditches, trees that were one way in winter and one way in spring. Ways that you lay or laughed or walked. Ways I prepared for meeting you. These have all been true. There's no question about these. But I have no answer about why. No answer for myself, much less for you.

When you smile your mouth reminds me of your wife's.

That might be what you see but that has nothing to do with the truth.

I saw no hope.

I told no one until the thing was settled but already they knew. I gave my notice. Lord Walter asked me to think again. He said there were people he knew and then he said the job would keep.

I put straw on the pits. I got my uniform. I tied the last of the dahlias. Collected my wages. Cycled down the castle avenue without looking right or left. At home I washed in the starry yard, put on my uniform and called for her. I walked to her door and knocked. The stock was still in flower. They asked me in and ignored the uniform. We walked across the town and back. Sat on the low wall until Sunday came.

The night before he left we danced at the town hall. Sneering, I said, 'Why don't you wear your uniform tonight?' For once I saw the pain and it frightened me. I drew back from saying any more, afraid I might have said too much.

What did we do? We danced every dance while the music was playing. The music of fiddle, melodeon, piano and drum. We swung with the crowd without hearing the music. I was stunned by the speed with which certainty had arrived. Danced to the waltzes when the waltzes were playing, nodding at faces that passed in the crowd. There was Robert MacWilliams and Christopher Power, faces that passed as we swung around. He kept his distance but this moment of passion lasted as long as the music was playing. And then the music stopped. The faces grew voices, the movement was over and bodies jostled towards the cloakrooms. We were part of the crowd again. Faces smiled. Mouths dribbled short ashy cigarettes. I handed in my ticket, took my coat and put it on before we walked down the stairs. Stepping out into the night, I felt neither cold nor warmth. Loud men shouted in Emily Square, peeling their bicycles from the layers against the wall. Girls laughed and waited, uncertain whether to go or stay.

We walked up Offaly Street towards the park. The cold, hard park with its shiny brown bark and its thinly frosted grass.

'Would you not bring me home this once?' I said.

'What did you say?'

'Would you not bring me home? This once.'

I brought you . . . home.

Instead of passion there was panic. He saw how easy the whole thing could have been. How simple. But he dared not recognise it. Too late for that. And I dared not say anything. Isn't that the way it was that night? Whatever our bodies did, no matter how easily, could have been done much better a thousand times after that. And whatever it was that they failed to do could be changed if there was time and ease. They did their work. The sweat of terror made the bodies slide together. It might have smelt of ecstasy but we were terrified. Our bodies ground on because it meant we had nothing to say and less time to think. And he was thinking, as I was, how this might have happened before and how easily it could have been another day on which we'd rise and go to work and come back home and go to bed. Had I not said all that? The truth was evident but there was no place for it now. I stayed and watched him dress. Had this been some kind of sweet, pale honeymoon?

We walked to the station. Him in his uniform. Me in my dancing dress. There were others there in their regalia. Their wives and sweethearts dressed for the day.

Mick Lawlor. William Wall.

I kissed him then. There on the top platform outside the stationmaster's house. We leaned against the iron footbridge and kissed. He saw, again, how easy life can be. His body hard between my twisted skirts. Until the train began to move.

Outside the station, in the silence after he had gone, I heard somebody whistle, a young shop boy on his bicycle. A song the band had played the night before: 'Night and the stars are gleaming, tender and true, Dearest my heart is dreaming, dreaming of you.' The walls closed in. I saw the throng. I smelt his sweat and I heard the music clearer than when it played. Every sense I'd stifled came alive. His smell, his touch, his taste, flowed from every pore and left me sick.

I woke up. It was another day. I had to work. I realised he had gone. I dressed and walked to the shop. Where was he now?

Still in Dublin? Halfway across the sea? Somewhere in England? Certainly no further than that. I expected him to come lumbering into the shop, embarrassed, saying he had talked with Lord Walter and things had been worked out. He was going back to gardening. He was looking for a cottage in Kilkea. It might take time but then we'd move.

I was in the bakery when one of the girls called to me. There was a man in the shop wanting to talk to me. I recognise him. Noel Lambe. He says Frank has left a key with him. He'll be keeping an eye on the cottage – sleeping there now and again. He's to give me anything I want. I'm to go there any time I want. I can stay there if I like. That's what he's been told to tell me. I have only to let him know. Any time. All as matter of fact as that.

I carry bread from bakery to shop. I chat. I clean the windows in the street.

I wake up. It's another day. I have to work. I wait and wait.

Little things that never bothered me before begin to bother me now. The weight of these boots. The way the collar scuffs my neck. The task of writing and what to say and how to say it.

'We have arrived here safely and we are training. It's not as bad as you might think. I suppose Noel told you what I said about the house. Whatever is there that you might want is yours to take.'

I don't mention moving in. I try to come to that from several ways but I can't.

I sit out in the barrack yard and try to think of other things to write. I look at the nail of moon caught on the edge of a hawthorn bush. Beyond it the lake water is dark. Darker than the Griese. But the thorn reminds me of a turn on the castle avenue. This is England. That was home. I start thinking of fields. I think of how she nested in the hollows of my body. I think of how I wound my arms around her and nested in the hollows of her body. Her breast was in the hollow of my hand. There was a particular smell from her hair. Maybe of apples or rain. I started to say that to her and then some people passed and we went back to our bicycles and she tossed my hair with her fingers.

I don't mention any of this in my letter. This has happened. She knows that. Why write it? I tell her the food is good and the lads here are a decent crowd.

I wake and it's another day. I walk to work. I stop at his gate and notice that Noel has scuffled all the weeds. They lie in neat piles along the edge of grass. Today he will come and burn them.

I wake. This is not another day.

We cross the English Channel. It's not as bad as people say. They tell us Ypres was the worst but they tell us too that English, Irish, Germans, sang together at Christmas time. I write and tell her this.

'A happy, happy New Year.'

I am surprised at what I've written. I leave it so.

I wake and it is spring. The snow melts into isolated spots of snowdrop. The crocuses in purple-yellow dot the ground around the apple bark. And then it snows again in wintry narcissi. The evenings lengthen, carts of dung arrive from the countryside and back between the creaking hinges of town gates. Young girls I last saw as children walk with boys, out the Dublin Road to Ardscull and back.

And then it is summer. I tend his garden in the evenings. Noel comes and cuts the grass. The roses rear above the walls, sweet pea rambles across the gable wall. I wash and clean the floors. I open drawers and find his shirts in neat lines. They smell of winter. I hang them on the line and it gives me pleasure to see them threshing in the warm wind. I leave them out overnight and tell myself as I walk to work that he is home. I almost see the smoke from his chimney. That evening I fold the shirts and put them back inside their drawers.

Noel comes and limes the walls. We sit in the kitchen talking. The sun seems caught on the hills of Laois, unable to sink. It throws a long bolster of light across the table. I ask Noel if he knows why he went. 'If you don't know, no one does,' he says. His words give me some feeling of closeness to Frank. I know what he says is true. If I don't know, he doesn't know himself. And it doesn't matter, anyway. All that matters is that next summer the three of us will sit here and then the pair of us.

His letters come. I write to him. I read his words.

We heard a story down the line today about two blokes who were sentenced for desertion. They were strapped to the wheels of a gun and shot. I don't write about that kind of thing. We hear these stories, we talk about them, but I don't write of that. I write and say things are going well. I say the weather is improving. I am glad to hear the garden is doing well and glad about the lime. The cottage needed that. I mention people I know, fellows I've met – Larry Kelly and Stephen Mealy.

In April we were at Ypres. The gas crept like stink from a tomb. We passed these men lying in the grass. Their eyes were bandaged. We could hear their screams long after we had lost sight of them. Somebody said, you can't fight that bastard gas. I didn't write of that.

I remember the autumn by its fruit. I picked the low apples. Noel climbed for the high. I came home one afternoon and found a basket left at my digs, a basket of pears sent from the castle. I walked with the other girls on October Sundays. To Bert Bridge, to the Moat of Ardscull.

At Christmas I went home to Fraughan Hill. The house smelt of damp timber and the fire shot sparks across the stone floor. I told my mother about Frank. She smiled and said nothing. On the morning I left she said, 'You'll be all right.'

We had an Easter of daffodils. They trembled and shivered. I picked some and put them in a vase on his table. I left them there, even when the petals nodded, frizzled, stumbled and fell. I left them for a very long time.

There were other things I didn't write about. I met this chap with his fingers cut so deep that they hardly seemed to be a part of him. I asked him how this happened: stretcher bearing. No stretchers left. He and the others carried the wounded on sheets of corrugated iron. He lost the use of his hands but he went on carrying with stretcher sacks tied around his neck. He told me he had carried a man two miles to the medic. Already there were thirty or forty bodies surrounding the trestle table where he worked. Still men, men screaming. The medic worked on, his vest blood-soaked. The bodies came and went, the dead and the dying. The rest were shipped further back.

The funerals begin. In the afternoon the shop shutters bang. Small cards with scrawled words appear all over the town, on doors in Barrack Street, in Leinster Street, around the square.

I break the last branch of bloom from his lilac tree and take it home. The scent fills my room for three nights and then the bells fall apart.

One afternoon while we were marching, very close to the front, we saw a horse galloping towards us. His innards were trailing like a second tail. Then these men appeared. They came in twos and threes, the walking wounded. They came without rifles, many of them shirtless. They reminded me of people I had seen at grave sides, people deep in shock. They ignored us and went on walking, sometimes linking like drunken men on the Barrow Bridge, stupefied beyond recognition. Further along the track I saw a piece of flesh. I recognised it. Torn from the horse's belly. We went on marching.

Later, lying in a trench, waiting for the whistle, I thought about all this and then I thought of her. I knew then I would write and tell her everything – but first about the horse, the wounded, the raving mad.

His laburnum flowers fall, their golden rain scattering the grass. I get more letters from him now, full of the things he sees, the things he smells, the sounds of shells and guns and human voices. He tells me everything.

'My darling, Last week, Sunday I think, we came upon this village. It's hard to believe but it's still in one piece. It was raining when we marched in, far back from the lines. A bit like Ballitore on a wet evening. No one about. Four of us went to this little café place and sat there drinking wine. We stayed there while it got dark. You get used to wine. It's nothing like the pint of stout in Maher's but better than a lot of things I've drunk out here.

'There was this woman behind the counter. She sat there the whole afternoon and evening. She was sewing. When it got dark she lit a lamp and I could have sworn she was you. I know what you're thinking, so much for all this wine, but I swear, with the light and the colour of her hair, it could have been you. I was just sitting there watching her, and thinking to myself that I've forgotten a lot about you. About the way you look.

'The clearest memories I have are of the parts of you I saw the least. Your face only came back to me in her face and hair in the light of the lamp. You must get a photograph taken and send it to me. Then I can remember all of you. Like I say, there's parts of you I have no trouble remembering at all.

'I know what you're saying to yourself – this fellow is getting very forward.

'I've been thinking, too, about the things I'm looking forward

215

to going back to. I made a list of them the other day. November mornings cycling out to Kilkea was the first. And then the blossoms in the castle yard. And summer evenings coming in the road when the cuckoo is raising a row in the fields. These are going to be the same as they always were. I've noticed that. No matter what changes for me over the years, no matter what sort of time I'm going through, these things always keep their magic for me.

'There's other things that will never be the same. And the things between us, they'll never be the same, only better.'

I went down to Carlow to have that picture taken. It was a Wednesday afternoon, a half-day in Athy. I took my bicycle and went alone. I was put standing in front of a tree painted on canvas.

I spent one night in a shell hole, out in no-man's-land. The artillery went on firing, the thunder never stopped. I lay there with my companion, a dead machine gunner.

When I got the photograph I put it in an envelope and sent it off to him with a letter I had written but would never dare to read.

'My dearest Frank, I've had the photograph taken and I enclose it here. I cycled to Carlow to have it done. The man there was very nice. He said all the girls are having it done. I went down on my birthday. Imagine, I am twenty-six. The photograph came on the train this evening and I collected it on my way home. I shouldn't say this, but I like it. I hope you do too. Is this the way you remember me or the part of me you've forgotten?

'It's terrible to hear what you have told me about the war. Everything is quiet here now. Sometimes I think the worse the things you write about the better it is. I feel nothing will happen to you while these things are in your letters.

'Every week now some house in the town has a black ribbon on the door and the telegram boy from the post office is dreaded when he appears in any street.

'After I read your letter, your last letter, I laid it out on the bed in your room and took off all my clothes and stood in front of your mirror and looked at myself. I was thinking of how little we've seen of one another's bodies and thinking about what you said about being different. I think you're right. But I was thinking, too, that the braver and bolder you get in your letters, the harder it is for me to be any way bold in mine. And to think I was the one was always wishing you'd do those things to me when we were out walking the Carlow Road. Now I can only wish you were here to touch and kiss me the way I know you're thinking when you write your letters. You have so little time and I have all the time in the world. Don't worry, I was on my own in the house when I did that.

'I wait every day for your letters. I keep them all. I think, sometimes, you must be out of the war, the way you write such long and lovely letters. Everything here is waiting for you. Noel has the garden in fine order. The house is shining inside and out. I've painted the gate bright red. I hope you won't mind that. Everything is ready – the house, the garden, me, my body. Everything is waiting for you.

'I love you.'

I heard of a stretcher bearer who went out seven times yesterday. Each time he brought back a wounded man. The eighth time he was killed.

'My darling, I was thinking today about all the flowers I've put in that cracked jug on your kitchen table since you went away. Crocuses and snowdrops; lilacs and dog daisies and cornflowers and roses; water irises and wallflowers and dahlias now. I've picked them everywhere. Out the Barrow line, at

217

Mullaghcreelan and Ardscull. In your garden and along the roadside out past Bray. I even brought a spray of fuchsia from Fraughan Hill.

'I wonder what flowers will be in it when you come home. Whenever it is, even in the depth of winter, I'll have flowers in it for you.'

We push to a new front line. For a time there's relief. Something new promises, but then this line, these trenches, become the same as all the others. We have been in them before or someone else has. Our lines weave. Here we are at the front line, a mile away some other uniforms are moving cautiously.

There are always stories here. New stories come with every telegram. With every corpse a story comes. One week there are four men from Barrack Street, four doors with black ribbons, eight windows with the curtains tightly drawn. Schoolchildren walk from the other end of the town to gawk. They have never seen so much death before.

I begin to fear for something. It seems there is nothing to stop this rush of dying, nothing to say the next black ribbon won't be fastened to his door. I have to get away. I leave early and travel with Noel, on his cart, to Castledermot. I walk from there. I stop to throw a penny into the Lerr at Hamilton Bridge. I wish for luck and life. For him.

Near the top of Crop Hill I meet my father taking a horse down to the forge. I walk with him. A shire horse. Brandy.

'This is the heaviest horse we've ever had,' he says. 'And he's as quiet as a lamb. Do you remember Bess when you were small? I used to put you on her back.'

I remember. Black, brown, grey and bay with a star on her forehead. 'She'd be nothing to this fellow,' my father says. Skin and bone. The huge feather-feet fall as lightly as a bird's. The horse steps daintily until we reach the open forge. I stand and

218

wait. I rename the bits of harness that my father taught us all: the cheekpiece, the blinker, the browband, the peak, the haims, the pad, the loin strap, the crupper strap, the quarter strap, the breeching strap, the bellyband, the girth, the trace bar, the rein, the bit, the noseband. I have remembered every one. I repeat them to my father and he and the blacksmith clap. The horse turns and shifts uneasily.

Walking back, my father questions me as he did when we were children.

'Would you give a horse a long drink, now, after a hot day's work?'

'No.'

'And which comes first, the food or drink?'

'The drink.'

He laughs. 'You remember well, I taught you well. I doubt your sisters would remember the half of it.' And without pausing he says: 'What about this chap of yours?'

I tell him almost everything, but not the important things.

'You'll find it hard, the two of youse, when he comes back. Things like that are all very well until they look like being permanent. Can you deal with that? The sneers and the priest coming twenty times to your door? That'll be the easiest part. Have you the stomach for all that? Has he?'

'We have now,' I say. 'He mightn't have had a while ago, but we both have now.'

'Well,' my father says, 'if you're bent on staying with him and if the pair of youse are in love, you'll be all right. You've nothing to worry about in your mother nor me.'

I laugh and say: 'Doesn't news travel fast?'

'Faster than you'd think,' he says, and we walk on laughing and I'm so happy that I've come back here.

I get back to Athy on Sunday night. I sit in your kitchen and put things in order in my mind. You have my photograph. I have your house. Your wife has nothing. I smile.

219

The summer passes. Every weekend I walk or cycle someplace. Sometimes with Noel, sometimes with girls from work, sometimes on my own. I walk around Kilkea a lot. There and in your house is where I find it easiest to be with you. I talk to you all the time. I take plants from the fields and tell you what they are. I point the differences between the spear thistle and the creeping thistle. This is the evening primrose and this is the hawk's-beard. My father told me those. There are places where I can talk to you and say things I may never say to your face.

The summer ends and then the autumn.

I never wonder at his luck in being alive. I believe he will never die. Always he has some stories in the post of death, of bravery, of miracles.

'We went back to that village, to that café I wrote about. The woman is still there. She hasn't changed. She hasn't aged. She wore a brighter blouse this time. I took it as a sign. I have to laugh to think that someone like me, who never looked up from the ground, is seeing signs. And out here of all places. But I believe that nothing that has happened – no torn limb, no frantic horse, no soldier screaming, no shell that leaves me in an open grave with corpses all around – can come between us.

'The woman in the café lives, she dresses brightly, she smiles, I suppose she loves. All this a few miles from the front. She is the same as she was and so are you.'

'I have to write to tell you this. Today in the shop some women were talking about someone they'd heard was killed. One of them turned and said: "And how's your Frank?" I could have cried. "Your Frank." I laughed and said you were fine, that you'd be all right.

'And this woman said: "Of course he will, hasn't he you to come home to? Why wouldn't he be?" I think that was the happiest minute of my life. And you do have me. And I have you.

And every night now I leave a space for you beside me and every morning I wake up in your space.'

The summer has passed and the autumn. Sometimes I wonder at my luck at being alive, at escaping without a scratch. Sometimes I am convinced I will never die.

His letters come. I find them on the windowsill in the hall when I get home from work. The envelope is always fat and full of paper, sometimes a dried flower that I put into a book I keep. Sometimes I send a pressed flower back. But never one from his garden. Always wild flowers.

'Today is my birthday. I'm writing this in a garden or what remains of it. It's a garden on the edge of a town and it looks down across a valley. It's like looking out from the clear patch on the side of Mullaghcreelan, down across the castle and the houses in Kilkea. But here there's no village, just a clear valley of fields, without a tree. There's a river in the bed of the valley, as wide and cool as the Griese.

'I was here last spring when the place was paved with flowers. I prefer it now. It has the bite of home. We're billeted here but I've taken my blanket out into this garden to sleep. You get used to sleeping under the sky but here it's quiet. If the wind blows right, there isn't even a muffle of the guns.

'Lying under a tree at the end of the garden, I remember nights when we were out the Barrow line and, strange enough or maybe it isn't, I remember our last night. Our only night inside. My only regret is that the nights were too few and the distance seems so far. But not too far. This is the quietest, the happiest birthday of my life.

'I love you.'

I carried that letter to work with me and read it in the yard when things were quiet. I carried it home and that evening I went and sat in the room where we had lain and I read it and read it again. I wanted to write something like that but now, at such a distance from him, I could feel his passion flowing and mine was drowned.

'I've been thinking hard about things, now that I have the chance to. I thought maybe it was the great hate that made everything seem in its right place. But that can't be it because there's little or no hate here. None of us feels hate for whoever is behind the big guns. We feel panic sometimes and we feel helpless for men that are dying in the dark, men we can hear shouting and can't reach, and we feel disgust at what the human body can look like, but we feel no hate. I've never felt as free of hate. I think it's the pain all around us that makes other feelings so important. That's what it is – the pain.

'Then the other feelings are more important than they were. You see a man get hit. You see the blood draining out of him the way we'd drain a lake. You see the life going with it. You look, when you have the time, and you see these things. You see a skin disappear and another one replacing it. You know the man is changing in a way you never get to understand but you recognise the change. It can happen as sudden as a dam bursting or it can be as slow as a summer evening. But you know death is coming on, it's like a mist. You see it and you don't. And you think about the other things that are draining out of this man. The love he wanted to talk about. And you realise there's no other time than the time we have now. You lie in a trench and as fast as anything you're somewhere else.

'I'm back with you on the haycocks out the Carlow Road or in a field at Mullaghcreelan but this time I don't talk on and on. This time I kiss you and touch you and I forget the shells and the bullets and the mist that's always hanging over us.'

I read his letters. I keep them till I've finished my meal and then I take them across to his cottage and I read them in his room. I sit in his kitchen and write these letters in my head, letters I've been making up all day at work. Letters about the parts of me he barely touched. I write about the feelings and when he must do these things and how. But when it comes to writing the letters down, putting them on paper, they seem foolish. They never seem to have the ease of his.

And so I write: 'Everything here is as it was. Noel has all your apples in. They're laid out on the scullery floor on sheets of newspaper. The ones that weren't ripe are in the kitchen window. They catch whatever sun there is and I come and check on them in the evening.

'Noel laughs and says I should move in altogether and be done with it. The girls in work laugh too when I talk about you. "You're twenty-six," they say. "You'd better settle down. Get the house and then he'll have to take you!" I laugh at that. I think I'll wait. Do you want me to wait? Will it be as easy when you get back here?'

I ask the question more of myself than him but I am pleased when his answer comes in a torrent of words I wish he had used when he was here. His words explore each part of me.

'I want you to know these things. I came out here to take stock, to gather strength for going back. I have no fear of that. I don't care about the mouths that mouth. I care for our mouths and for the way they meet each other. For the way they meet strange parts of the body and don't find them strange at all.

'If a man here can be twisted, be hung from a stump or blown onto the top of a wall and left for days, he loses his life. We lose our respect for the unimportances. We put this aside and carry on surviving and when this war is over we put it aside and return to living.

'For me that means going back to the castle, cycling out in all weathers, working hard. It has nothing to do with what people say.

223

'For me it's getting back to the cottage. It has nothing to do with where the cottage is.

'For me it means my body and yours – the dry smell of your hair, the wet smell of me in you, the dark smell of the shadows your breasts make in the lamplight, the clean smell of us standing naked together wherever we want it to be. None of this worries me because I've been doing this for the last months, years, and so, I know, have you. We know each other's bodies. They will meet like friends and rampant lovers who don't hesitate. They will find their way without more than the slightest touch to guide them.'

When I touch, my touch is of his hands.

'The thing I miss, apart from you, is trees. I'd love to climb a tree again and feel the particular way a tree is. There are no trees where we are now, only the occasional stump.

'I feel myself growing surer each week. I see men that we buried reappear. These are men without legs. Men whose heads are found elsewhere. I see men running, men I know to be dead. They go on running in the smoke, their faces dead. They fall eventually but by then the life is gone out of them. I see a man running on one leg. For a long time he thinks there are two and he goes on running perfectly. And then he sees and he falls, crying, and we leave him there. We go on running because we have two legs under us and we want to keep them there.

'We rest against a parapet of flesh, of men gorged each into the next. I hate all these things – the shells, the gas, the buried and unburied dead – but it's the rain, puddled, dammed and trapped in trenches that hurts the most. It seeps in through the boots, through the ankles and the knees. Joints ache. Coats, soaked and muddy, dry and melt and dry again. Fresh shell holes smell of powder and then of rain. The water appears like holy wells around our feet. It comes from nowhere. We hear of thousands, hundreds of thousands, dying. We see them. We see the enemy from time to time but I hate only the rain.

'The lists go up on every side.

'We find a pair of legs, their owner is running somewhere, running on into the smoke.'

'My darling, I have read and read your letter until every page is tattered from turning and carrying. I don't care to leave it anywhere that someone might see it, so I bring it everywhere with me.

'When I read where you had written about me being your wife, I stopped. It was like a dream. Had I been asleep and missed out on that? I wondered. And then I realised what you were saying and that was even better. You say that since the night when we slept here I have been your wife. For me I have been your wife since very early on.

'And when you wrote all those things you think about, I knew exactly how you felt and I did what you asked. It was a sunny afternoon and I cycled out to the bridge at Kilkea and crossed the two fields and lay in that place where you asked me to and I knew you were there. It was the way you wrote it would be.

'When you come back that will be the first place we will go together. I love you more than everything and I often think that this war, this separation, was worth it after all because I know you're not gone.

'I love you, my darling. Mary Lloyd that now thinks of herself as Mary Kinsella.'

When we went forward we had blackened faces. It was night. We cut through wire. There were fewer flares than usual – a blessing. We came upon them suddenly, three young men, much younger than we were. They threw up their arms and we bayoneted them. Very little time to stop. We went through their uniforms. Then up and on across another no-man's-land. More muck, more sockets in the earth and legs and fingers pointing nowhere. Then up and on.

I thought I saw a level spray of bullets. I couldn't have but I thought I did. It started away to my left and neatly mowed through two of us. I was running, the other man was crouching. It tore my legs from just above the knees, it shot his head away. His lungs released a flow of air, a belch out through his open neck and he went down.

I thought of how the pain was less than I expected. I thought of how passion seemed less possible without my legs. I tried to picture her pushing me about in some stiff chair, lifting me like a bladder onto our bed. I was a different man and the future took on a different sense; it drained of any colour.

I had suspected this all along. I could look now and weigh the options for myself. And I could go on looking because by then I was dead. My body was half sitting, my open eyes stared straight ahead as my comrades raced by.

Of course the letter came to her. I could only laugh. And then they brought him home. She followed him along the street, between her brothers. He came in a box off the evening train, down past the shuttered windows and back again in the morning. Through the welcoming gates. She followed him and I followed to the top of the bridge and watched from there.

An army grave. She'd be buried with her own. I knew his grave was far too small. There was no crevice where I might knead my body between the earth and skin. I wished they'd left his bits in France. To have him lying at the head of the street while I pressed my naked self against the cold wet window as if he was there, out there, beyond it.

I set myself to live within the bounds that I had set myself. I turned myself on you but reaching back became a crime.

I have become content with naming things that marked our

226

past, reverting to my former self: daffodil, wild violet, primrose, the cherry tree, bluebell, lilac, the golden rain, the marigold, the apple fruit, the rusting dahlias underneath.

His wife was there behind the hearse. One wife.

I saw no hope beyond the bounds that I had set myself and that is why I despise the angle now. I see the possibilities when they are gone.

If you can touch, then touch me now.

Daffodil, primrose, wild violet, the cherry tree, bluebell, lilac, the golden rain.

Across the street the laburnum bends, a kind of light.

The marigold, the apple fruit, the rusting dahlias underneath.

I press myself against the window and watch the ghostly dancers pass.

Frank Alcock.
Martin Hyland.
John Byrne.
Mick Lawlor.
Willie Tierney.
William Wall.
Owen Kelly.
Thomas Fox.
Stephen Mealy.
Joseph Hickey.
Larry Kelly.

Patrick Leonard.
Martin Moloney.
Robert MacWilliams.
Martin Maher.
Christopher Power.
Laurence Dooley.
Thomas Ellard.
Norman Hannon.
John Hannon.
Henry Hannon.
Frank Kinsella.
And Mary Lloyd.

I push my naked body through the glass and join the dismal dead who pass.

BIOGRAPHICAL NOTES

MICHAEL CARRAGHER

b. 1953 in south Armagh. Educated at Violet Hill College, Newry, and Trinity College Dublin, where he read Geography, Economics and Psychology. After a brief career as a civil servant in Belfast and Stormont, he was features editor of a motorcycle magazine in Dublin, and currently manages a motorcycle shop in Galway city. He has been writing short stories since 1981 and has been published in the *Irish Press*'s 'New Irish Writing', *Passages*, and the *Belfast Review*. His very first published story ('New Irish Writing', 1984) was shortlisted for a Hennessy Literary Award. He has given readings of his work, at the 1990 Galway Arts Festival and elsewhere.

EMMA COOKE

b. 1934 in Portarlington, County Laois. Educated at Alexandra College, Dublin, and the Mary Immaculate Training College, Limerick, where she studied Philosophy. Has been involved in community affairs and adult education since the mid-1960s, and since the early 1970s has been an active member of writers' workshops, including the Listowel Writers' Week, where for two successive years she conducted its short-story workshop. In 1989 she was awarded second place in the RTE Radio 1 Francis MacManus Award. Her work has been widely published in many magazines and anthologies in Ireland, Britain and the United States, and in translation in Germany and Denmark. She has published one collection of short stories (*Female Forms*, Poolbeg Press, 1980) and two novels (*A Single Sensation*, Poolbeg Press, 1981; and *Eve's Apple*, Blackstaff Press, 1985). Currently lives in Killaloe, County Clare, where she helped to found the Killaloe Writers' Group.

CIARÁN FOLAN

b. 1956 in Newtowncashel, County Longford. Educated at University College Galway, from where he graduated with a B.Sc. Currently teaches Science in Dublin. In 1987 he won the RTE Radio 1 Francis MacManus Award. His stories have been published in the *Irish Press*'s 'New Irish Writing' and the *London Magazine*.

231

DAPHNE GLAZER

b. Sheffield. Educated at Hull University, where she read English and German, and after graduating, taught German in Nigeria for five years. Currently works as a further education college lecturer in Hull, teaching German and conducting writers' workshops. She has co-tutored various writing courses with Zoe Fairbairns, Linda Anderson and Gary Armitage. Her work has been widely published in a variety of anthologies, magazines, journals and newspapers, including *Forms of Narrative* (Cambridge University Press, 1990), *God Gives Nuts To Those Who Have No Teeth* (Heinemann, 1990), *Critical Quarterly, New Statesman and Society, Spare Rib*, and the *Guardian*. Her stories have also been broadcast on BBC Radio 4. Her novel *Three Women* was published by Judy Piatkus in 1984 and Sumach Press is due to publish her first full collection of short stories in 1992.

SIMON KORNER

b. 1957. Educated at Lewes Priory Comprehensive School, and Trinity College, Cambridge. Teaches part-time at two inner-city colleges in London. The two stories published in this anthology are part of a series of linked semi-autobiographical pieces. He is currently working on a novel.

JIM MCCARTHY

b. 1954 in Waterford. Educated at the Christian Brothers' School, Tramore, and has lived in Dublin for the past twenty years, where he currently works in the engineering section of Telecom Éireann. In 1983 he was the recipient of a Hennessy Literary Award. Had a series of feature articles published in the *Evening Press* between 1981 and 1985, and his stories have appeared in the *Irish Press, Cyphers, The Salmon, Nutshell* and *Passages*. His play *Choosing* was broadcast on RTE Radio 1 in 1986.

JOHN MACKENNA

b. 1952 in Castledermot, County Kildare. Educated at St Clement's College, Limerick, and University College Dublin, where he read English and History. Currently works as a senior producer in RTE. Winner of a Hennessy Literary Award in 1983, the 1986 Leitrim Guardian Award, and a C. Day-Lewis Fiction Award in 1989 and 1990. Has had three books published: *The Occasional Optimist* (Winter Wood Books,

1976); *Castledermot and Kilkea* (Winter Wood Books, 1982); *The Lost Village* (Stephen Scroop Press, 1985). He has also edited two books by the Quaker diarist Mary Leadbeater, *The Annals of Ballitore* (Stephen Scroop Press, 1986) and *Cottage Biography* (Stephen Scroop Press, 1987).

GEORGE MCWHIRTER
b. 1939 in Belfast. Educated at Grosvenor High School, Queen's University Belfast, and the University of British Columbia. Lived in Spain from 1965 to 1966, when he moved to Canada, where he is currently professor and head of the Creative Writing Department at the University of British Columbia, Vancouver, teaching literary translation. His first book, *Catalan Poems* (Oberon Press), shared the Commonwealth Poetry Prize with Chinus Achebe's *Cry, Soul Brother* in 1972; his novel *Cage* (Oberon Press) won the 1987 Ethel Wilson Prize for Fiction, BC Book Awards; and his translation of *The Selected Poems of José Emilio Pacheco* (New Directions) was awarded the F.R. Scott Prize for Translation by the League of Canadian Poets and the F.R. Scott Foundation in 1987. His poetry, short stories and translations have been widely anthologised, and in all he has published three novels, five collections of poetry, three collections of short stories, and one of translation.

AISLING MAGUIRE
b. 1958 in Dublin. Educated at the Sacred Heart Convent, Mount Anville, and University College Dublin, where she read English. Has taught adults on community education projects and now works as a journalist in Dublin. Has had stories published in the *Irish Times*, the *Irish Press*, the *Sunday Tribune*, and *Panurge*. Her stories have also been anthologised in *Raven Introductions 4*, *The Dolmen Book of Irish Christmas Stories*, *The Blackstaff Book of Short Stories* (1988), and *Forgiveness: Ireland's Best Contemporary Short Stories*.

GERARDINE MEANEY
b. 1962 in Waterford. Educated at the Presentation School, Kilkenny, and University College Dublin. Was a junior research fellow at the Institute of Irish Studies, Queen's University Belfast (1988–9), taught at Trinity College Dublin (1989–90), and currently teaches English and Women's Studies at University College Dublin. She won a Hennessy Literary Award in 1987. Her stories have been published in the *Irish Press*'s 'New Irish Writing', the *Midland Review*, the *North Dakota*

Quarterly, the *Sweeping Beauties* (Attic Press, 1989) and *Wildish Things* (Attic Press, 1989). A feminist critic and theorist, she has contributed a pamphlet to the Attic Press LIP series, *Sex and Nation: Women in Irish Culture and Politics* (1991) and a book on feminist theory and women's writing is forthcoming.

ÉILÍS NÍ DHUIBHNE

b. 1954 in Dublin. Educated at Scoil Bhríde, Scoil Chaitríona, and University College Dublin, from which she holds a BA in English and a Ph.D. in Irish Folklore. She works as an assistant keeper in the National Library of Ireland and lectures on Irish Folklore in the People's College and occasionally at UCD. She has won various awards and scholarships, including a UCD English Prize in 1971, a Listowel Writers' Week Award in 1989 and an Arts Council Bursary in Literature in 1986. Her poetry and short stories have been published in a variety of journals and newspapers, including the *Irish Press*, the *Irish Times*, the *Sunday Tribune*, *Poetry Ireland Review*, *Cyphers*, *The Salmon*, and anthologised in collections such as *Best Short Stories 1986* (Heinemann), *Territories of the Voice* (Virago), *The Blackstaff Book of Short Stories* (1988) and *Frauen in Irland* (DTV). She has published a collection of short stories, *Blood and Water* (Attic Press, 1988), a novel, *The Bray House* (Attic Press, 1990; shortlisted for the Irish Book Awards), and a children's book, *The Uncommon Cormorant* (Poolbeg Press, 1990; shortlisted for the Bisto Awards). A new collection of short stories and another children's book are due for publication in autumn 1991.

HARRIET O'CARROLL

b. 1941 in Callan, County Kilkenny. Educated at St Mary's College, Arklow, University College Dublin and the Mater Hospital School of Physiotherapy. Has lived in England, Denmark and various parts of Ireland. Has been a three-times winner of the Maxwell House/Arlen House short story competition for Irish women writers and won the 1981 International Year of the Disabled short story competition sponsored by the Mental Health Association of Ireland. She was a joint prizewinner of the 1988 O.Z. Whitehead Playwriting competition. Has had radio plays and short stories broadcast by the BBC and RTE, and has written some episodes of the RTE series, *Glenroe* and *Fair City*. Her short stories have been published in the *Irish Times*, *The Blackstaff Book of Short Stories* (1988) and *Territories of the Voice: Contemporary Irish Women Writers* (Virago/Beacon Press).

EDWARD POWER

b. 1951 in Mooncoin, County Kilkenny. Educated locally to secondary level. Has worked as literature officer at Waterford's Garter Lane Arts Centre, and is currently editor of *Riverine* literary magazine. One of his stories was shortlisted for a Hennessy Literary Award in 1987 and in 1990 he was awarded joint first place in a competition organised by Kilkenny County Council in conjunction with The Book Centre and Radio Kilkenny. He has received scholarships and bursaries to attend Listowel Writers' Week, University College Galway's National Writers' Workshop and the Hewitt International Summer School. Has had poetry, short stories, reviews and articles published in a variety of magazines and journals, including the *Irish Press*'s 'New Irish Writing', *Poetry Ireland Review*, *The Salmon*, *Cyphers*, the *Sunday Tribune*, *Passages* and *Rostrum*.

PATRICK SEMPLE

b. 1939 in Wexford. Educated at the King's Hospital, Dublin, and Trinity College Dublin, where he read Philosophy and Theology, and the University of Chicago. A Church of Ireland clergyman, he has worked in Belfast and Laois, and has been the Church of Ireland Adult Education Officer. He is currently rector of Donoughmore and Dunlavin, County Wicklow. Has had short stories broadcast on RTE Radio 1.

JANET SHEPPERSON

b. 1954 in Edinburgh. Educated at George Watson's College, Edinburgh, and Aberdeen University, where she read English and won the Calder Verse Prize in 1976. Came to live in Belfast in 1977, where she has held a variety of jobs. She has been shortlisted for a Hennessy Literary Award and has won a prize in the Bridport Arts Centre Poetry Competition. Her poetry and short stories have been widely published, including the *Irish Press*'s 'New Irish Writing', the *Sunday Tribune*, *Passages*, *Fortnight*, *The Salmon*, *Poetry Review*, *Stand*, *Poetry Wales*, the *Honest Ulsterman*, *Trio Poetry 5* (Blackstaff Press, 1987), and *The Blackstaff Book of Short Stories* (1988). She has given readings and participates in the Arts Council of Northern Ireland's Writers in Schools series.

MONICA TRACEY

b. 1931 in Lisburn, County Antrim. Educated at the Sacred Heart of Mary Convent, Lisburn, and Queen's University Belfast, where she read French. Has lived in France and Germany, and taught in Enniskillen,

Belfast, and Newcastle upon Tyne, where she currently lives. Started to write in 1988, when she had to give up teaching because she was suffering from ME. Has had stories and articles published in *Cat World* and the *Guardian*.

OTHER TITLES
from
BLACKSTAFF PRESS

FLORRIE'S GIRLS
MAEVE KELLY

Ripe for fun and life, eighteen-year-old Cos arrives
in postwar London to begin her training at a small
hospital run by nuns. Dreaming of the Irish home
she has left behind, she consoles herself with the
thought that she is doing something noble. But a
student nurse, she finds, is at once the lowest worm
in creation and the cornerstone of the hospital –
and the burden of human suffering is not
an easy one to bear.

Together with her vivacious colleagues – Binks and
the irrepressible Hanley – Cos discovers survival is
a tricky business. Dodging the wrath of Sister
Maguire, teasing young doctors, stealing time to
chat to patients, they learn that laughter, friendship
and as irreverent a detachment as they can manage
are their lifelines.

Tender and funny, *Florrie's Girls* vividly captures
the innocence and anguish of a young woman
learning to grow and love, caught between duty
and temptation.

'The burning injustices, horrors, friction and
agitations of hospital life are all recorded by Cos in
a spirit of bravado . . . Maeve Kelly writes with
assurance . . . and shows a strong feeling for the
quirkiness of everyday events.'
Times Literary Supplement

198 x 129mm; 256pp; 0 85640 465 9; pb
£4.95

THE CHARNEL HOUSE
EAMONN MC GRATH

Set in Ardeevan sanatorium in the 1950s, when tuberculosis was still a major cause of death in Ireland, *The Charnel House* is a powerful study of the twilight existence of the chronically and terminally ill.

Bringing together a wide and varied set of characters – Richard Cogley and his sister Eileen, the eccentric Commander Barnwell, young lovers Vincent and Lily, hospital joker Arty Byrne, homosexual Phil Turner, and the embittered Frank O'Shea – Eamonn Mc Grath charts their relationships as they confront pain and death, creating a deeply felt examination of the nature of suffering and the unexpected strength of the human spirit.

'Remarkably vivid . . . moving without ever being sentimental . . . Mc Grath writes with . . . delicacy and generous openness'
(Julian Symons, *Sunday Times*, reviewing Eamonn Mc Grath's first novel, *Honour Thy Father*, also available from Blackstaff Press)

198 x 129mm; 240pp; 0 85640 447 0; pb
£5.95

MY COUSIN JUSTIN
MARGARET BARRINGTON

'As I watched my husband and my cousin, I realized for the first time that . . . each was as badly mutilated as if he had lost an arm or a leg. What they had lost was more because one could not see it. The scars of war lay on their souls, and old wounds ache.'

Moving from the shelter of her Anglo-Irish upbringing and the claustrophobic intensity of her relationship with her cousin Justin Thorauld, Loulie Delahaie becomes embroiled in the merciless world of Dublin journalism and revolutionary politics. There she is swept into a headlong love affair with Egan O'Doherty, a gunman on the run from the Black and Tans.

The bitter violence of the Irish Civil War and the dark shadows it casts over Loulie, Justin and Egan are powerfully caught in this absorbing story of passion and deceit.

'it has fire and movement'
Manchester Guardian

'there is wit in the telling of this story . . . a rich and juicy wit which it is impossible to resist'
Tribune

198 x 129mm; 288pp; 0 85640 456 X; pb
£4.95

TOLD IN GATH
MAX WRIGHT

The story of Max Wright's early experiences with the Plymouth Brethren has now been told, and not exclusively in Gath, and published, not necessarily in the streets of Askelon. If the daughters of the Philistines don't rejoice, they ought to. I'm convinced that many readers will rejoice. They will certainly laugh; this is a witty account, full of good jokes and wonderfully funny stories. They may perhaps weep too (I did) for the book describes, feelingly and with gruesome accuracy, the physical and spiritual discomfort, the wilful ignorance, the abuse of language, the distortion of logic and often the sheer malpractice into which fundamentalist religion can suck whole groups of potentially good and intelligent people.

Any account of the Brethren is bound to be compared with Edmund Gosse's, and indeed *Father and Son* will always have its place. But Max Wright has brought the subject up to date; not so much factually, for things have changed very little, as in approach: he is more honest than Gosse and less stately. But he is equally serious.

Told in Gath is an important book. The Brethren were always testifying to something or other; I testify to this.
Patricia Beer
author of
Mrs Beer's House

198 x 129mm; 208pp; 0 85640 449 7; hb
£11.95

198 x 129mm; 208pp; 0 85640 439 X; pb
£5.95

THE MIDDLE OF MY JOURNEY
JOHN BOYD

'I perceived the job of being a producer – the name itself is significant – to being a kind of midwife. You persuaded, pummelled, encouraged, pacified, pleaded, cajoled ordinary and extraordinary people to give birth to their thoughts by speaking them into a microphone.'

Appointed as a radio producer by the BBC in Belfast in 1946, John Boyd found himself at odds with the 'literary apartheid' and conservatism then governing broadcasting. But over the next twenty years, Boyd's quiet but determined work behind the scenes – bringing the voices of writers like Frank O'Connor, Louis MacNeice and Philip Larkin to a wider audience – made him one of the BBC's most influential regional producers.

Covering those years of intense activity, this second volume of autobiography from John Boyd paints a vibrant picture of creative and artistic life in Belfast.

'This man of calm and honest judgement'
Benedict Kiely, *Irish Times*

198 x 129mm; 240pp; 0 85640 438 1; pb
£5.95

NIGHTFALL AND OTHER STORIES
DANIEL CORKERY
edited by
FRANCIS DOHERTY

'That terrible promiscuity of rock, the little stony
fields that only centuries of labour had salvaged
from them, the unremitting toil they demanded, the
poor return, the niggard scheme of living; and then
the ancient face on the pillow, the gathering of
greedy descendants – he had known it all before;
for years the knowledge of how much of a piece it
all was had kept his mind uneasy.'
from 'The Priest'

Passionately committed to the idea of a unique but
vulnerable Irish identity, Daniel Corkery was
nevertheless clear-eyed and unsentimental in his
observation of peasants and poor town-dwellers.
Widely recognised as among the finest Irish writing
of this century, his masterly short stories, of which
twenty are presented here, spring from this tension
and from his sense of an unknowable mystery at the
heart of common experience.

'The simplicity of the writing at times reminds you
of Hemingway, but it has a warmth and passion
that Papa rarely showed. Powerful, elemental
themes – exile, death, blindness, loss – are dealt
with in flexible words that add to the pathos of
what is being written about.'
Irish News

198 x 129mm; 224pp; 0 85640 414 4; pb
£1.50

THINE IN STORM AND CALM
AN AMANDA MCKITTRICK ROS READER
edited by
FRANK ORMSBY

Under the sway of the 'magical and delicious
intoxication' of language, Ulsterwoman Amanda
McKittrick Ros wrote novels and poems which
burst upon an astonished literary world unaccus-
tomed to her style of ornate embellishment and
enthusiastic alliteration. Numbering Mark Twain
and Aldous Huxley among her stunned admirers,
she rapidly established herself at the turn of the
century as a literary celebrity and cult figure.

This highly entertaining selection by Frank Ormsby
presents characteristically unrestrained writing
from her major novels, *Irene Iddesleigh*, *Delina
Delaney* and *Helen Huddleson*, together with poems
and, for good measure, some of her quite terrifying
letters to critics, solicitors and other enemies.

'Amanda Ros was Northern Ireland's answer to
William McGonagall of Dundee, Poet and
Tragedian. What he did in verse, she did in prose;
and the results are equally hilarious – unconscious
humour raised to a level of genius.'
Brian Fallon, *Irish Times*

198 x 129mm; 192pp; 0 85640 408 X; pb
£0.50

ORDERING BLACKSTAFF BOOKS

All Blackstaff Press books are available through bookshops. In the case of difficulty, however, orders can be made directly to the publisher. Indicate clearly the title and number of copies required and send order with your name and address to:

CASH SALES

Blackstaff Press Limited
3 Galway Park
Dundonald
Belfast BT16 0AN
Northern Ireland

Please enclose a remittance to the value of the cover price plus: £1.00 for the first book plus 60p per copy for each additional book ordered to cover postage and packing. Payment should be made in sterling by UK personal cheque, postal order, sterling draft or international money order, made payable to Blackstaff Press Limited. Access, Visa, Mastercard and Eurocard are also accepted.

Applicable only in the UK and Republic of Ireland
Full catalogue available on request